SUDDEN LOVE

He put out his arms to hold Taryna again; and when she would have resisted him, he swept her masterfully close to him. She tried to resist, but it was too late. Already that ecstasy was creeping over her again, sapping her will, so that she could only cling to him and feel her mouth go soft beneath his.

Later, she wondered why, why did he love her? And then she knew! Michael thought that she was very rich. He was making love to her because of her money. But could any man make her feel as Michael had done and yet be a hypocrite?

"I've got to hate him," Taryna said aloud.

Yet even as she tried to whip up her anger, she knew it was hopeless. She loved him. She felt herself quiver with a sudden delight at the very memory of his kisses. Whatever he did, whatever he said, she would still go on loving him!

LIGHTS
OF
LOVE

Barbara Cartland

PYRAMID BOOKS
NEW YORK

LIGHTS OF LOVE

A PYRAMID BOOK

Pyramid edition published March 1973
  Third printing, September 1973

© Barbara McCorquodale 1958
© Barbara Cartland 1969

All Rights Reserved

ISBN 0-515-02965-3

All of the characters in this book are purely imaginary and
have no relation whatsoever to any living person.

Printed in the United States of America

Pyramid Books are published by Pyramid Communications,
Inc. Its trademarks, consisting of the word "Pyramid" and the
portrayal of a pyramid, are registered in the United States
Patent Office.

Pyramid Communications, Inc.,
919 Third Avenue,
New York, New York 10022

1

"Taryna!"

A young voice called the name; then the door was burst open and a girl came hurrying into the room.

"I thought I'd never get here!" she exclaimed. "I got mixed up in an accident and the policeman took hours writing down the details."

Taryna looked up from the suitcase she was packing.

"Oh, Kit, not again!"

Kit nodded her fair head.

"Yes, again," she said. "That's the third bicycle this term."

Taryna laughed.

"You really are incorrigible," she said. "I should think the insurance company will refuse to take a risk on you in future."

"What else can they expect with seven thousand undergraduates milling around Cambridge?" Kit asked. "But actually it was a lorry driver's fault!"

"Not you, of course!" Taryna said with mock seriousness.

"Of course not," Kit replied airily, flinging her gown on the floor and settling herself comfortably in an armchair.

"Don't let's talk about it," she said. "It bores me. Next year I shall be able to have a car."

"Then Heaven help all of us!" Taryna exclaimed.

"What worried me while the policeman was sucking his pencil and trying to spell was that I might miss you," Kit went on, ignoring her friend's exclamation. "I knew you had said something about leaving on the afternoon train."

"Oh, I've decided to go on the later one," Taryna replied. "I didn't get any of my packing done last night."

"Were you at a party?" Kit enquired.

Taryna shook her head.

"No, I was working."

"On the last night of term!" Kit exclaimed. "Really, Taryna, you never think of anything but work."

"It sounds rather awful," Taryna said apologetically. "But, you see, I may not have a chance to study much in the vac."

"Sounds interesting," Kit said. "What are you going to do?"

"Do?" Taryna enquired. "Oh, get a job, of course,"

"A job! What sort of job?" Kit sat up suddenly and stared at her friend.

Taryna looked reflective.

"I don't really know. Last vac I served in a shop. I made about five pounds a week, but it was terribly hard work and one of the girls was telling me that if one is a waitress one gets much more with tips."

"But, you'd hate it," Kit said. "Can you imagine serving up meat and two veg to ghastly commercial travellers who shout 'Hi, miss,' at you?"

"I wouldn't really mind that if the money was good," Taryna answered.

"Is it so important—the money, I mean?"

Taryna turned away to look out of the window on to the quiet courtyard below. Her face was in profile. It was a lovely face, Kit thought suddenly, with its tiny, delicate features, the dark hair waving back from an oval forehead. It was a face that had a kind of spiritual beauty.

"Yes, it is very important," Taryna said after a

6

moment, slowly, as if the words were drawn from her. "Mummy and Daddy have made such sacrifices to send me here. Oh, I know I won a scholarship; but that doesn't pay for everything, and, naturally, if I hadn't come to Cambridge I should be earning money and giving them something every week."

"But, Taryna, surely your father has a salary?" Kit exclaimed.

"But of course," Taryna replied. "As Vicar of an East End parish, which is very poor and very ill endowed, he has the magnificent sum of four hundred pounds a year left when he has paid the rates on the Vicarage, and the various other things to which he is compelled to contribute. And, of course, we must not forget his income tax, which is levied not only on his stipend but on the Easter collections as well."

There was a sudden bitterness in Taryna's voice and impulsively Kit jumped to her feet and ran across the room.

"Oh, Taryna, I'm sorry," she said, putting her arm round her friend. "I oughtn't to ask such questions. I'm thoughtless and spoilt—spoilt by too much money. If only you'd let me help."

"Now, Kit, we've had this argument before. As you've always told me, I have my pride!"

Taryna was laughing again as she turned from the window and went to the chest-of-drawers to collect more clothes for her suitcase.

"I know," Kit said wistfully. "You are the biggest bore I know on self-respect and not taking a meal off someone who wants to give it to you, and paying your own way, and all those tiresome, old-fashioned things which nobody even thinks about nowadays."

"Except the Grazebrooks," Taryna added. "They are all very particular—Father, Mother, Donald, Edwina and me. As you say, we have our pride."

She struck an attitude and picking up a white lawn collar which she had just taken from a drawer, put it on her head.

"Can't you see me in my café," she said. "Oh, sir, do have a little of the shepherd's pie made of the left-overs of yesterday's dishes. It's quite delicious."

Kit suddenly gave a scream. It was so shrill and so unexpected that Taryna dropped the lawn collar and stared at her in astonishment.

"Kit, what's the matter? Has something stung you?"

"No, I've got an idea," Kit said almost breathlessly. "Listen, Taryna! Oh, listen to me. I've got a job for you."

"A job?" Taryna asked.

"Yes! And, please, Taryna, say you'll listen to me. It's the best idea I've ever had."

"What is it?" Taryna asked suspiciously.

"Now, listen while I start from the very beginning," Kit said. "You know how miserable I am at home. I've told you about it often enough."

"Yes, I know what you have told me," Taryna agreed. "But I have never quite believed it."

"Well, I promise you it's the truth, the whole truth," Kit answered. "I hate my stepmother and she hates me. Father's always too busy to worry about me, and to be really honest I loathe the idea of going back. I shan't know what to do with myself until term starts again in October. I only came to Cambridge to get away from home."

"Poor Kit," Taryna smiled sympathetically.

"It's no use being sympathetic. I've got to face it and you haven't," Kit said. "And what I have just thought of is, why shouldn't you come with me? I had a letter from my stepmother only two days ago saying that she was very busy and it would be a good idea if I got a nice friend to come and stay with me. Do you see?"

8

"I don't know that your stepmother would consider me nice," Taryna said. "But if you are inviting me to stay, Kit, thank you, but I've got to get a job."

"But that is your job, don't you understand? I'll pay you to come with me. Oh, please, Taryna, don't be stuffy about this. I mean it. It will not only be a job for you, but it will be the salvation of me."

"Don't be silly, Kit. Find yourself a nice friend and ask her to stay."

"But I haven't got any friends except you, you know that. You're the only person I'm really fond of here."

"But it doesn't have to be a friend from Cambridge," Taryna said. "What about all those people you know in London?"

"They are all my stepmother's friends, and most of the girls are stuck-up idiots. I hate them all. If you want to know the truth I felt they were looking down on me."

"Kit, that's stupid!"

"It's true," Kit said with a sudden passion. "Do you suppose I'm so half-witted that I don't know what they think of us—jumped-up rich people. Oh, I know father can buy himself anything he wants—houses, yachts, cars, aeroplanes. But money doesn't buy you a place in Society—not in real Society at any rate. And if my stepmother's thick-skinned, I'm not. I heard what people were saying, I saw the way they looked at me, I know what they felt."

"Oh, Kit, you mustn't talk like this. I'm sure it isn't true. You're so pretty, so gay, you . . . you have everything."

"Everything!" Kit cried. "You talk about everything; you who have got a family who loves you and cares what you do and wants to have you with them. Me, I've got nothing but money! Money Money! And that's a cold thing to love and kiss I can tell you."

9

There was a sudden break in Kit's voice; and watching her, the tears came into Taryna's big dark eyes.

"I hate you to be miserable, Kit," she said sympathetically. "You know I'd help if I could."

"You can help me if you want to," Kit answered. "Come back to that hell I call my home! Come and see what I have to suffer! Come and help me to be brave when my stepmother sneers at me and the servants are cheeky and there's nothing to do but to try and climb into the society of people who don't want you."

"But, Kit . . ." Taryna said.

"Don't say 'but'; don't give me your sympathy; do something, if you really care for me."

"I do care, you know that," Taryna said.

Kit gave an impatient little stamp of her foot and put her handkerchief to her eyes.

"A fine way you've got of showing it," she said. "You'd rather go off and work in a café than help me."

"What exactly do you want me to do?" Taryna said.

"I want you to come home with me. I'll pay you whatever you like—ten pounds, twenty pounds a week—so long as you'll come."

"But I couldn't take your money," Taryna exclaimed.

"Why not?" Kit asked tensely. "You'll take other people's. Is my money tainted or something that you won't touch it?"

"Oh, Kit, Kit. Don't talk to me like that."

"I'm sorry, Taryna, but money has always prevented me from having anything I've wanted in life, and now it's preventing my having you."

Kit suddenly burst into tears. They ran down her cheeks, welling out of her big eyes in a kind of flood.

"Oh, don't, don't," Taryna begged. "Stop crying, Kit.

I'll do anything you like if only you won't cry like that. I can't bear it."

The tears were checked and then in a voice that was broken a little, Kit said:

"You promise? You promise you'll come with me?"

"I'll try . . . no, I promise," Taryna said quickly, as it seemed that Kit would start sobbing again.

It was as if the sun came through the cloud. Almost instantaneously there was a smile on Kit's red lips and a sudden twinkle in her eyes although her lashes were still wet. She blew her small, tip-tilted nose with a decisive gesture.

"You promised," she said triumphantly.

"Yes, I know," Taryna answered ruefully. "I'll come and stay with you, but I won't take your money."

"You will take it," Kit exclaimed. "Otherwise I shall spend it all on buying you a diamond brooch or something equally useless that you don't want."

"Very well," Taryna agreed resignedly. "You shall pay me five pounds a week and I shall stay with you for three weeks. After that I shall look for a job."

"I shan't let you," Kit said. "And once you see all you have to do, you'll understand that you can't get away."

"Well, we'll see," Taryna replied. "But, mind you, I don't really want your money."

"You don't want it, but your father and mother do, and Donald and Edwina—don't deny that."

"No, I can't deny it," Taryna said. "All right, Kit, you win. But I don't suppose your stepmother will be pleased to see me."

"Wait a minute, I have an idea!" Kit exclaimed. "An absolutely marvellous idea. I'm going to tell my stepmother that you're somebody of great importance, somebody she'd like me to know. Now, Taryna, don't look so disapproving. I know Irene and you don't. She's the biggest snob who ever stepped."

"In which case," Taryna smiled, "she's not going to be very impressed with the daughter of a struggling vicar."

"She won't know he's a struggling vicar unless you tell her so," Kit answered. "After all. Grazebrook is a very nice name."

Taryna's chin went up in a little unconscious gesture.

"It's a family which has contributed quite a lot to the history of England at one time or another."

"Well, there you are," Kit said triumphantly. "We'll tell her that and we'll tell her about your grandmother, the one you're named after. The Countess Taryna . . . What was her name?"

"Pavtoysky," Taryna replied. "But that's not going to impress her very much. White Russians were two a penny after the revolution. My grandmother came over here and tried to get a job as a housemaid, which was how my grandfather met her."

"Oh, keep those skeletons in the cupboard, please," Kit said laughingly. "We'll tell Irene that your grandmother was a White Russian and a close personal friend of the Tzar."

"Her father was A.D.C. to the Emperor," Taryna corrected.

"Better and better," Kit approved.

"But even that is not going to make me into a Society girl," Taryna said.

"Oh yes it is," Kit corrected. "I am going to tell her that you're very rich; that your family live in Canada—that will at any rate prevent our having to produce them—and that you've come to Cambridge just to fill in the time before you start spending your millions of dollars."

12

"Oh, how ridiculous you are!" Taryna laughed. "As if anyone would believe that."

"Why shouldn't they?" Kit asked. "And Irene is awfully stupid."

"Even she is not stupid enough to think I am rich when she sees my clothes," Taryna mocked.

Kit put her fingers to her mouth.

"I never thought of that. How stupid of me! It's quite true; Irene and that stuck-up lady's maid of hers will be snooping round the labels on your suits almost as soon as you get into the house."

"Well, there you are," said Taryna. "Tell the truth and shame the devil, as the old woman used to say who cleaned out my father's church."

"No, wait! I've got another idea," Kit said. "I shall tell Irene that you were sailing for Canada, your luggage had gone ahead, and just as you were getting on the train to go to Liverpool I stopped you and made you come home with me."

"And how is that going to help?" Taryna asked sarcastically. "The suit I'm wearing cost exactly five-pounds-ten three years ago. Even your stepmother is not going to believe it's Hardy Amies."

"The suit that you're wearing is going to come from Hardy Amies," Kit replied, "because I bought it there myself."

"Now, Kit . . ." Taryna began. Kit drowned her words.

"Don't you see that, if your clothes have gone on to Canada, you must wear mine. We're the same size exactly, and actually I've got a lot of new things that Irene has never seen, so we can pack one suitcase for you at any rate—the sort of things you would take with you for one night. Oh, Taryna! It's all so easy. I've thought it all out and it's no use making objections."

"Well, I have every intention of making objections,"

13

Taryna cried. "I am not going to deceive your step-mother. I am not going to lie."

"Please, please," Kit begged. "Just to please me; just to make things easier. If I go back saying I've brought a friend from Cambridge, she'll start asking questions at once. Who are you? Where do you come from? And then she'll look down her nose and sniff and be awfully snooty to you. And when she gets me alone, she'll say it's just a waste of money for me to be here if I can't make the sort of friends that she and Father would like me to have."

Kit threw out her arms.

"Taryna, save me from that. I had so much of it last holidays, it made me utterly miserable. I swore I'd never go home again. But I've nowhere else to go."

Kit's blue eyes filled with tears again, and then, as Taryna didn't speak, she went on:

"When my mother was alive, it was so different. Father was different then, too—far more approachable, far kinder. I even loved him, although I was frightened of him. Nothing mattered as long as Mummy was there."

Kit gave a deep sigh.

"And then," she went on, "when she died, every-thing changed. Father just worked and worked and got richer and richer, and I was alone day after day, week after week, with only the servants. I had nannies, governesses, tutors and games instructors, but none of them stopped me from feeling lonely or from knowing that when Mummy died the only thing that mattered had gone out of my life."

The tears ran down Kit's cheeks. Without heeding them she went on:

"It's bitter, isn't it?" You want to be with your family and yet you can't afford to be with them. I can

14

afford anything in the world, but money can't buy back my mother from wherever she is now."

Taryna moved swiftly and put her arms round Kit.

"I will come with you," she said comfortingly. "Perhaps I'm being absurd and selfish to have scruples. I'll do what you want. You must try and be happy Kit. Your mother wouldn't like to see you so miserable when there's so much happiness in the world if only you could find it."

Kit hugged Taryna and wiped her eyes.

"Now, we've got to make plans," she said practically.

Taryna looked at her half-full suitcase.

"I would much rather tell the truth," she said.

"And if you do, it will make things unbearable," Kit retorted "No, you must do as I say. You must be the daughter of a rich Canadian. Your mother can be English so that will account for your accent. Father goes to America a lot, but I've never heard of his going to Canada, so that will eliminate any possibility that he might have met your father. You've come to England because you want to get a degree. But, of course, you're not going to be a doctor, or anything like that. You're just going back to enjoy yourself."

"This is going to be an awfully difficult rôle for me to play," Taryna said.

"Oh, don't worry. Once Irene is impressed by you she won't ask too many questions. She's so selfish she only thinks about herself. If she asks anything uncomfortable, just turn it aside by asking her about her jewels or her clothes. That's about the only thing she's interested in besides Society."

"Well, I certainly know nothing about the latter."

"That won't matter, don't you see?" Kit said. "You don't know anybody in England because you have only been here two terms."

15

"And I know rather less about Canada. Where am I supposed to live when I'm out there?"

"Oh, in Montreal," Kit replied. "You know that freshman with the red hair. She comes from Montreal. Her name's McCall."

"Well, if we can't take her for local colour I don't see that helps much," Taryna smiled.

"Don't make any more objections, Taryna."

"What am I to do with my clothes?"

"Why not send them to your home as luggage in advance?" Kit suggested.

"That's the right expression," Taryna said. "I shall be following them in a very short time." There was a pause and then she said suddenly: "But your stepmother. What will she think? What is she really like?"

"I'll show you what she's like," Kit replied.

She pulled open the door and Taryna heard her running down the passage to the room of one of the other undergraduates. She sighed and then said aloud:

"Am I doing wrong? Ought I to refuse to do this?"

She felt indecisive and very hesitant to take up the rôle which Kit had designed for her. And yet, at the same time, she had loved the fair-haired girl from the moment they had first met on Cambridge Station.

Taryna had been feeling shy and nervous that eventful day in October. She had come to Cambridge having won a scholarship, but was fully conscious of what sacrifices her time there would entail from her father and mother.

She had been elated and excited at the thought of continuing her studies at Girton; and yet, when she stepped out on to Cambridge Station platform, she had felt her own insignificance and inadequacy. She was only a little girl after all, an ignorant little girl who knew nothing and would doubtless fail and return home ignominiously.

And then she had seen a pair of bright blue eyes looking into hers, a smile on a pair of very red lips, and heard a voice say:

"I see you are going to Girton. Are you a freshman too?"

Taryna's eyes travelled to the label on the suitcase of the girl who had spoken to her, and in that moment a friendship was born. They had clung to each other amongst the sea of strange faces, of strange customs, and the indifference of a busy, bustling world to two young women who knew nobody and nothing.

And then gradually Taryna had found herself beginning to love the irrepressible Kit, with her moods of wild gaiety and deep depression, with her generous impulses and fierce dislikes, and with her background of unlimited money which she loathed and despised.

Kit was a type of person whom Taryna had never in her whole life met before. And perhaps it was because they were, strangely enough, in some ways very much alike, that they became, as far as Cambridge was concerned, inseparable.

Taryna had more balance. She had, too, a deep, underlying faith which was lacking in Kit. And one thing was very obvious—they were utterly content to be in each other's company.

Kit came hurrying back into the room.

"I knew Millicent had the *Tatler*," she said. "Last week's edition has a photograph of Irene in it. Here it is. You asked me what she looked like. You can see her quite clearly."

She opened the paper and plonked it down on the table. Taryna bent forward to look. It was a flashlight snap taken at a ball. The caption read:

The beautiful Mrs. Walter Newbury at supper with Mr. Michael Tarrant.

Taryna looked closely. Mrs. Newbury was certainly

17

very good-looking and very elaborately dressed. It was a hard face, she thought, and yet perhaps she was being unfair and it was difficult to see the truth in a press photograph. Kit's stepmother obviously had good features.

The cost of her dress alone would have kept the Grazebrook family for a year, Taryna told herself, and then stifled the thought because it was envious.

She looked from Mrs. Newbury to her companion—a lean, handsome-faced young man with a square jaw and high cheek-bones. It was somehow an arresting face, and almost involuntarily Taryna asked:

"Who is Michael Tarrant?"

Kit shrugged her shoulders.

"One of Irene's hangers-on, I suppose. Ever since they first married, Irene has insisted on having what she calls 'boy-friends'. There used to be rows about it at first, then Father gave up caring. I don't think he cares about anything now but making money. And so scroungers and spongers play the part of lounge lizards to poor, lonely, misunderstood Mrs. Newbury."

Kit gave a sharp laugh that had no humour in it.

"Oh, she gets lots of sympathy, I assure you. The sympathy flows very smoothly when its engendered by Father's best champagne and his biggest cigars."

"Don't, Kit! Don't!"

Taryna spoke sharply. Kit turned to look at her wide-eyed.

"What's the matter?"

"I hate the way you're talking," Taryna said. "It spoils you. All that bitterness; it's eating into you. It's like poison. Stop it, Kit. You are not to think such things."

"But they are true," Kit insisted.

"How do you know? This man, for instance. He doesn't look like that. Look at his face."

18

"I don't want to look at it," Kit replied petulantly. "If he's out with Irene, I know exactly what he's like. You wait."

"I don't believe it," Taryna said.

She spoke in a low voice almost to herself.

"You'll find out that I am speaking the truth," Kit said. "Now come on. The car is coming for me at three o'clock. I refused to do that beastly journey again. It means changing in London and with all the luggage I've got it's quite impossible. So I told them to send the Rolls."

Taryna shut her suitcase.

"Kit, I'm frightened. Don't make me do it."

"You promised," Kit said. "You can't back out now."

"I shall have to ring Mummy and explain what I am doing," Taryna said. "They will be expecting me. I was going to stay at home for two or three nights at any rate." She gave a sigh and added: "But I daresay they won't mind. Donald's got the measles and my aunt Christine is there at the moment. Even one more mouth makes a lot of extra work."

"Send them your first week's wages," Kit said.

She put her hand in the pocket of her coat and brought out a well-stocked notecase.

"I have just cashed a cheque so as to be able to tip the porters," she said. "And I was going to pay a bill at the booksellers", but that can wait. Here's a five-pound note. It's easier to send by post."

She held it out to Taryna who put her hands behind her back.

"I can't take it from you, Kit."

"Very well then," Kit replied. "I will telephone the florist and tell them to send your mother five pounds' worth of flowers. I know she'll be thrilled."

19

She turned resolutely towards the door just as Taryna put out her hand to stop her.

"No, Kit! No! I believe you really would do it, and I just can't bear such a waste of money."

Taryna took the money from Kit, kissed her lightly on the cheek, and then went to the writing-desk. She wrote a few lines and slipped the five-pound note into an envelope and addressed it to her mother.

"And now I am going downstairs to telephone," she said.

"And I am going to pack," Kit told her. She picked her gown up off the floor and slung it over her shoulders.

"I'm really looking forward to the vac now," she said "It's going to be simply wonderful to have you there."

She went from the room as Taryna opened her bag to find some money for the telephone call. With her purse in her hand she turned towards the door, then hesitated.

The *Tatler* was still lying open on the table. Slowly, irresistibly she found herself drawn towards it. She stood looking down at the two people seated at supper—the elegant, sophisticated woman and the young man, with his lean face and deep set eyes.

"He looks intelligent," Taryna thought. Could he really be as bad as Kit had described? A scrounger; a hanger-on of rich people?

She felt suddenly sick and disgusted at the thought. With an angry little gesture she shut the *Tatler,* then carried it across the room and thrust it into the waste-paper basket.

That was the right place for it if it portrayed people who are wasters, who are no good to anyone—not even to themselves.

2

"I wish I hadn't come!"

Taryna almost said the words as the car turned off
the road through lodge-flanked gates and started the
journey towards the house which she could see in the
distance.

She had been carried away by Kit's pleading. Now
she saw how mad she had been to consent to this wild
scheme. But it was too late. Already the house was in
sight—long, low, dazzlingly white and far bigger than
Taryna had ever anticipated.

"I'm frightened," she said to Kit in a whisper, so that
the chauffeur could not overhear what she said.

"Nonsense!" Kit answered. "It's going to be fun."

The house, which was called Earlywood, was built in
Italian style, with pillars, a balcony in front of the
first-floor windows, and a low, flat roof. At the same
time it was so enormous that it inspired awe rather than
admiration. Because it was painted white and perhaps
because everything around it had been planted and
grown for effect, it made Taryna feel that she was
looking at a poster rather than at something real that
could in any circumstances be called a home.

A footman in livery ran down the steps to open the
door of the car.

"Come on," Kit said impatiently.

She jumped out and Taryna followed her. She had a
startled impression of a big, square hall where everything seemed to shine. The floor, the furniture, looking-

21

glasses, silver, brass—everything reflecting and re-reflecting until her eyes were dazzled with it.

"Is my father at home, Morris?" she heard Kit ask the butler.

"Mr. Newbury is in London, Miss Kit. Madam is down by the swimming-pool."

"Did she get my message saying Miss Grazebrook would be accompanying me?" Kit asked.

"Yes, Miss Kit. I took the message down to her myself. She said Miss Grazebrook was to have the Lilac Room, near your own."

"That will be all right," Kit said. "Come on, Taryna."

She led the way into a long room which seemed to run half the length of the house. It was beautiful, and yet there was something over-luxurious, over-expensive about it. It was not just because her eye was accustomed to simpler things, Taryna thought. It was because the brocade on the sofas was too rich, the silk curtains too thick, the cushions of such expensive embroidery that they might have been museum pieces. The rugs, the furniture and the pictures all gave the same impression.

Kit watched her looking round.

"Father says antiques are an investment," she said after a moment.

There was a bitter note in her voice which made Taryna avoid her eyes. She could not understand anyone furnishing a home simply in order that its value might increase in the years to come.

"We will walk down to the swimming-pool," Kit said reflectively, "so that Irene will see you looking so smart. And then we will change into something light and comfortable. I've got an awfully pretty cotton dress upstairs which she's never seen."

Taryna suddenly took hold of the back of a chair.

22

"Let me go, Kit," she begged. "It's been amusing to come here and rather fun planning it all. But now I've got cold feet. I want to go back to the Vicarage in Bermondsey, to see the worn stair carpet, the faded covers, the peeling paint, and to know I am home. I want to be myself. I don't feel rich or important."

"Take a look at yourself," Kit said.

She put an arm round Taryna's shoulders and drew her to one of the long Queen Anne mirrors which were set between the french windows.

Taryna looked. She saw an exquisite little face with delicate features and a pointed chin. That was herself all right, but the rest obviously belonged to someone else. The smart little red hat trimmed with soft feathers set so jauntily on her dark hair screamed Bond Street in every line. The suit of red featherweight tweed—with a blouse, gloves and bag to tone with its brown velvet buttons—gave her a figure which might have come out of a women's magazine.

"Lawks a mercy on us, this is none of I," Taryna quoted, and Kit laughed.

"The beautiful and rich Miss Grazebrook!" she said. "Do you really believe that anyone won't accept that when they look at you?"

To be honest, Taryna couldn't say no. It was, indeed, hard to recognise herself. Kit's clothes transformed her. The shapeless suit she had worn for so long had hidden her slim hips, her tiny waist and the soft swelling curves of her young breasts. Here in the mirror she could see how clothes could alter people completely.

"Come along," Kit said. "We have got to impress Irene."

Speechless, because she felt she could not argue any more, Taryna followed her on to the terrace outside the window. There were steps which led into a garden

23

ablaze with flowers—roses in every conceivable colour, long herbaceous borders so vivid that they took one's breath away, and a fragrance as intoxicating as the sunshine itself.

"I have never seen anything so beautiful," Taryna said.

"Father had them laid out at great expense," Kit answered, and again there was that hard, metallic note in her voice.

They walked along paths which twisted between flowering shrubs and through a cunningly contrived water garden until they reached the swimming-pool.

It was bigger and bluer than any private pool Taryna had ever seen. Around it, in front of a pavilion which looked like something from Hollywood, there were Li-los on which one could lie to dry after a bathe.

A radiogram was playing soft music. There was the tinkle of ice in long drinks which a man was bringing from the pavilion towards a woman lying in the sun.

"Hi, Irene!"

Kit's voice rang out and the woman looked up. She was beautiful, there was no mistaking that. Very fair with vividly blue eyes, she wore an almost classically cut bathing-dress of white satin laced with blue ribbons.

Languidly she sat up. Her lips were vividly pink against her pale face; her toe-nails were painted the same colour.

"So you are back," she said in a voice which was curiously at variance with her beauty. It was an ugly voice and yet the slight drawl with which she enunciated her words had a somewhat unpleasant attraction about it.

"She is like a beautiful cat," Taryna thought suddenly as she followed Kit round the pool.

24

"Yes, here we are," Kit said. "And this is my friend, Taryna Grazebrook."

Irene held out her hand. Despite the sunshine the fingers were cold.

"I am so glad you could come and stay with Kit," Irene said graciously. "I got her message to say that you were really returning to Canada but that she had persuaded you to pay us a visit."

"It is very kind of you to have me," Taryna said a little shyly.

"The more, the merrier! That's the motto in this house," a voice said from behind.

Taryna started. She had forgotten the man she had just glimpsed carrying the drinks. Now she looked at him and almost uttered an exclamation.

He was so like the photograph in the *Tatler* and yet, at the same time, so much better looking. His skin was of a golden brown. It looked at if he must have spent hours and hours lying in the sunshine. His eyes were dark and had a twinkle in them, and his mouth was very firm above a square chin.

"He's nice," Taryna thought instinctively, and then remembered what Kit had told her and felt a sudden distrust that was almost disgust sweep over her.

"Your drink," Michael Tarrant said, setting it down in front of Irene almost ceremoniously. "Do you girls want anything?"

"Of course," Kit replied. "I want a really well-shaken cocktail and so does Taryna. But first we are going to change."

"Kit tells me that your father is very important in Canada," Irene said.

Taryna felt herself blush.

"I don't know what to say to that," she answered.

"But of course he is," Kit said. "Taryna's so modest about him. But when you're not all listening I promise

25

you we indulge in the old childish game of 'my father's richer than yours' and Taryna always wins. It isn't fair."

"You'll have to tell Walter to pull up his socks," Irene drawled. "A little competition might do him good."

"What part of Canada do you come from?" Michael Tarrant asked.

"You're not allowed to ask questions until you've been introduced," Kit told him. "May I present Mr. Tarrant—Miss Grazebrook. Taryna—Michael."

"How do you do?" Michael said in an amused voice, holding out his hand.

Taryna took it. There was something about the touch of him that was warm and comforting. Despite herself she found some of her fear evaporating. All the same, her heart was beating quickly as Irene asked her yet another question.

"Were you sailing on the *Empress of Britain*?"

"Of course she was, in the royal suite," Kit answered for her. "That's why her luggage has all gone to Liverpool. But it doesn't matter. She's the same size as I am and we often exchange our clothes."

"If they are in the mess that yours usually are when you come back from Cambridge, I'm sorry for Miss Grazebrook," Irene said crushingly.

"Well, I'm going to find her something cool to wear now," Kit replied. "Mind that cocktail is ready for us when we return."

"I won't forget," Michael Tarrant answered.

Taryna turned away quickly. She had the feeling that he was trying to be nice, but she didn't want to respond to it. And yet, as she walked round the swimming-pool again, she was, without looking back, vividly conscious that his eyes were following her.

What was he thinking? she wondered. Was he speculating as to how rich she was? Or perhaps being afraid she was another sponger come to chisel in on his pitch?

She felt her lip curl in sudden disdain. How she hated men like that! She thought of how hard her father worked, of his too thin frame and lined face after a long week in the parish. She thought of the calls on him day and night, the times when he must turn out in the rain or snow to go to someone who was dying. He couldn't afford a car. He would often have to trudge miles if it was too late for the buses to be running.

For a moment she didn't see the flower-filled garden or hear the birds singing in the bushes. Instead she could hear her mother saying: "I'm sorry, darling. You'll just have to make those shoes do for another few months. I simply can't spare the money for any more." Shoes that let the water in, shoes that, when she sat down, she tucked under the chair for fear that someone should see their cracks.

What did people like these know of life where the necessity of buying new shoes meant going without necessities so as to save up for them carefully, penny by penny?

They reached the house and Taryna shook herself free of her thoughts.

"Come and see my room," Kit said. "It's really rather pretty."

They raced up the stairs. Kit's bedroom was exquisite. All shades of pink, with a small four-poster bed covered in eau-de-nil satin.

"Oh, Kit! Let's tell the truth," Taryna begged. "I know I'm going to be caught out. I didn't like the look on Mr. Tarrant's face when he asked what part of Canada I came from."

"Don't worry about him," Kit replied. "He's just like all the other tame cats Irene has. There's Billy; he's completely half-witted and wouldn't know where

27

Canada is on the map if you asked him quickly. Eric's very nearly as bad, except he has travelled a bit when he was in the Army. And, of course, he manages to get himself invited to Nassau every year. There's always someone ready to pay his fare."

"Somehow I shouldn't have thought Mr. Tarrant was like that," Taryna said.

"Call him Michael," Kit admonished. "I never attempt to remember their surnames. They're just Irene's good-time boys and as such they are only entitled to a Christian name—unless, of course, you prefer to call them all 'darling' as she does."

"Aren't you being a bit unfair?" Taryna asked. "Your stepmother seemed quite nice."

"Nice!" Kit gave a little laugh which had no humour in it. "You don't know her yet. Oh, she'll be nice enough to you as long as she thinks you're important. I sent her a long and very complicated message over the telephone; but Miss Bailey, she's one of the secretaries, took it down in shorthand, so I knew she'd get it word for word."

"I wish you hadn't," Taryna said.

"It's done," Kit said triumphantly. "Now let's see what you're going to wear."

.   .   .   .   .

A quarter of an hour later they walked back to the swimming-pool. Taryna was wearing a dress of coral-coloured tussore with an enormously wide skirt flaring out over a number of petticoats. It made her waist look very small and showed up the white unsuntanned beauty of her neck and arms.

Kit was in blue. A dress which became her fairness far better than the coral could ever have done.

"I love bright colours, that's why I buy them," she

said. "But I know really I ought to stick to blues and greens though they always seem somehow insipid."

"Not for you," Taryna smiled. "They do something to your eyes. But all the same, I'm glad you bought this flame-coloured dress." She touched it with appreciative fingers. "It's one of the prettiest dresses I've ever seen."

"You ought always to wear that colour," Kit said.

"I know," Taryna answered. "But it's not very serviceable."

She almost regretted the words as soon as she had spoken them. They somehow jarred, reminding her all too vividly of the dress she ought to be wearing, ornamented with a plastic apron while she helped her mother prepare the meals.

They had arrived at the swimming-pool and Kit's young voice went echoing across the water.

"Here we are, and where's my cocktail?"

Their arrival obviously interrupted the two people sitting beside the pool. Michael's face had been very close to Irene's. It seemed to Taryna that they both started a little and drew quickly away from each other. Yet, with scarcely a pause, Michael Tarrant jumped to his feet.

"It's on the ice," he called. "I've mixed you something scintillating, seductive and inspiring."

"It had better be good after that," Kit said gaily.

"It is," Michael answered.

"Michael shakes a better cocktail than anyone else I've ever known," Irene said, and managed to make the remark sound possessively intimate.

"She's in love with him," Taryna thought, watching her.

There was no doubt at all that Irene was watching Michael as he went into the pavilion and she followed him with her eyes as he came back.

"She's beautiful," Taryna thought, and yet knew on

29

closer scrutiny that the adjective did not really describe Irene. She was not exactly beautiful, but she did give an impression of it. Yet there was something commonplace about her face; something, too, that was lacking.

It was difficult to know what it was because it was hard to remember anything save that the effect of her was breathtaking. Everything was so elegant, from the very last hair on her head to the very smallest nail on her hand. Everything was groomed and polished and curled and trimmed until the finished product was almost perfection.

"Now try this."

Michael was standing at Taryna's shoulder and she looked up at him. For a moment she met his eyes. She had a very queer sensation as if looking into her face he was seeking something. She was not certain what it was, but she was afraid. Her eyes fell before his.

"Mmm! This is good," Kit exclaimed. "What is it?"

"Passion fruit, gin and a secret ingredient of my own," Michael answered. "I shan't tell you what it is because I'm thinking of patenting it. I shall call it 'Michael's Kiss,' or something equally nauseating, which will undoubtedly make it sell!"

"It might really be a success," Irene said.

"If you would launch it for me it would undoubtedly sweep the world," Michael answered.

She gave him a look from under her dark lashes which said all too clearly that she was quite willing to do her part in helping him. And then before he could reply Kit said in an unnaturally sharp voice:

"Where's Father? Why isn't he home?"

"I expect he's busy," Irene drawled. "After all, making money takes up quite a lot of one's time."

"So it appears," Kit answered.

She gave Michael almost a venomous look as she spoke and then got to her feet.

"Come on, Taryna. I want to show you the rest of the garden."

She walked off leaving Taryna to follow her. It was quite obvious that Kit was being rude; but Taryna did not miss the tiny, almost imperceptible shrug of Irene's shoulders or the way her eyebrows went up as if to imply that such uncouthness was something which must be expected.

They were hardly out of earshot before Taryna said: "Why did you do it?"

"Do what?" Kit asked.

"Speak like that. It sounded awful."

"I meant it to," Kit retorted sullenly. "Do you suppose I'm such a fool that I can't see what they are up to? Irene's in love with Michael. She's prepared to pour out Father's money and he's prepared to take it. It makes me sick."

"I think she's just got under your skin." Taryna said. "You oughtn't to let yourself mind about this, Kit. It will spoil you. Forget about your stepmother. Accept her as just another person and don't let anything she says or does hurt you."

"But it does hurt me, don't you understand? It does and I can't help it," Kit replied stamping her foot.

Taryna slipped her arm through Kit's and gave it a little sympathetic squeeze.

"I'm so glad you came here with me," Kit went on. "Can't you understand that everything is going to be much better because you're here? It's when I have to bear it alone, when I have no-one to talk to, I can't stand it."

"But you have your . . ." Taryna began, only to have the last word taken out of her mouth by a cry from Kit.

"Father!" she called, and ran from Taryna's side across the garden.

31

A man was coming down the steps from the house. He was dressed in a dark suit as if he had just come from the office. He was small, rather stout and grey headed, and Taryna felt a sudden pang of disappointment.

She had somehow expected Kit's father to be good-looking, someone who would be a pair to the exquisite Irene. This man was middle-aged and ugly. What was more, as she drew nearer she had the almost instantaneous feeling that she did not like him. Why, she could not think.

"Father, this is Taryna," Kit was saying.

A heavy hand was held out towards Taryna.

"I am very glad to welcome any friend of my daughter's," Mr. Newbury said.

There was something in his voice, a faint intonation, very faint and yet quite obviously there, which told Taryna he was not English.

"It is so kind of you to have me," Taryna said quickly, trying to smile, forcing herself to be friendly against some invisible barrier which seemed to stand between her and the man facing her.

His eyes rested on her face. They were cold, dark and shrewd. She had a feeling that he was trying to look into her, to see more than appeared on the surface.

"Kit tells us very little about Cambridge," he said. "Now you will be able to inform us how she is doing and what she is doing in the scholastic world."

"I think she is working quite hard," Taryna said quickly.

Kit gave a little cry of laughter.

"Don't you believe her. I'm doing nothing of the sort, but I am enjoying myself. I'd much rather be at Girton than having to trail round London as Irene wanted me to do. I loathe débutante balls, and I hate the young men who attend them even more."

Mr. Newbury smiled and looked at Taryna.

"Does she take after me in that she likes work?" he asked. "Or is she just running away from a world which she feels unsympathetic?"

He left the question in mid air and turned towards the swimming-pool.

"I am going to find Irene," he said.

"She's by the pool . . . with Michael," Kit said.

There was just a little pause before she accented the name. Her father looked at her with a faint smile.

"That was what I expected," he said, and walked away.

Taryna watched him go for a moment and then turned towards Kit who was looking after her father. There was an emptiness in her expression, a sudden wistful drooping of her lips as if she had been disappointed.

"He has failed her," Taryna thought suddenly, and felt a wave of compassion towards her friend. For the first time she began to understand that Kit's complaints had not been without foundation. She began to see that the situation was far more complicated than she had imagined. "She wants to be loved," Taryna thought, "and no-one, not even her father, loves her very much."

Impulsively she put her arm round Kit's shoulders.

"Come and show me more of the house," she said. "I'm full of curiosity."

Kit brightened up immediately. It was as if she wanted to persuade herself, as well as Taryna, that the house was worth seeing, that her possessions really were worth while.

They looked at the drawing-room, the library stacked with books all beautifully bound in ornate and tooled leather, but which Taryna felt had never been read. They looked at the great ballroom which Kit said

33

Mr. Newbury had built only five years ago to please Irene. It was decorated in gold and yellow and the chandeliers hanging from the ceiling had been copied from those at Versailles.

They looked at the dining-room, which had been brought just as it was from one of the wonderful *Schlosses* in Austria belonging to the Emperor Franz Joseph. They inspected, too, the music-room, the card-room, the map-room and several little ante-rooms which opened out of them or led from one part of the house to another.

"These are the secretaries' rooms," Kit said as they came down the passage from the billiard-room.

"How many secretaries does your father keep?" Taryna asked.

"Three here," a voice said from behind them. "But a great many more in London."

Both girls started.

"Oh, it's you, Mr. Corea!" Kit exclaimed, as a thin, white-faced little man with glasses came from a room on the further side of the passage.

"I didn't know you were back, Miss Kit," he said. "Has Cambridge come down for the Long Vacation?"

"Yes, today," Kit answered. "And you knew that quite well because you always know everything."

"I am flattered," Mr. Corea replied, bowing with an irony which was inescapable.

"This is my friend, Miss Grazebrook," Kit said. "But don't pretend you didn't know she was coming, because I'm quite sure Miss Bailey showed you my message before she had it taken to my stepmother."

"How do you do, Miss Grazebrook?" Mr. Corea said. "Miss Kit and I are, you will have gathered, old enemies."

He bowed and disappeared as quickly as he had

34

come, closing the door of the room he had entered almost silently behind him.

"Brr!"

Kit gave herself a little shake.

"That's Father's chief secretary. Now you see what he's like. The slimy toad!"

"Hush!" Taryna said, afraid that he would hear. But Kit only shrugged her shoulders.

"He knows what I think about him," she retorted. "And if he didn't, his spies would tell him. He has his ear to every keyhole in the house. There's nothing goes on that he doesn't know. When I was a child and I was naughty, he always told Father before my governess had time to do so. He knew, you see. He always knows."

She walked quickly down the passage and Taryna followed her.

"Let's get away from here," she said. "If I'd known I was going to meet Corea, I wouldn't have come."

"You hate too many people," Taryna admonished.

"So would you if you lived in this house for long," Kit replied.

For once Taryna felt that she was not exaggerating and it was almost in silence that she followed Kit upstairs.

She walked through one of the bedroom windows and on to the balcony. There was a magnificent view which stretched away as far as the eye could see. Green trees and the glitter of water here and there, tiny villages, and far, far away in the distance the sudden shimmer of what might be the sea.

Taryna drew a deep breath. Beauty always moved her wherever she found it. Sometimes she thought it was her Russian blood which made her respond to every mood, to every facet of beauty in whatever guise it came to her.

Then she looked from the view down into the garden below. Mr. Newbury was walking back from the swimming-pool, his arm linked with Irene's. Behind them, carrying some magazines, was Michael Tarrant.

"Look at the lackey in attendance," Kit said in a jeering voice.

"That was what he looked like," Taryna thought. And yet, at the same time, she resented that he should put himself in such a position. Of all the people she had met so far at Earlywood, he was the only one whom she could believe was capable of better things.

"A lackey!" Kit repeated.

She turned from the balcony and they went back into the room.

"Now they have come away, shall we go down to the swimming-pool?" she asked.

"It will be rather fun," Taryna answered cautiously.

"Come on then," Kit cried.

They ran along the passages to their rooms. Kit tossed Taryna a bathing-dress. It only took her a few minutes to undress and put it on. It fitted her slim body tightly and there was a white cap to pull over her dark hair.

"It's easier to change in the house," Kit shouted from her bedroom. "You'll find a bathing-wrap in one of the cupboards."

A few seconds later they sped across the garden. The pool was cool and quiet. Taryna climbed up on the diving-board; the water below shimmered iridescently in the evening sun. She knew it would be warm and yet she paused a moment before she committed her body to it, longing for it and yet half dreading that moment when she must disappear beneath the shining surface into the blue depths below.

Then with a little quick intake of her breath she dived. Down, down she went, feeling at that moment as

36

if she could go on for ever, as if everything was left behind, as if she set off on a new adventure. And then she came to the surface.

The sun glittered against her wet eyelashes. She shook her head to clear her vision, and then, to her astonishment, found herself looking straight into the face of Michael Tarrant. He was in the water beside her, his face and shoulders incredibly brown, his eyes twinkling as he saw her astonishment.

"I, too, wanted another swim," he said simply.

"We wanted to have the pool to ourselves," Kit shouted rudely from the far end.

"You must try not to be selfish," he retorted.

"I like that from you!" Kit spluttered.

Michael turned to Taryna.

"Am I really intruding?" he asked.

She had a feeling that his question was entirely sincere and because it embarrassed her she didn't know what to say. She felt herself begin to blush, her eyes flickered before his. He had a disconcerting way of looking right into one, she thought, almost as if he wanted to know what you were thinking.

She realised that he was waiting for the answer to his question.

"No ... of course you're not," she stammered, and swam quickly away from him towards Kit as if she were in need of protection.

Michael climbed out of the water then dived in again in a manner which brought a gasp of admiration even from Kit's lips.

"Where did you learn to do that?" she asked.

"In my travels," he retorted.

"But you're good, terribly good."

"I'm flattered you should say so."

"Will you teach me?" Kit asked.

"Of course," he answered.

37

He showed her several times, but she was clumsy beside him. His thin body had a wiry grace which made it appear as if he was flying through the air.

"It takes a lot of practice," he said. "And this pool isn't really deep enough. One wants a tropical sea."

"So that's where you learned to dive like that," Kit said. "The West Indies?"

"I'm not telling you," he answered. "You're far too curious." He looked across the pool at Taryna. "Don't you want to try it too?"

"I'm not good enough," Taryna replied. "I haven't had much chance of swimming."

"Let me show you a few simple dives," he suggested, but Taryna shook her head.

She did not know why, but she was suddenly shy of him. She did not wish him to touch her as he had touched Kit, to place her hands together, to stand beside her on the narrow diving-board so that their bodies were touching.

"Once more," Michael said to Kit, "and then we must go in. We mustn't be late for dinner."

As if the shadow of Irene suddenly descended upon them, Kit said quickly:

"No, I won't do it any more."

She pulled off her bathing cap, shaking her head to free her hair. Taryna ran to get the wraps which they had put down at the far end of the pool. She swung hers over her shoulders, holding the other out for Kit.

"I'll race you back to the house," Kit said, slipping on the loose towelling slippers she had worn to cross the garden.

She started off before Taryna was ready. The back of one of her slippers had got folded in and she had to stoop and adjust it before it would have been possible for her to run. As she stood there, Michael swam across the bath and putting his hands on the marble surround pulled himself a little out of the water.

"Taryna!" he said.

She turned to look at him, surprised to find his face just below her, only a foot or so away.

"Yes?" she answered.

"Let me teach you tomorrow," he said. "I'd like to."

"Perhaps," she answered. "But I don't think I'm good enough to do these complicated dives. I might hurt myself."

"I wouldn't let you."

There was something in the way he said it which made her look at him enquiringly.

"I'll look after you," he said softly. "That is one thing of which you can be quite certain."

Her eyes met his, something passed between them, something so strong and electric that she felt her heart give a sudden leap.

For a moment it seemed almost as if he held her captive, and then suddenly Taryna began to run—running faster than she had ever run in her life before.

3

Taryna awoke and lay watching the sun seeping through the curtains to make a golden pool of light on the pale carpet.

"What is wrong with the atmosphere here?" she wondered.

She had asked herself the same question at dinner last night. There had been three outside guests and it ought to have been a gay and enjoyable meal, and yet somehow there was an undercurrent of discomfort and she could not explain.

Was it Mr. Newbury, sitting stolid at the end of the table, who cast an atmosphere of restraint over the party? No-one could have accused Irene of not contributing her best. Wearing a gown of pale-blue satin which seemed to scream "Paris" with every movement she made, she was certainly breathtaking when she came into the drawing-room before dinner. Aquamarines and diamonds glistened at her neck and on her wrists, and she carried a stole of white mink just in case the evening grew chilly.

Taryna frankly stared at her. She had never seen anyone at close quarters before who wore such lovely clothes or such gorgeous jewellery. She had felt rather over-powering herself until Irene came into the room.

Kit had dressed her in a gown of vivid green chiffon and had insisted that she wore round her neck a tiny necklace of diamonds.

40

"I shall look as if I am going to a ball," Taryna had protested.

"Wait until you have seen Irene," Kit had answered, and Taryna realised that one could never feel too dressed up when Mrs. Newbury was around.

The guests—three business men—paid Irene rather heavy and ponderous compliments, but Taryna could not help noticing that it was to Michael that Irene turned as if for approval.

"Do you like my new dress, Michael?" she asked deliberately, and with a little inflection of her voice which seemed to say, for all to hear, that it was his opinion that really mattered.

"I like all your dresses," he answered. "Or should I say that Pierre Balmain's taste is admirable?"

Irene pouted.

"You never give me credit for anything," she said.

"Don't I?" he asked.

She looked at him and a look passed between them which suddenly made Taryna feel angry. "Must he flirt with Irene in front of her husband?" she asked herself, and then wondered if she really need worry about Mr. Newbury's feelings.

He seemed quite oblivious of anything except his conversation with one of his visitors. He had a cigar between his lips and one of his hands was thrust deep into the pocket of his dinner-jacket. "He looks like a gangster," Taryna thought, and then was ashamed of criticising Kit's father.

After dinner when the ladies had gone back to the drawing-room Kit threw herself down in a chair and said:

"Well, that was heavy weather! Not that Father's friends are ever anything but bores."

"You certainly didn't put yourself out to be nice to them," Irene said sharply.

41

"But I did," Kit replied with widened eyes. "I talked about the political situation, or rather I listened. I was instructed on the niceties of the economic crisis; and I believe we also touched on hunting and shooting."

"You know what I mean," Irene said crossly. "It's always the same. You never do pull your weight."

"Perhaps if Taryna and I had someone better to talk to than Father's bores and your A.D.C.'s we might do better," Kit said rudely.

Irene got up and walked across to the table in search of a cigarette. She found one and put it between her red lips and then she said:

"What you want is polish. A Season in London would do far more for you than messing about at Cambridge."

"I'm not taken in by that sort of talk," Kit said. "You want to meet all the mothers who are launching débutantes. You want to be in on the Season, and the only way you can get there is with my help. Well, nothing doing."

"I think you're an odious and extremely spoilt child," Irene said. She shut the cigarette-box down with a bang and walked from the room, slamming the door behind her.

Taryna looked at Kit.

"Oh, I know I'm rude," Kit said wearily. "But I hate her. She's always getting at me. Not because she cares a damn what happens to me one way or the other; she just thinks I might be a social asset to her."

"I wonder if you are being rather unkind?" Taryna asked.

"One couldn't really be unkind to Irene," Kit said. "She's got a skin like a rhinoceros."

"I don't think anyone has that really," Taryna answered. "Most people can be hurt, and pretty badly, even if they don't show it. Try being nice to her for a change."

"I won't," Kit said stubbornly. And then she laughed. "So you're trying your proselytizing on me. You're too good for me, Taryna, that's the truth. I'm bad in lots of ways, and I like being bad. Irene's just a silly snob and not worth worrying about."

"You've got to live with her," Taryna said gently. "It would be much better if you could be friends."

"How could I be friends with that stupid, dressed-up clothes-horse?" Kit answered.

Taryna gave a little sigh. She loved Kit, but she knew that when she was in one of these obstinate moods nothing would change her.

Unfortunately there was no more time to talk. The men left the dining-room and joined them, and Irene returned from wherever she had gone in her temper. Everyone was talking, so Taryna slipped through one of the french windows and on to the terrace outside.

It was growing dusk. There was a great red glow in the sky where the sun had sunk to rest. It was still possible to see the garden, the flowers folding their petals, the bats swooping low over the lawns.

"Well, what do you think of it all?" a voice asked beside her.

She looked round. Michael stood there and she had not heard him come across the terrace to her side.

"It's lovely! Absolutely lovely!" she said.

"The peace, the view or the people?"

"Perhaps all three," she answered a little lamely.

"That isn't quite the truth, is it?" Michael enquired. "And I was certain you were a truthful person."

"Why should you think that?" Taryna asked.

"Because of your eyes," he answered. "Aren't eyes supposed to be the windows of the soul?"

43

He spoke mockingly, but Taryna answered him seriously.

"I'm not certain that eyes are always as truthful as people think," she answered. "I remember a girl at school who used to tell most astounding lies, and she always looked you straight in the face."

"And yet I'm sure that I can tell your character by your eyes," Michael said. "And also by your mouth."

"My mouth!"

Taryna was surprised.

"Yes," he answered. "It's a very attractive mouth, but when you are amused it twitches just a little at the corners, and when you are frightened it tightens a little."

Taryna turned her head away from him. It was somehow embarrassing to hear him say such things in his low, deep voice.

"You must have been watching me very closely," she said lightly. "I suppose I should feel honoured."

"Tell me about yourself," he suggested. "What do you think of Montreal?"

Taryna stirred quickly.

"I think one always imagines that one's home is the most wonderful place in the world," she answered, evading the question.

"That's true," he agreed. "So long as you have a home."

"Hasn't everyone?" she enquired.

He shook his head.

"I haven't. My mother died many years ago and my father was killed in a motor accident two months ago."

"I am sorry," Taryna said simply.

"It leaves a gap, doesn't it?" Michael asked, and she knew that though his words were simple there was a pain and regret behind them. "And yet I suppose some people would say it has its compensations," he went on.

44

"Now I can do what I like, go where I like. There's no-one to care."

"Only your friends," Taryna corrected.

"Perhaps I haven't got any," he said. "Or shall we say only a few? I have been too much of a rolling stone." There was a pause for a moment and then he added: "But you are being very clever and very feminine and making me talk about myself when I wanted to talk about you."

"I'm not interested in myself," Taryna said quickly. "Tell me where you have been and what you have seen."

He shook his head, his eyes laughing at her.

"No, you don't evade me like that. Tell me what your family consists of."

"I have a father, a mother, a brother of sixteen and a sister of ten," Taryna replied.

"Is your brother at school in Canada?"

This was a difficult question, but Taryna told the truth.

"No, he is at school in England."

"How wise! There's no better education than one can find in the old country," Michael said. "And now, answer my first question. What do you think of this place?"

Somehow, almost as if he compelled her, Taryna found herself answering.

"It is very luxurious and magnificent."

"Yes?" he prompted. "Go on."

"What more do you want me to say?"

"What are your impressions? What did you think of dinner tonight, for instance?"

"Why are you questioning me like this?" Taryna asked. "I think you are trying to make me disloyal or critical of my host and hostess. I have always been

45

brought up to believe that one doesn't eat a man's salt and then insult him."

She spoke a little heatedly and Michael threw back his head and laughed.

"Well done," he cried. "And, incidentally, you have answered my question."

"What do you mean?"

"So you have noticed that things are not as smooth, as pleasant as they should be?"

"I am not saying anything," Taryna retorted. "You are trying to push me into a corner and I should have thought that you were the last person to criticise Mr. and Mrs. Newbury's hospitality."

She spoke without thinking and then realised exactly what she had implied. The words had slipped out, and impulsively she put out her hand.

"I am sorry," she said. "I didn't mean that. It sounds terribly rude and I didn't mean it."

Michael did not look particularly angry. The expression on his face was somehow appraising.

"You're no fool," he said, and turned without a word and left her.

Taryna stood on the terrace feeling her heart beating quickly. How could she have been so rude? she asked herself, and felt the blood rising in her cheeks from sheer embarrassment. And then, before she could move, Kit came running from the drawing-room to her side.

"Come and play Canasta," she said. "Irene wants you to make up a table."

There was no time for conversation, no time for more introspection. Taryna followed Kit inside and was thankful to see that she was not expected to sit next to Michael.

She avoided his eyes when they said good night, but nevertheless she had found it difficult to sleep when

46

finally she got to bed. She could not think what had come over her. It was very seldom she was rude or unkind to anyone, but that had been definitely not only rude but a blow beneath the belt, and she was ashamed of it.

When finally she fell asleep, she dreamed wild and incoherent dreams in which she was striving to reach something which remained persistently, terrifyingly out of reach.

"I must somehow try and make amends," Taryna thought now as she lay thinking of what had passed. She wondered if she should apologise, but felt that was completely impossible. Perhaps Kit was right when she said he didn't matter. And yet, somehow, Taryna, could not help feeling that he did.

The door opened and Kit barged into the room.

"Are you awake?"

"Yes, of course I am," Taryna answered. "What time is breakfast?"

"Oh, any time that you ring," Kit replied. "I thought I would come in here and have breakfast with you."

"I'd love that," Taryna smiled. "Shall I draw the curtains?"

"No, I'll do it," Kit said. "Just ring the bell by your side. We are never called. We just wait until we wake. It was one of Irene's ideas. She likes her beauty sleep."

She drew the curtains and the sunlight came flooding into the room. It turned Kit's hair to gold. She looked very young and sweet in a pale-blue satin dressing-gown trimmed with a quilted collar and cuffs.

"Shall we have breakfast in here or out on the balcony?" Kit said.

"Oh, on the balcony. That would be lovely," Taryna exclaimed.

She jumped out of bed and slipped into a dressing-gown that Kit had lent her. It was almost a replica of

47

the one Kit was wearing herself save that it was in a soft shade of pink with a collar and pocket of aquamarine blue, and there were tiny, high-heeled mules to match.

"Wasn't it a deadly evening?" Kit asked as they walked on to the balcony to wait for their breakfast to be brought up to them.

"I enjoyed it," Taryna replied.

"But you couldn't have," Kit exclaimed. "Father's business friends are always bores."

"What are we going to do today?" Taryna asked to change the subject.

"We are going to have a swim nice and early before anyone else gets there," Kit answered. "And after that we will play tennis."

She stretched her hands above her head.

"Well, I'm glad in some ways not to be going to some boring lecture. But if you weren't here, I should be longing to be back at Cambridge."

"Don't you think you're a little ungrateful? You've got so much," Taryna said quietly.

Kit looked over the balcony to the garden below. Her eyes went out farther towards the view. The horizon was obscured by the morning mist, but it was still transcendingly beautiful.

"It depends what you want," Kit said at length. "I want a real home, not something that's just been bought for me."

"Real homes are made by love, not hate," Taryna said.

"And whom am I supposed to love?" Kit asked.

Taryna made a little gesture with her hands. It was no use saying the obvious. Kit hated everyone here and there was nothing to do but to hope that gradually she could see things differently.

"There you are, you see," Kit said triumphantly, as

if she had scored a point. "Now, here's breakfast, and thank goodness for it."

Taryna was as hungry as Kit was, but she could not help enjoying, too, the silver tea-pot, polished until she could see her face in it; paper-thin china; a choice of three dishes; the golden yellow butter from a Jersey herd; and the lawn tray cloth, lace edged, with napkins to match.

She almost felt inclined to get up and shake Kit and make her see that, although she lacked love and a mother, there were still compensations in being waited on and having beauty in every shape and form around her.

Kit put down her cup.

"I'm going to put on my bathing-dress," she said. "It's nice in the swimming-pool in the early morning before a lot of other tiresome people get there."

"I won't be long," Taryna promised.

She went to the dressing-table and brushed her hair. However busy she was, she always found time to do that. It was thick and naturally wavy and dark as the proverbial raven's wing.

"You have inherited it from your Russian grand-mother," her mother had often said, and she was amazingly like the portrait which hung in her father's study.

How lonely and frightened the Countess Taryna must have been when she fled from Russia, leaving everything that was dear and familiar behind her and ar-riving in England penniless and unknown! That must have been worse than anything she or Kit had ever been called upon to endure, Taryna thought now; and then, because the face looking back at her from the looking-glass was so serious, she smiled.

"I am becoming a bore in the way that I count my blessings," she said, and laughed out loud.

She found that the bathing-dress she had worn the day before had been replaced by another. It was white and fitted her perfectly. There were red shoes to go with it, a red cap and a towelling dressing-gown that was also trimmed with red.

Carrying the cap in her hand, Taryna opened her bedroom door. As she did so a maid came out of a room on the other side of the corridor.

"I was just coming to find you, miss," she said. "Mrs. Newbury would like to speak to you."

She opened the door behind her and Taryna went in. There was a colossal bed in an alcove at the far end of it, raised on steps. Shaped like a shell, it was covered in white satin and the bedspread was of white satin fringed with gold.

The whole room was white and gold but there was too much of it. The furniture was all exquisite examples of eighteenth-century design, but in such preponderance that one was almost overwhelmed. There were white sofas and white chairs and a white carpet, which made one afraid to walk on it.

And in the centre of the huge bed Irene sat looking exactly like a pearl in an oyster. She wore a diaphanous nightgown which did nothing to conceal her figure, and her lips were very red as she lay back against the enormous cushions covered with antique lace.

"What are you and Kit doing today?" she asked.

"We were just going down to swim," Taryna answered.

"Well, I have asked some people to lunch, so you have got to be here. Will you tell Kit that? She has a maddening habit of going off in the car somewhere without telling me."

"Yes, of course I'll tell her."

Taryna tried to smile reassuringly at Irene, but the latter did not seem to notice.

"If you are going downstairs, take this message to the secretary," she said. "And tell Miss Bailey to ring up at once, otherwise we shall be thirteen."

"I'll tell her," Taryna replied.

She walked towards the bed, took the piece of paper from Irene's hand.

"It's quite hard work arranging these things," Irene said in a complaining voice. "And I never get any help from Kit. I'm a fool to go on slaving for her."

"I'm sure she's grateful, really," Taryna smiled.

Irene looked at her sharply.

"You know she's nothing of the sort. What's the point of having all that money if she doesn't make use of it in the proper way? If she's not careful, the only people she'll meet are undesirable fortune-hunters, and then there'll be a nice fuss."

Taryna felt uncomfortable.

"I'll go and give your message to Miss Bailey," she said.

"And tell her to hurry," Irene added.

"I will."

Taryna hurried from the room, thankful to get away from an argument about Kit. She ran down the front stairs trying to remember in which direction the secretaries' rooms had been when Kit had shown them to her the day before. She would have asked a footman, but as it was so early there didn't seem to be anyone about.

Then she remembered. Past the music-room, turn right and then left. Yes, there were the secretaries' rooms and the room opposite out of which Mr. Corea had come so silently and startled her.

She put her hand on the door. As she did so, she heard the sound of voices, men's voices, talking. For a moment she hesitated. If Mr. Newbury was in conference or interviewing anyone he might be annoyed if she came bursting in. It was his voice that was talking, and now another man. And then, suddenly, she heard the voice of a woman. She was saying something quite trivial, but there was a burst of laughter. Mr. Newbury spoke again and the woman replied.

Taryna stood as if turned to stone. She could hardly believe her ears. She must be dreaming. And then she heard, at the same time, the tap of the typewriter. Someone else was speaking, too, now, another man. She recognised his voice. It was the man who had sat next to her at dinner last night, and as she listened to what he was saying she knew she was not dreaming, she was not mad. She heard her own voice repeating a remark that she herself had made last night.

She stood and listened. It was somehow impossible for her to do anything else. Words and phrases came to her ears, and she knew she was listening to a repeat of exactly what had been said the night before. The conversation at dinner.

"We will leave you now."

It was Irene's voice speaking.

"And don't be long, Walter. I know what you men are like when you settle down to the port."

Those had been the words which, Taryna remembered, had taken Irene, Kit and herself from the dining-room.

There was the sound of chairs being pushed back.

"I promise you, my dear, that we shall be all anxiety to join you."

A door closed and then Mr. Newbury went on:

"Move up to this end of the table, gentlemen, Brigadier, will you have some nuts?"

"No, thank you."

There was a moment's pause and then:

"I see you are not taking any port, Michael. I wonder if you would do me a favour? Just slip down to

the garage and see if you can find some papers I left in the pocket of my car this afternoon. I would have asked one of the servants to do it, but they are rather private and I'd rather nobody saw them."

"Yes, of course."

It was Michael's voice.

"You were using the Cadillac, I think," he continued.

"That's right. And they're in the pocket at the back. I can't think how I was so silly as to forget them. They certainly shouldn't be left lying about."

"That's all right. You trust me—at least, I hope so."

There was laughter in Michael's voice. A door shut.

"That was a good excuse to get rid of him," Mr. Newbury said. *"We shall be able to talk later when my wife has retired to bed, but there's one point I wanted to make and that is . . ."*

"Miss Grazebrook! Is there anything I can do for you?"

Taryna swung round hastily. Mr. Corea, with his eyes staring at her from behind his thick glasses, had come from his room on the other side of the passage.

"I . . . I was trying to . . . find Miss Bailey." Taryna stammered, wondering how long he had been there.

"Have you a message for her?" Mr. Corea asked.

"Yes. Mrs. Newbury sent me with this."

Taryna held out the piece of paper. Mr. Corea glanced at it.

"A message for Major Davidson, I see. I will telephone immediately. Miss Baily is, I think, engaged."

"I . . . I wasn't certain in which room she worked."

"There was no reason why you should know, Miss Grazebrook, as you only arrived yesterday."

"No, no, of course not," Taryna agreed.

"That will be all right then. I will see to everything, you can be certain of that," Mr. Corea said.

Somehow Taryna felt there was a vague threat in his words, and yet the one thing she didn't want was to talk with him any further. She turned and hurried away down the corridor, and when she thought she was out of sight she started to run.

She ran through the house and into the garden. Only then did she stop for a moment as if to still the frightened beating of her heart. It seemed ridiculous, and yet it had been a shock to hear her own voice, to listen to the dinner-table conversation, and to be surprised by Mr. Corea.

What did it all mean? She paused for a moment against the roses to think it out. A tape-recorder under the table! She had heard of such things but never imagined them happening. One of the men at Cambridge had explained to her one night one of the methods used in Russia for keeping a check on the comrades who might feel a little revolutionary. They had laughed at the time and said how embarrassing it would be if all their conversations were recorded.

"Fancy thinking that every time you made love to a girl some civil servant was going to file it away for future reference."

The undergraduates had laughed.

"Where you're concerned it would be almost impossible to avoid a breach of promise case every week," someone had suggested.

They had all laughed again. It had all seemed so impossible, a kind of fantasy that happened in other countries and not in this. And yet it had happened last night, here, in Earlywood—in a house filled with ordinary people like herself.

She must have been dreaming. And yet she knew she had not. And why had Michael been sent away? If only Mr. Corea had not come out at that moment. And then suddenly Taryna shivered. She didn't want to know Mr. Newbury's secrets. She didn't want to hear what she wasn't meant to hear. It was best to keep away from it all. And yet, at the same time, she could not help feeling curious.

She had reached the swimming-pool without knowing her feet had been carrying her there.

"Come on slow-coach," Kit called. "Where have you been all this time?"

"The most extraordinary thing has happened, Kit," Taryna replied. "Your stepmother sent me with a message to Miss Bailey, and when I got there I sort of hesitated at the door and I heard . . . Oh, what do you think I heard?"

"I can't think," Kit answered. "Tell me."

"Yes, tell me, too," a voice said from the swimming-pool.

Taryna looked down, startled. Michael was in the water and she had not noticed him. She had not expected to find him there. She had only seen Kit, who was sunbathing in front of the pavilion.

Faced by the question, she stood there irresolute. In a flash she realised that she should never have said anything to Kit. After all, it was her father's secret. It would be indelicate, to say the least of it, to reveal what she had not been intended to know but had just stumbled upon by chance.

She felt the colour coming quickly into her face. She wished that she could undo the sentences she had already spoken.

"Go on," Kit said. "What did you hear?"

Taryna looked down into Michael's eyes. He was waiting with an expression she could not fathom on his sunburnt face. He was somehow alert, somehow anxious to know what she had to say.

55

Why had they got rid of him? What was to be said that he was not to hear? And why had he been trusted with papers that were too secret for the servants to handle?

Taryna felt herself shiver. There was more in this than she had imagined, and it was stupid of her to be so ready to blurt out her surprise at hearing her own voice. If she told Kit about it, she must tell her in secret, must tell her when Michael was not there.

She realised they were both waiting.

"It was nothing," she said lamely. "I took a message for Mrs. Newbury. She was afraid that we might be thirteen for lunch."

"Oh, Taryna! That wasn't what you were going to say," Kit said accusingly. "You were going to tell me something really interesting. It's only that tiresome Michael that stopped you. Go away, Michael. I can't think why I can never have the pool to myself."

"Aren't you being rather selfish?" he asked. "And besides, I'm longing to hear what Taryna heard."

"It was ... nothing," Taryna stammered. "Absolutely nothing. I took the message, at least I tried to take it to Miss Bailey, but Mr. Corea came out of his room and said that he would give it to her."

Michael turned and swam away down the pool.

"I can quite see I'm not wanted," he said, "and I'd hate to prevent the prattling of little girlish secrets."

Taryna sat down on the Li-lo beside Kit. She felt shaken and almost afraid.

"Oh, pay no attention to him," Kit said. "I hate people who tease, don't you? What were you going to tell me?"

"Nothing," Taryna said. "Really, nothing at all."

Kit got up and pulled her cap over her curls.

"You're being horribly mysterious, Taryna," she

said. "And I think Michael's to blame. Never mind, let's swim. It's going to be scorching later on."

She dived into the water at the side of the pool. Taryna sat for a moment watching her swim towards the shallow end where Michael was sitting on the edge splashing his feet in the water. Then, feeling she must make an effort, she threw aside her bathing-wrap and climbed slowly on to the diving-board.

She had reached the top when she realised that Michael had followed her. He must have swum very quickly down the pool, and yet he did not appear in the least hurried as he raised himself to stand just beside her on the diving-plank.

"Changed your mind about a lesson?" he asked.

"No," she answered almost petulantly. "And if you want to dive, go first. It makes me nervous to have someone waiting behind me."

"Very well, if that's how you want it," he said, passing her so that for a moment their bodies touched.

She felt the coldness of him against her arm and hip and then he stopped, looking down at her.

"You're a bad liar, aren't you?" he asked.

"I don't know what you mean," she answered unsteadily.

"I think you do," he replied.

He seemed to fly through the air as gracefully as a swallow in flight, and disappeared into the blue water below. After some seconds Taryna followed him, feeling that she was clumsy and inert beside such perfection of movement.

She swam across the pool slowly. She was about half way from the end when suddenly in the pavilion the telephone shrilled loudly. Kit, who was sitting at the far end of the bath, looked towards Michael who was climbing up to the diving-board again.

"Are you going to answer it?" she asked.

57

"Why should I?" he replied. "It's very unlikely to be for me."

"Oh, bother you," Kit muttered.

She got to her feet and walked through the glass doors of the pavilion. Everything she said seemed to echo across the water.

"Hello! . . . Oh, hello, Father! . . . Yes, yes, of course. We'd love it . . . Yes, I'll tell Taryna. What time do we leave? . . . About three o'clock. That will be perfect . . . Yes, Michael's here. Is he coming? . . . But of course she will . . . Oh, thank you. It sounds wonderful."

Kit put the receiver back and came running out to the pool.

"Listen, Taryna," she said. "It's too wonderful, too exciting. We are all going to Deauville tonight. We're going in the yacht. When we get there, we're to stay at the hotel—it's more comfortable."

"Deauville!" Taryna said in a dazed voice.

"Yes, isn't it exciting?"

"B . . . but I . . . I can't," Taryna said, reaching for the side of the pool and beginning to walk up the stone steps which led out of the water.

"Don't be silly," Kit answered. "Of course you're coming with us. Father wanted you to come particularly."

"Perhaps she's frightened of being sea-sick," Michael said.

Kit glanced at him scornfully over her shoulder.

"You're coming too. Irene particularly wants you. That's a surprise, isn't it?"

"I am very gratified," Michael replied in a mocking voice.

"I thought you would be," Kit said, and turned away from him. "Now, Taryna, don't be absurd. You'll love it. The yacht is wonderful, it is really."

58

"But, Kit, how can I? My clothes!"

"I know they are on the sea, but there's always mine," Kit answered. "There's really no difference between staying here and coming to Deauville."

"But I can't let you pay for me if I'm going to the hotel," Taryna protested.

"Don't be ridiculous," Kit answered and added in a louder voice: "But of course, if you want to, you can pay for yourself." She had her back to Michael. She gave Taryna a warning frown as she spoke.

"Yes, of course," Taryna managed to say. "It's very kind of your father. I . . . I've never been to Deauville."

"You'll enjoy every moment of it," Kit said.

She seemed radiant.

"Come on, let's get back to the house."

She gave Taryna a warning glance and then whispered in a voice that was vibrant with excitement:

"I've got something absolutely thrilling to tell you!"

4

Taryna said nothing until they were out of earshot of the swimming-pool, and then, even as she realised that Kit was bubbling over, she said:

"Don't you realise that to go to France I shall need a passport?"

Kit put her hands up to her face.

"Oh! I never thought of that. Haven't you got one?"

"I have as a matter of fact," Taryna answered. "I tried to get a job last summer taking out some children to Israel to join their mother. But at the last moment the people backed out. I think they thought I was too young."

"Well, if you've got a passport that's all that matters," Kit said.

"Don't be silly," Taryna replied. "You know I'm supposed to be Canadian. Mine is an ordinary British passport, and I happen to know that as a Canadian I couldn't get a British passport unless I could prove that my father had been born in this country."

Kit stood still for a moment biting her lip. Taryna watched her with a little amused smile. She knew only too well that Kit's fertile imagination was hard at work trying to churn out some reasonable explanation from what was obviously an impossible situation.

"I've got it!" Kit cried suddenly.

"I'm quite certain you haven't," Taryna answered. "But what is it?"

"We needn't worry in the slightest," Kit cried. "Mr.

Corea sees to all passports, tickets, and things like that. Neither Father nor Irene ever trouble their heads with anything so mundane. I shall tell the little man that you got your passport in a very hush-hush manner and tell him to say nothing to Irene about it because it's a secret. His lips will be sealed from that moment. He hates Irene."

"He's not likely to believe that sort of nonsense," Taryna laughed.

"Oh, but he is," Kit answered. "And it isn't nonsense. Mr. Corea will think that you've got your passport by some underground method such as he uses himself."

"Uses himself!" Taryna repeated. "What do you mean?"

"Well, I know that he can get passports for people by some illegal method of his own," Kit said a little defensively.

"I don't believe it," Taryna challenged.

"But it's true," Kit asserted. "One day Father was talking to him in the library and they didn't know I was there. They were discussing a Czech friend of Father's who was in trouble of some sort. And Father said to Mr. Corea: 'Get him a passport at once, and mind it's better than the last one you produced.'

" 'I was sorry about that, but the man who usually does them was ill.' Mr. Corea told him.

" 'I don't want excuses,' Father bellowed. 'All I ask for is efficiency. Get me that passport, and mind it's foolproof.' "

Taryna looked at her friend with startled eyes.

"Do you think Mr. Corea arranges for passports to be forged?"

"I'm sure of it," Kit answered. "But don't look so innocent, Taryna. You know it was done for all sorts of people in the war, and we forged the French and

61

German ones for our spies. I was reading a book about it only a few weeks ago; all about one of those women agents who were dropped over German-occupied France. You don't suppose her passport was anything but forged?"

"No, of course not," Taryna said hesitantly. "But I wouldn't like anyone to think that I am a woman agent."

"They won't," Kit promised. "I've got the whole story now at my finger-tips. Your father didn't want you to come to England. He made an awful fuss and threatened to take your passport away; and so by some clever means of your own, which we needn't go into, you managed to get a British passport just in case your Canadian one was confiscated."

"He won't believe it," Taryna said flatly.

"He will, it's a jolly good story," Kit contradicted. "Besides, being a twister himself he'll expect other people to be the same. You know, on the theory of 'set a thief to catch a thief.' "

"I think it's rather terrifying," Taryna said. "And somehow I don't want to be embroiled in things like that."

"But you're not," Kit pointed out. "If the worst comes to the worst, we can always tell the truth. It will infuriate Irene to think she's been taken in, but nobody else will care a hoot."

Taryna had a sudden vision of Michael looking down at her and saying that she had honest eyes. Then deliberately she thrust the thought away from her.

"Well, in for a penny in for a pound, I suppose," she said grudgingly. "But it only goes to show that Daddy's right when he says that one lie always leads to another one. I'm beginning to wonder now what is the truth and what isn't."

"The truth is that you're coming to Deauville with

me," Kit said. "And we're going in the yacht. That's what I want to tell you about."

"The yacht!" Taryna repeated. "Is that why you're looking so happy."

"Yes, that's exactly why I'm looking so happy," Kit replied.

"It's a man," Taryna guessed. "Why haven't you told me about him?"

Kit looked over her shoulder.

"Because I was afraid," she said. "Because I felt that even you wouldn't understand. But now you're going to meet him; and when you do, you will realise why I am so excited and why I am in love."

Kit said the last words in a whisper as if they were too precious to be said aloud.

"Oh, Kit, you're not in love with someone unsuitable are you?" Taryna asked.

"It depends what you mean by unsuitable," Kit said in a hard voice. "Don't tell me you're going to be like all the others. Like Father, who only thinks about money; and Irene, who only thinks about social standards and blue blood, and all that bunk. I'm in love with a real man, and I think—only I'm not sure—that he's in love with me."

"Who is he?" Taryna asked.

They had reached the low wall which bordered the water garden. They were in sight of the house, but it was impossible for anyone to overhear what they were saying. Taryna sat down.

"Tell me all about this, Kit," she said. "I don't know why you haven't told me about it before."

"I've wanted to," Kit answered. "I very nearly blurted it out more than once, but then I was afraid. Have you ever had anything in your life so exciting that you were afraid lest anyone else might know about it and so destroy it? That's what I feel about my love for Jock."

"What is his name?" Taryna asked.

"Jock MacDonald," Kit said. "And he's the mate on my father's yacht."

"The mate!" Taryna repeated. "Kit, you'll never be allowed to marry him!"

"That is what I was afraid you'd say," Kit answered. "But if he loves me, as I think he does, then I'm going to marry him."

For the first time since she had known Kit, Taryna noticed the firmness of her chin and the way that her lips could tighten into a hard line when her will-power was aroused. She put up her hand and laid it on her friend's arm.

"I want you to be happy, Kit," she said. "That is all I want, you know that. Tell me about this man."

"It was during last holidays that I got to know him," Kit said. "We went on a cruise in the Mediterranean, visiting the Balearic Islands, Sicily, Capri, and all the places of that sort."

She made a little grimace.

"At first I was hideously bored," she went on. "Irene had Billy to amuse her, and Father seemed to be working the whole time, dictating letters, sending cablegrams—in fact we hardly saw him."

Taryna could see the picture all too clearly.

"I felt the odd one out, as I always do," Kit continued; "but then when I was lying about on the deck I began to notice the mate. He looked different from the other crew. Anyway, he was much better-looking. I got into the habit of finding excuses to talk to him. I used to slip up on to the bridge when the captain wasn't there, and Jock always seemed to be on deck after dinner when the others were sitting in the saloon. Suddenly I realised that I was in love with him."

"And he's in love with you?"

"He hasn't said so," Kit said. "But I know in my heart he is. He's always very careful to be polite, to talk to me as if I were just the boss's daughter, but underneath I am sure he loves me. I have seen it in his eyes. One can't mistake that sort of thing."

"But, Kit! If you haven't seen him since Easter . . ."

"I've written to him," Kit said, "and he's answered my letters. Rather stiff, polite replies which would tell me very little if I didn't know him. I'm going to break down that Scottish reserve and I'm going to marry him."

"It sounds rather crazy," Taryna said. "You don't know what he's really like, and you know that you will have to fight not only Irene but your father. He'll never stand for your marrying someone who is . . ."

"His servant," Kit put in. "Yes, I know. That's what Jock said when we were talking about things once. "I'm your father's servant," he said, and I knew he was warning me that that was the way my family would look at it."

"Don't be in a hurry," Taryna begged.

"Hurry!" Kit cried. "Do you think it is a hurry when I haven't seen him for nearly three months? And I was wondering how I could possibly make the excuse to go down to Southampton. No, I have not been in a hurry, but this is too wonderful. Tonight I shall be seeing him, and even if we don't sleep in the yacht when we get to Deauville, Jock will be there in the harbour."

Taryna looked over Kit's head towards the house. White and dazzling, it stood for opulence and money, and in contrast she thought of the smallness of a mate's pay.

"What will your father do if you marry without his consent?" she asked.

"Cut me off with the proverbial shilling, I suppose," Kit answered lightly. "It wouldn't worry me."

"You have never known what it is to be poor," Taryna said. "You've never had to cook and make an appetising meal out of the cheapest cuts of meat and vegetables that are tired and shop-soiled so they are a penny or so cheaper. You've never had to wonder whether you could afford to have the roof mended or whether you'll have to go without a winter coat; and a thousand and one problems like that. You wouldn't even begin to know about them."

"I could learn," Kit said stubbornly. "I'm not as stupid as all that."

"It's not a question of stupidity," Taryna said. She stared at the house again and then she said: "I don't want to marry a man who has a lot of money. I don't want riches like you have. But, Kit, I'm afraid of living in poverty all my life. I hate it. It's degrading; it pulls one down; it takes everything that is beautiful and gives in exchange nothing but disillusionment."

Kit stared at her spellbound.

"Taryna, you've never talked like this before."

"Perhaps I haven't been honest then," Taryna said. "I've heard you abusing your money, finding fault with your home; and although I don't for a moment doubt that we are a much happier family, for my father and mother love each other and we are all very close to each other, at the same time, the poverty such as we endure would destroy the love of any people who aren't saints."

She gave what was almost a sob.

"That is what my father and mother are—saints, in many ways. And yet I have known my mother rail against the Ecclesiastical Commissioners because the

66

stipend is so small. I have seen the tears in her eyes when, because she just hasn't got the money, she has had to refuse to buy me a new dress that I have wanted so very badly. I have seen the pain in her expression when my father has pushed away his plate at mealtimes because the cheap dish, which was all that we could afford, was too unappetising to be edible."

There were tears in Taryna's eyes as she finished speaking. Kit was silent, and then she said slowly:

"I hadn't thought of things like that. I just thought it would mean living in a small house, perhaps doing the cooking. And I wouldn't mind doing that for someone I loved."

"You would mind when the kitchen was dirty and you had to scrub the floor yourself," Taryna told her. "And when the gas or the electricity bill was so big that you had to keep economising week after week until you hardly dared cook anything! You would mind when the paint peeled off the walls and you couldn't afford to have them redecorated."

Her voice was scornful as she added:

"You're thinking of one of those super American kitchens where you whisk round in an elegant apron before polished stoves and built-in cupboards, and even the refuse is taken away by some super machine. You're not going to get anything like that on a mate's pay."

"Father couldn't take all my money away from me," Kit retorted. "My mother left me some."

"And how do you know that Jock McDonald will want to live on your money?" Taryna asked. "If he's a decent man, he'll refuse; he'll want to earn his own way."

Kit put her hands up to her eyes.

"Taryna, I never thought you'd fail me," she said.

"This is my whole life and now you're trying to destroy it, to spoil my happiness before it's even begun."

Taryna gave a little cry.

"I don't mean to do that, Kit, I promise you. It's only that I think you've got to face this not only with your heart but with your brain. You've got to use your common sense. You can't just rush into something."

"The only rushing I am doing," Kit said a little unsteadily, "is to the chance of seeing Jock again. Perhaps when we meet he won't care for me any more—there's always that possibility."

There was something so piteous in her face that Taryna could only try to reassure her.

"If he really loves you, he won't have forgotten," she said gently.

"He does love me; I am sure he does," Kit cried. "Oh, Taryna! I love him so much."

It was obvious that she spoke from the very depths of her heart, and out of kindness Taryna forbore to say any more.

"Let's go back to the house and dress," Kit suggested. "And we've got to put out what things we want packed."

She tried to speak gaily, but it was obvious that some of the sparkle and the excitement had gone. She was more sober, less sure of herself, and Taryna felt guilty because it was her fault that some of the thrill of anticipation had gone.

They reached the house and went up to Taryna's bedroom.

"Now give me your passport," Kit said with a slight return of her eagerness.

"It's lucky I brought it," Taryna answered. "I very nearly sent it home in my suitcase and then I thought that it might get lost on the train or something. I was so thrilled to have a passport that I kept it by me as a sort of talisman, believing that one day, by some lucky chance, I should get abroad."

"You've never been abroad before?" Kit asked.

Taryna shook her head.

"No," she answered. "That is why I wanted so much to take those children to Israel. But I suppose it was my inexperience that frightened their parents off."

She pulled a cheap leather writing-case out of a drawer.

"It's in here," she said, "with the work I ought to be doing and which I haven't looked at since I arrived."

"You won't have much time for studying at Deauville," Kit smiled.

"I shall have to make time," Taryna answered. "I daren't get behind if I'm going to get my degree."

"What are you going to be when you've got it?" Kit asked.

"A teacher, I think," Taryna answered, "if I can get a grant so that I can go to a training college when I finish at Girton."

"You'll get married long before that," Kit said positively.

Taryna shook her head.

"No," she answered. "I don't think I am the marrying kind. As I've told you, I am afraid of poverty, and I'm not likely to meet any millionaires."

She was joking, but Kit took her seriously.

"You will meet plenty with us," she said. "I can warn you that they are all poisonous."

"I suppose we all want the opposite of what we have," Taryna said.

"Yes, I suppose that's true," Kit answered. "Therefore I want love and poverty and you want riches and security."

"I want love, too," Taryna said quickly. "I suppose everyone wants it more than anything else in the world.

69

But for some of us it isn't possible to find the right person and that is why I shall have to work. A career will somehow make up for a husband—at least I hope so."

"It won't, you know," Kit said frankly. "I don't believe that anything can make up for love. That's why I am going to grasp it while I have the chance."

"But you say he hasn't asked you to marry him," Taryna said.

"He will," Kit replied confidently. She glanced across the room and saw her reflection in the mirror on the dressing-table. "He will," she repeated. "Whatever anybody says, whatever the opposition, I am not going to let him escape me now I have found him."

There was a knock at the door.

"Come in," Taryna said.

It was Kit's maid who entered.

"What are you going to take with you to Deauville, miss?" she said. "And what am I to pack for Miss Grazebrook? I shall have to get started. They say that the boxes are to be downstairs by half-past two."

"Come on quickly," Kit said.

She took Taryna by the hand and dragged her along the passage to her room. There a number of smart white suitcases lay open on the floor and Kit, running to the wardrobe, started to pull out dress after dress which she flung on the bed in two piles.

"Pack those for Miss Grazebrook and these for me," she said to the maid. "Don't forget the hats to go with them, the belts, bags and shoes. The cotton dresses nearly all have cardigans to match. You weren't here last summer, were you? Otherwise you would remember."

"No, but Rosa says she'll help me," the maid answered. "She told me there were loads of bits and pieces that I must remember to put in."

"We shall want fur wraps for evening," Kit said. "And warm coats for the daytime. You will find those in the other room. You had better pack a blue and a white one for Miss Grazebrook and a pink and a green for me."

"I shan't get them all into these suitcases," the maid replied.

"Then send for some more," Kit ordered. "There are plenty in the boxroom."

Taryna stared at the pile of clothes, feeling as if she was in a dream. Cotton dresses, silk ones, sweaters and skirts, smart woollen suits, bathing clothes and wraps—there seemed to be no end to the pile of things which Kit was allotting to her.

"Isn't it lucky we are the same size?" Kit asked suddenly. "It's funny when you think about it, because although our measurements are the same and you can even wear my shoes, we are so utterly opposite in appearance."

She put out her hand and touched Taryna's hair.

"Black and gold, that's what we are together. We will back every horse that carries those colours at the races. Now, let's go and dress and then I will take your passport down to Mr. Corea."

She gave Taryna a warning glance as she spoke, not to say anything in front of the maid. Taryna walked slowly back to her bedroom and shut the door. Picking up the passport from where she had laid it on her dressing-table, she looked at her own photograph and the description of herself.

"This is wrong," she said. "I oughtn't to be doing this."

And yet somehow it was hard to protest when she longed, as she had never longed for anything before, to go abroad with Kit.

"Deauville," She whispered the word to herself and it seemed to have a magic sound.

Somehow she couldn't regret the pretence which had brought her here, the masquerade which was making it possible for her, unless Kit was over-optimistic, to accompany the Newburys across the Channel to one of the most luxurious playgrounds of Europe.

She was still staring at the passport a few minutes later when Kit burst into the room.

"Oh, Taryna, you're not changed yet!" she said. "Here, give me the passport. That's what I am looking for. I am going to take it to Mr. Corea."

"I'd better wait until you get back to know what I am to wear," Taryna replied. "If Mr. Corea doesn't believe your story, I shall be taking the train to London."

"He'll believe it," Kit smiled.

She kissed Taryna on the cheek as she passed and then sped from the room like some busy humming-bird.

Taryna took off her bathing-wrap and started to put on the exquisite, lace-trimmed underclothes which Kit had provided for her. Then she went to the wardrobe and looked at the dresses hanging there.

There was one of white linen with a little short coatee to match trimmed with blue. It somehow seemed vaguely nautical and Taryna put it on.

She was just ready when Kit came back into the room.

"He never turned a hair," she said, shutting the door quickly behind her. "I told him your father was a very difficult man and even threatened to cut you off from your inheritance. I said on no account to tell Irene this, and he was delighted to feel he was doing her down. He even looked quite human and said: 'I make it a practice, Miss Kit, never to confide in anyone.'"

72

Kit mimicked Mr. Corea's voice and Taryna could not help laughing.

"Anyway, it's all right. And as he never bothers Father with things of that sort, no-one will know your guilty secret except little Corea himself."

"I don't like lying even to him," Taryna complained. At the same time, she could not help feeling her heart leap with excitement to know it was all right; she could go to Deauville. She could sail tonight with Kit, and for the first time in her life she could see a foreign shore.

"There's only one thing I must do," she said quickly. "And that's to let Mummy and Daddy know where I am going. Will it be all right for me to telephone?"

Kit looked horrified.

"But you can't telephone from here," she replied. "The secretaries listen in to all the conversations."

"Why should they do that?" Taryna asked.

"I don't know," Kit answered, "but they do. I have seen them doing it. Besides, Father has known about things that I have never told him which I have discussed on the telephone with my friends."

Taryna thought of the tape-recorder playing back the conversation at the dinner-table. After that it was not surprising that the secretaries were instructed to listen in to telephone conversations.

"But I must let Mummy know," she said.

"We've got time to slip down to the village before lunch," Kit told her. "I'll go and fetch a car so that nobody will ask questions. Meet me half-way down the drive in about three minutes' time."

"Shall I come with you?" Taryna asked.

"No, it's better if I go alone," Kit replied. "You don't know how nosy people can be in this house."

She was gone as she finished speaking. Taryna gave a little sigh. There seemed to be such a lot of mysteries, she thought, and wondered if there was a quite reasonable explanation to all of them.

She still could not get over hearing her own voice speaking from behind the closed door of the secretaries' office. Surely it very unusual for any man to take a record of what was said at his own dinner-table?

She tried to remember exactly who the three men were who had come to dinner. The one who had sat next to her had been Sir William someone or other. Another had been a brigadier and the third she was quite certain had the mundane name of Hopkinson.

It was no use puzzling over it, Taryna thought. She was not likely to find the answer, and really it was none of her business.

She went down the stairs, let herself out of the front door and hurrying down the steps started walking briskly down the drive. She hadn't gone far before Kit overtook her.

"Jump in," she said, opening the door of a smart two-seater American roadster.

Taryna did as she was told.

"Did you see anyone?" Kit asked.

"Nobody except one of the footmen," Taryna answered.

"That's all right," Kit said. "I was only afraid you'd run into Irene or Michael. We couldn't say we were going out to telephone and they would know there was nothing we could possibly want to buy in the village."

"I don't see why not," Taryna answered. "We could say I wanted some ribbon or a stamp, or something."

"Stamps are provided by Morris, the butler, and Irene's maid has stores of buttons and ribbons and all that sort of thing in case we should ever need them."

Taryna laughed.

"It's so ridiculous," she said, "that we can't go to the village without there being a court-martial."

Kit laughed too, but added soberly:

"That's what it really amounts to. There are always so many questions as to what I am doing and why I am doing it. It's only because everybody else hasn't got enough to do."

"That seems to be a very sensible explanation," Taryna said.

"There's the telephone box," Kit exclaimed, braking suddenly just as they got to the edge of the village.

Taryna got out.

"I tell you what I'll do," Kit said. "I'll go down the road and turn round. I'll also buy some acid drops at the village shop. I can't help feeling that's one thing they won't have in the house. It's as good an excuse as any if we're really pressed for an explanation."

"All right," Taryna answered.

She went into the telephone box and got her money ready. Then she asked the operator for the Vicarage number. She could hear the bell ringing, ringing. That was usual, she thought. The telephone was in her father's study and her mother would be in the kitchen at this time of day and it would take some time before she heard it.

At last the receiver was taken off. Her mother's voice said: "Hello!"

"Hello, Mummy!" Taryna called, only to be interrupted by the operator.

"Press button A," she called.

Taryna did as she was told.

"Mummy! It's Taryna," she cried.

"Hello, darling! I was hoping so much you would ring up. Are you enjoying yourself?"

"Yes, I am having a wonderful time," Taryna answered. "And, Mummy, what do you think? We're going to Deauville this afternoon."

"To Deauville!"

75

Mrs. Grazebrook sounded surprised.

"Yes, Mr. Newbury is taking us over in his yacht."

"Taryna, what about your clothes? I'm sure you haven't got the right things to wear for a place like that."

"It's quite all right, don't worry," Taryna said. "Kit and I are the same size and she's lending me everything I want."

"I wondered why you had sent back nearly all your clothes," Mrs. Grazebrook told her. "I couldn't imagine what you were wearing."

"Kit's got so many things. Anything extra that I require she lets me take out of her wardrobe."

Taryna felt herself blushing. It was one thing to pretend to strangers; quite another thing to pretend to her mother.

"Then that's all right," Mrs. Grazebrook said, and she sounded relieved. "I have been worrying about you and I would have sent you back that money; it was sweet of you, darling, to send it. But we seem to be terribly hard up at the moment. Donald has had to have quite a lot of special food since he's been ill, and you know how he loves fruit."

"Yes, I know, Mummy, and I'm perfectly all right and don't want anything. In fact, I hope to be able to send you something more ... I ... I've got a sort of job here."

Taryna felt she couldn't tell her mother that she was taking money from her best friend. She felt sure that her father would not let her accept it. He might be poor, but he had a tremendous amount of pride.

"How splendid! But don't worry about us," Mrs. Grazebrook said. "We shall manage. Anyway, you will want what you earn. There will be people for you to tip."

76

"That's quite all right; it's all arranged," Taryna said.

"What about your bathing dress? Won't you want that?"

Taryna had a vision of the old, cheap bathing dress she had worn for nearly five summers. It had been mended and it had lost its colour. The mere thought of having to wear it at Deauville made her shudder.

"No, it's all right, Mummy. I can borrow one of Kit's."

"Well, mind you thank them for having you and giving you such a wonderful time," Mrs. Grazebrook said. "We are so glad for your sake. Daddy was saying only last night what a wonderful opportunity it is for you to stay with people who have money and not to have to rush straight from Cambridge into a job."

"I'm enjoying every minute of it," Taryna said. "Give my love to Donald and Edwina."

"I will," her mother promised.

"Give Daddy a big kiss for me. And don't do too much, will you, Mummy?"

"I'll try not to."

There was a faint hint of amusement in Mrs. Grazebrook's voice.

"Goodbye, darling, and God bless you."

Taryna put down the receiver. She could see just a little of her face in the looking-glass which decorated the wall of the telephone box. She looked into her own eyes and felt ashamed.

If her mother could see her now wearing Kit's white linen suit. If she knew the lies she had told and the pretence she was keeping up of being somebody rich and important, she would have been miserable.

"She must never know," Taryna vowed, and then, opening the door of the telephone box, she slipped out into the sunshine.

For a moment she thought the road was empty and then she saw that a little to the right, under the shade of some trees, a car was waiting. It was an open grey car and seated at the wheel was Michael. Taryna stared at him stupidly as he got out and walked towards her.

"Shall I give you a lift home?" he asked.

"No . . . no, thank you. Kit will be picking me up in a moment."

"Yes, I saw her further down the village and wondered what she'd done with you. Then as I passed the telephone box I felt I couldn't be mistaken. Was it a very urgent message?"

Taryna felt herself stiffen. It was one thing to be embarrassed by meeting him; yet another to realise that he was frankly and quite unashamedly curious.

"I suddenly remembered something I hadn't done," she said. "And the person to whom I wanted to speak might have gone out by the time I got back to the house."

"So that was how it was," he smiled.

"Yes, that's how it was," she replied.

They were fencing, she thought, and somehow she was not afraid but rather exhilarated by the fact.

"Are you looking forward to the sea voyage?" he enquired.

"Very much."

"Are you a good sailor?"

"I . . ." Taryna realised just in time that she was going to say she didn't know. She bit back the words almost as they reached her lips and substituted: "It depends on the sea. It ought to be calm enough tonight, at any ate."

"That's just what I was thinking," Michael said. "If you'll come up on deck after dinner, I will show you the lights of old England. They can be very beautiful, as I expect you know."

78

"Yes, of course," Taryna said a little lamely.

She was not quite certain what he was talking about and with a sense of relief she saw Kit coming speeding down the village street in a cloud of dust. She drew up with a shriek of brakes.

"Sorry to have been so long," she said, and then saw Michael. "What are you doing here?"

"The same as you, I suppose," Michael answered.

"You're spying on us," Kit said, "and I won't have it. It's nothing to do with you what we do or where we go."

Taryna looked in consternation from Kit's angry face to Michael's astonished one. "He is genuinely surprised," she thought to herself, and wished that Kit had not flown at him so impulsively.

"I came down to the village to buy myself some razor blades," Michael said. "If I have inadvertently stumbled on something that I should not know, then I can only say that my actions were quite innocent and it was not my intention to offend in any way."

"Well, we came for some acid drops," Kit suggested. "And if you don't believe me, they are here beside me on the seat."

"But I do believe you," Michael said blandly. "Why shouldn't I?"

Taryna got into Kit's car.

"Don't say any more," she whispered beneath her breath.

Kit slammed in the gear and drove off without looking at Michael again.

"It's always the same," she said furiously. "Irene makes her young men spy on me just for the pleasure of making me realise I am only a child who should ask before I do anything or go anywhere."

"I'm sure you are wrong this time," Taryna said.

"You don't understand," Kit retorted. "If you stay

with us long enough you'll see what I mean about Irene. I hate her, and I hate Michael as well."

Taryna was silent. She was feeling that she ought to be able to echo those sentiments; she ought to be able to say that she, too, hated Michael and that she was afraid of him. But somehow she couldn't force the words to her lips.

She wondered what he had meant by his offer to show her the lights! And she certainly didn't hate him.

5

Taryna stood in her cabin listening to the sound of the water lapping against the sides of the ship. They were moving very slowly because Mr. Newbury had said that they would take most of the night crossing the Channel so that the ladies would not be awoken too early when the ship tied up in Trouville harbour.

"We have to tie up in Trouville," Kit had told her, "as Deauville has no harbour. But there is only a mile or so between the towns. Unfortunately Irene thinks Trouville is noisy, so we can't stay on the yacht but have to go to a hotel!"

As far as Taryna was concerned she didn't mind how early she was awoken or where she stayed once they arrived. She could hardly believe that the voyage had really begun, that England was left behind and that ahead of her lay France.

All the time they had been driving down to Southampton she had felt that something must happen to prevent their getting to France. It seemed impossible that at last all her dreams were coming true and that she was on her way abroad.

The journey was conducted with the luxury that coloured everything arranged by Mr. Newbury. Kit, Taryna, Irene and Michael went into one Rolls. Mr. Newbury followed in another with Mr. Corea and his chief secretary. There were two other cars following behind filled with servants and luggage. There was Irene's maid, and Kit's, who was also to look after

Taryna. There was Mr. Newbury's valet; there was the second chef, who apparently always accompanied them when they went to sea; and two footmen who acted as stewards, besides the permanent staff who were always aboard the yacht.

"If they only knew how strange this all is to me," Taryna thought as she saw the smart luggage which Kit had lent her with dozens of other suitcases, dressing-cases and hat-boxes on the quay at Southampton.

There were a great many ships in the harbour and Taryna had a sudden longing to go aboard one of the great liners and sail across the Atlantic. How wonderful it would be if she really could visit Canada! As if her thoughts had been spoken aloud, a voice beside her said:

"Are you feeling homesick?"

It was Michael who had asked the question, but for a moment she did not understand what he meant.

"Why should I be?" she asked.

"I thought you had that nostalgic look in your eyes as you stared at the *Queen Elizabeth*," he said.

"Is that . . ." she began, only to check the question, knowing that in her travels backwards and forwards across the Atlantic she was certain to have seen the *Queen Elizabeth* before.

"Yes, that's the *Queen Elizabeth*," he answered, as if she had completed the question. "Didn't you recognise her?"

"Not for the moment," Taryna replied with an air of indifference. "But then I'm never very good at recognising ships."

She turned away quickly, frightened of what more Michael might say to her, and a few minutes later was walking aboard the *Heron*.

It was the most wonderful yacht that Taryna had

ever seen—although she told herself that was no criterion as she had seen very few.

To begin with, she had never expected Mr. Newbury's private yacht to be so big. It seemed to her the size of a smaller liner. Secondly, everything about her was so dazzlingly white. Despite her resolution to appear *blasé* Taryna could not help exclaiming:

"It's lovely! Really lovely!"

Kit gave her a warning glance, but Mr. Newbury seemed gratified.

"It's comfortable, I'll say that for it," he said. "It ought to be, seeing what it costs."

"Father always gets his money's worth," Kit remarked with a mocking note in her voice, but there was not so much bitterness there as usual. She was looking quickly round the deck, searching, as Taryna knew only too well, for someone she was longing to see, a familiar face about which she had been dreaming.

"Well, personally I loathe the sea," Irene said petulantly. "You promise me, Walter, that we're not going to start until dinner?"

"No, of course not," Mr. Newbury replied. "We won't start until you are ready to go to bed; and if you take a sleeping draught, you won't know a thing until you find yourself on the other side of the Channel."

Irene disappeared below. Taryna leant against the rail watching the sea-gulls swirling overhead, seeing the water, grey and dirty as it was in the harbour, transformed by the sunshine into the sea of gold.

She felt a thrill of excitement go through her. This was the beginning of adventure. Now at last things were happening in her life, which only yesterday had seemed so dull and depressing.

"Let's go and find our cabins," Kit said, and Taryna knew by the sound of her voice that she was disappointed. "I can't see him anywhere," she whispered as they went below.

"Perhaps he's ashore," Taryna suggested.

"I should have thought he would have been here to meet us," Kit said.

The cabins were as magnificent as the rest of the ship. Very prettily decorated, they had beds instead of bunks and little fitted dressing-tables with cunningly concealed lights and mirrors which showed to the very best advantage whoever was sitting at them. There was a bathroom opening off the cabin where Taryna was to sleep, a radio by her bed, and every form of heater and ventilator.

"I am sure I shall press the wrong button," she said laughingly, "and give myself a shower."

Kit put her finger to her lips.

"For goodness' sake don't look so delighted with everything. Remember you're rich, terribly rich. Your father has very likely got six yachts like this."

Taryna started to laugh.

"It's all so ridiculous!" she said. "I don't believe for one moment that anyone can be taken in by this silly game. I think I shall tell your father and stepmother the truth."

"If you do, I shall be surprised if you get as far as Deauville with us," Kit warned.

"You don't mean that really?" Taryna asked.

"Haven't you seen enough of Irene now to know that I am not exaggerating when I say she's the biggest snob that ever stepped?" Kit asked. "If she thought you were the daughter of an impoverished parson, she would refuse to let Father spend a penny on taking you anywhere. She'd say that you weren't a good influence on me and that I must make friends of my own class."

Kit laughed bitterly.

84

"That's a joke, isn't it? My own class! If I did that my friends would be barmaids or factory hands."

Taryna raised her eyebrows.

"Why do you say that?"

"Because it's true," Kit answered. "Irene would kill me if she knew I had said it, but my grandfather came to England from Europe without a penny in his pocket. He was a Czech, and he had only one asset. He didn't mind how hard he worked or what at as long as it brought him money. He started at five shillings a week sweeping the floor in a boot factory."

"You ought to be very proud of him," Taryna said.

"I am," Kit answered. "It's Irene who tries to pretend that Father's family were aristocrats, ruling over thousands of unwilling serfs. Gosh, she's such a fool!"

"Forget her," Taryna said briefly.

"That's just what I am trying to do," Kit answered. "I'm going to look round and see if I can find Jock. Are you coming?"

"I am going to stay here for a moment," Taryna replied. "I want to examine all the gadgets and pinch both them and myself to see if they are real."

Kit laughed and went from the cabin, shutting the door behind her.

Taryna walked to the port-hole and stood staring out. For a moment she was seeing only the view from the back windows of the Vicarage—the squalid houses, built too close together and sadly in need of repair; the rows of washing flapping in the breeze; the children shrieking at each other as they ran, tumbling and fighting, down the muddy streets; the thin, half-starved cats creeping round the refuse.

She gave a little sigh and turned away. If only her father and mother could be with her; if only she could give them even a part of this holiday, how much it

85

would mean! She thought of the endless calls at the front door:

"Can I have a word with the Vicar, please?"

"Will the Vicar come and see Gran? The doctor doesn't think she's got much longer."

"Will the Vicar speak for me?"

"Will the Vicar . . . ?"

"Will the Vicar . . . ?"

Endless, endless appeals, and none of them ever refused or turned away. And her mother, polishing, cleaning, cooking, hurrying out of the door with: "I shan't be long. It's the Mother's Union at three o'clock and I must go and see Mrs. Robinson as soon as it's over."

The telephone ringing, the door-bell ringing, people calling for her. Yet somehow Mrs. Grazebrook always remained smiling and sympathetic. No-one ever went away from the Vicarage without feeling that there was someone in the world who understood what they were suffering.

Taryna's hand caressed the back of a chair which must have cost more than the Grazebrooks spent in a month on food.

"Why is it so unfair?" she asked herself, and then knew that it wasn't. There was more happiness in that shabby, busy little Vicarage than in this magnificent, luxurious yacht. Happiness was what counted, happiness was what everyone was looking for, and money couldn't buy it.

"Nevertheless it helps to feel comfortable and pretty," Taryna whispered. She looked at herself in the mirror and realised what a difference Kit's clothes had made to her.

"Fine clothes" she told herself with a chuckle and ran up the companion-way. As she stepped on deck Kit appeared. Her eyes were shining.

She looked over her shoulder to be quite certain that everyone was out of earshot and said in a low voice:

"It's all right. He's here!"

"Was he pleased to see you?" Taryna said.

"I think so," Kit answered. "He's very Scottish. Nothing shows, if you know what I mean. But he must have been glad, because I was glad to see him."

Taryna privately thought that was poor logic, but she didn't say so and watched Kit's expressive little face, which seemed suddenly to have come to life.

"I love him," Kit said. "I'm sure of it. I was sure of it before, but I hadn't seen him for such a long time. Now that I have seen him again I know for certain."

"Oh, Kit! Don't jump to conclusions," Taryna begged. "It's all very well to say you love somebody even before you're quite certain you do love them. But love can show itself in very different ways."

"This is all of them," Kit said savagely.

"How can you be sure of that?" Taryna answered.

"I am sure," Kit replied. "And you'll know what I mean when you meet Jock. He's got something to do at the moment, but I think there will be a chance of speaking to him in about quarter-of-an-hour. We'll wait here and then we can go for'ard and see."

Taryna said nothing. She was afraid for Kit. She knew how much the girl had suffered from loneliness and from being unhappy at home. She could not help feeling that this was just the inevitable infatuation for the first man who seemed different from those who were thrust upon her.

"If only we had a chance of talking to each other," Kit said. "He's afraid of what the captain and the rest of the crew will say, and I'm afraid of Father and Irene. It's all so difficult. Perhaps we will get a chance of meeting when we get to Deauville."

Taryna privately thought that was unlikely. But

then, as she had never been to Deauville before, it was hard for her even to guess what sort of life they would lead there.

A quarter-of-an-hour later, Kit, having gone away to reconnoitre, came back.

"He's just for'ard, she said. "Come quickly. There's no-one about."

Taryna jumped up from her comfortable chair and followed Kit round the side of the ship. Standing on the deck she saw a thick-set, sunburnt young man. He was good-looking in a rough, almost rugged style, with deep-set blue eyes that were somehow unexpectedly inscrutible.

"This is my great friend, Jock," Kit was saying. "I have told her all about . . . us."

It seemed to Taryna that Jock McDonald stiffened himself.

"There's nothing to tell," he said a little stiffly.

"I know that," Taryna answered reassuringly.

He seemed to relax.

"Miss Kit is my employer's daughter," he said.

"Oh, don't start that, Jock," Kit burst out.

"Nevertheless it's true," Jock McDonald answered stoutly.

"Yes, I know it is," Kit said. "But it need not make any difference to us."

"It's bound to make a difference," he replied. "There will be trouble if I am seen talking too much to you on this voyage. I must go now."

"But, please, please . . ." Kit pleaded; but already he was gone, after a smart salute to his peaked cap which made Taryna realise how becoming uniform was to a man.

"Let him go," she said to Kit. "He knows what is best. You don't want to make trouble for him."

"No, no, of course not," Kit answered, subsiding

quickly. "It's just that I want to be with him. There's so much that we want to discuss."

"You can't do it now when he's busy," Taryna rebuked her. "You must remember that his good name matters just as much as yours."

"I never thought of that," Kit said.

"I don't want to preach at you," Taryna smiled, "but I think you are being rather selfish."

Kit squeezed her arm.

"I don't mind your preaching; it's when Irene does it that it gets my hackles up. And I know what you mean. I'll be more careful."

Taryna bent to kiss her cheek; but when she was alone in her cabin dressing for dinner she realised how hard it was going to be for Kit not only to conceal her feelings but to check her impulses.

"I hope he's nice," Taryna thought. "He must be for Kit's sake." She could not help seeing the wide gulf which lay between Kit's station in life and Jock McDonald's.

She could imagine Irene's horror when she learned what was happening, and she knew enough of Mr. Newbury by this time to realise that he would not be pleased.

She was thinking of him just as she finished dressing when there came a knock at the door.

"Come in," she called, thinking it was the maid, and then as the door opened she saw to her surprise it was Mr. Newbury.

"Can I come in?" he asked.

"Of course," Taryna answered.

He entered the cabin and shut the door carefully behind him.

"I have a favour to ask of you," he said.

"A favour!" Taryna echoed.

"Yes," he smiled. "Will you do something for me?"

"But of course," she replied. "Anything."

"It's quite a simple thing really," he answered. "You see, it's Kit's birthday next Thursday and I've bought her a little present. When we get to Trouville harbour the Customs officials will come aboard and sometimes they make quite a thorough search of the ship.

"Anyway, I don't want them to find Kit's present. It's not that I mind paying any Customs duties that there might be on it, but I don't want her to know what I have bought her. It's to be a surprise."

"But, of course, I understand that," Taryna said. "But what do you want me to do about it?"

"I want you to hide it somewhere amongst your things," he answered. "You are a guest and therefore they are not likely to be as interested in you as in me. It is owners of a yacht whom they suspect of carrying contraband diamonds or gun-running."

He laughed at his own joke.

"Yes, I'll hide it somewhere," Taryna said. "I don't know where, but I'm certain they won't find it."

"That is very kind of you," Mr. Newbury said. "And please, it's a secret from everybody—Irene and Michael besides Kit. I always make a point of pretending that I don't give birthday presents, then everyone is astonished when they get one."

"Oh, that's just like my father," Taryna said. "He always says that he hasn't had time and he can't afford ..." She hesitated a moment and then went on quickly: "... the time it would take to go shopping. And then on Christmas Day he has lovely presents for everyone."

"Well, I see he and I are two of a kind," Mr. Newbury smiled. "Thank you, Taryna. Hide it carefully."

He put a very small package into Taryna's hand. Somehow she had been expecting something much bigger and looked down at it almost in perplexity. It

90

was very light and carefully packed and sealed with several little blobs of sealing-wax.

"Thank-you," Mr. Newbury said again, and went from the cabin shutting the door behind him.

Taryna stood looking at the little parcel he had left in her hand. What could it be? she wondered. Jewellery, of course. But it was certainly very light and very small.

She looked round the cabin and wondered where would be the best place to hide anything. She remembered a detective story where things had been hidden in the toes of the heroine's shoes; but anything to do with clothes was ruled out by the fact that Ella, the maid, would handle everything she wore and might quite easily come upon it.

No, it would have to be a better place than that. There were cupboards and drawers fitted into the walls, but then cupboards and drawers were the first places where a Customs officer would look for anything that he wanted to examine.

Taryna stood thinking. It was much more difficult than she had thought at first to find a place of concealment that was not obvious, the sort of place in which you would conceal something.

Then she had an idea. Hanging from the rail on the washhand basin was the pink plastic sponge-bag in which Ella had packed the sponge and flannel which with her hairbrush, comb and toothbrush, were the only things of her own that she had brought with her from Cambridge.

The pink sponge-bag had actually been a present from Edwina, her sister, last Christmas. She had saved for it penny by penny and Taryna loved it because she knew that it had entailed endless small sacrifices on her sister's part to collect the two shillings and elevenpence which the bag had cost.

Ella had taken out the sponge and flannel and put them on the side of the basin. The sponge-bag hung empty. The plastic was not transparent and was thick enough to conceal inside the very small parcel that Mr. Newbury had given her. She pulled open the strings at the neck and slipped it in. Now nobody would know it contained anything. It swung very slightly from the chromium-plated rail

Taryna smiled to herself. "One should always conceal anything in the most obvious place, preferably where people can see it." Who was it who had said that? Or had she read it somewhere? Anyway, it was the best place she could think of to conceal Mr. Newbury's parcel.

With a start she realised that dinner must be ready. She had run from the cabin; and now, nearly three hours later, when she had come back to it again, her first thought was of Kit's present hidden in the plastic bag.

She touched it. It was there safely. And then as she stood listening to the water outside, she found herself remembering the words that Michael had said to her so much earlier in the day.

"I will show you the lights of England."

She had not been alone with him for one moment since they had come on aboard; and even if she had been, she felt somehow that he would not refer again to what he had said.

Had he meant it or had he just said it out of politeness and then perhaps regretted having given her such an invitation? She couldn't find the answer to the puzzle.

When they had all said good night in the big lounge, he had given her no meaning glance or conveyed anything in his voice.

"Good night, Taryna. Good night, Kit."

That was all, and she had come below, almost forgetting until this moment what he had suggested.

Irene had retired to bed about ten o'clock. Mr. Newbury had kept them up playing bridge. He enjoyed a game after dinner, he said, and Taryna had partnered him against Kit and Michael. She had made a number of mistakes as she was by no means an experienced player, and while Mr. Newbury had pointed out her faults he had been quite pleasant about them and not in any way annoyed at her stupidity.

She had really been concentrating too fiercely on the game to think of anything else. But now she remembered. Of course, it was ridiculous. She should go to bed at once as all the others would have done. It was late—nearly eleven o'clock. No-one would expect her to go up on deck now.

Slowly she started to undo the belt of her dress. It was a pretty dress, very full-skirted, of pale aquamarine blue lace with a waistband of sugar-pink velvet. She took it off and then put it on again. She would not sleep, she was sure of it. Why shouldn't she go up on deck and look for the lights herself?

It was not even as if she expected Michael to be there, she told herself. He had put the idea into her head, but he had forgotten about it. She had a sudden longing to miss nothing of this adventure. How tame to go to bed and go to sleep! She could sleep any time—but not now, not when there was so much to see.

She crossed to the wardrobe and took down one of the coats that Kit had lent her. It was a soft blue wool, very warm and comfortable. She slipped her arms into it and pulled it close round her body. She looked at herself in the glass and saw that her eyes were very bright.

"I am not going to meet anyone," Taryna said aloud.

"I am only going to look at the sea, just for a little while at any rate."

She turned out the lights of her cabin and walking noiselessly down the thick-carpeted corridor climbed the broad companion-way on to the deck above.

There was no-one about. She had not expected there would be. The ship was moving slowly through the darkness. She walked to the bow, felt the wind lift her hair gently from her forehead as she lent against the polished rail and looked back.

Very dimly she could see the outline of the coast; and then all along it, almost like fireflies in the darkness, she could see the lights. Lights on the cliffs, moving up and down as if they each had a certain individuality of their own; lights on the passing ships; and lights high overhead where some aeroplane was travelling slowly across the star-strewn sky.

They were very lovely, almost like a necklace encircling the safety and security that was Britain, Taryna thought. And then a voice at her elbow said:

"I said I would show them to you. Don't you think they are beautiful?"

She had not heard Michael come across the deck. But this time he did not startle her, as if she had known all the time that he would be there.

"Yes, they are lovely," she said. "So lovely that one can hardly believe they are real."

"But they are," he said. "And each of them represents a man and a woman and perhaps a child; a home, a person working, striving, struggling, trying to get somewhere; someone loving, living and dying. Each light means so much and every one of them British."

Taryna did not turn to look at him, but without thinking she said:

"I had no idea that you could think like that about it."

94

"Do I seem such a moron?" he said. "Or is it because you feel that men in my position should have no feelings about anything that does not concern money?"

"I didn't say that," she said.

"No, but you are thinking it."

"No, I'm not," Taryna contradicted. "I wasn't thinking about you at all at that moment. I was thinking of the lights. And then you put into words what I was feeling. I wasn't clever enough to think of that for myself."

"Your thoughts in words," he said gently. "So that was it?"

"Yes, that was it," she answered.

"And you don't want me to spoil them or this moment?"

It was a question and after a moment she said in what was almost a whisper:

"No, please don't."

They stood in silence for what seemed to Taryna a long time. A ship came out from the shelter of the land. It was a blaze of lights and it turned and went southwards and the little tug turned towards the north. Taryna drew a deep breath.

"It's almost like a fairyland."

"I thought that the first time I saw the lights of Monte Carlo," Michael said.

"I have never been to Monte Carlo," Taryna replied. "But I don't believe anything could be lovelier than this."

"Beauty to me is something which can be very lonely," Michael said. "I always want to be with someone. I want to feel that they are feeling what I feel, otherwise it is somehow incomplete. I long to say, 'Don't you feel this?' or, 'Don't you think this, too?'

Sometimes there's no-one to answer, only the wind and the sun, and they can both be very cold company."

"You must have been very lonely to speak like that," Taryna exclaimed.

"So lonely at times that I felt as if I couldn't bear it any more," Michael answered. "Then I have gone on, just because I have known that loneliness never really lasts; something, somebody, relieves it. And then one is excessively grateful because one realises the difference so acutely."

There was a note in his voice that told her he had suffered and she asked wonderingly:

"Is that why you wanted me to see the lights with you tonight?"

"I couldn't bear to look at them alone," Michael answered. "And I wanted you to be there too."

"That was kind of you."

"Kind!" There was a hint of laughter in his voice. "Do you think I am being kind?"

"Aren't you? I thought it was very kind of you to show me something I should never have known about otherwise."

"You are very innocent."

For the first time she turned to look at him. It was dark and yet she could see the outline of his face, the eyes deep-set and surprisingly he was not smiling at her.

"Innocent?" she queried. "In what way?"

"I don't understand you," he answered. "But I want to."

He was looking down at her, searching her face, and she was suddenly aware that the moon was rising and coming from behind the clouds. Her face must be almost clear to him while his was still in shadow.

She stood looking at him, trying to understand what he meant, trying, too, to understand some strange feeling within herself. It was almost a rising excitement, a sudden tenseness of her whole body, a kind of waiting as if she knew something was about to happen.

"You are very lovely!"

His voice was low and his words so surprising that they took her breath away.

Still she could only stare at him. Then, almost as if she tried to snap the spell which held her, she turned her head.

"You are talking nonsense."

Her voice sounded false even to herself.

"I am saying only the truth. You are lovely—lovelier than I imagined it possible for any girl to be."

"You can't have seen many then."

Taryna tried to speak lightly. It seemed to her that Michael had come a little nearer, his arm was against hers as she leaned over the rail.

"Taryna—the name suits you."

She did not answer. He had spoken her name almost as if it were a cry, and then had added the rest of the sentence.

"At this moment," he went on insistently, "we are in no-man's-land. Yesterday we were in England, tomorrow we shall be in France. Do you feel that we, too, are between the past and the future? Just you and I—Taryna and Michael!"

"The past and the future," Taryna repeated softly. "And yet we have no choice. The present must become the past."

"It also becomes the future," he said softly. "Do you wonder a little bit what that will bring?"

"I wonder, but I don't want to know," Taryna answered.

"Don't you? I should like to know. I am curious. And yet, at the same time, I have lived in the East long enough to be fatalistic. What is meant to be will be, and it's coming closer. Do you feel that?"

Taryna was not certain if it was a shiver of fear or of ecstasy that went through her.

"I don't know what you mean," she whispered.

"I think you do," he said. "It is coming closer, little Taryna. We cannot escape from it. Some things are too big—fate and love. We cannot run away from them."

"Do we want to?"

She did not know why she asked that, she only knew that he was casting a spell on her. He was mesmerising her, drawing her nearer to him and she could not escape from his voice, from the knowledge that he was there beside her.

"I don't want to," he answered. "But you may feel differently. I know, anyway, that there is no escape. This is fate and—love."

She felt his hand touch hers and turned in a sudden panic. But it was too late. His other arm was round her shoulders and drawing her close to him.

She made one indecisive movement as if to escape, and then his lips had touched hers and she felt him capture and hold her mouth. His kiss, fierce, possessive and wildly disturbing, made her prisoner.

6

For a moment Taryna felt almost numb with the surprise and shock. Then the pressure of Michael's lips, the hard strength of his arms, seemed to awaken within her a feeling she had never known before.

It was as if a flame shot through her body, leaving behind it a kind of tingling ecstasy which seemed to intensify until her whole being trembled at the wonder of it.

For a long, long time they stood locked together until Taryna felt as if the waters of a deep and wonderful sea closed over her head. She surrendered herself without thought, without being conscious of anything but the glory within herself.

Finally, with what was almost a little sigh, their lips parted, her head fell back against Michael's shoulder, and in the pale silver of the moonlight he looked down at her.

"My darling!"

He said the words aloud in a voice deep and moved with passion.

It was then that Taryna was suddenly aware of what had happened, and with a little inarticulate murmur she turned and hid her face against his shoulder.

He said nothing, but held her close. There was something so comforting in his strength and in the very nearness of him that she wanted to cling closer, to know that never again would she feel the loneliness of being one person.

"Taryna!"

She heard his voice, urgent, compelling. She raised her head a little as if to listen. She was too shy to meet his eyes.

"You are so adorable," he said. "From the very first moment I saw you I knew that you were the girl I had waited for all my life. Did you know what you looked like, I wonder? So young, so fresh, so utterly and completely desirable."

Slowly in Taryna's mind stirred the memory of that moment. Michael carrying the drinks to Irene, the luxury and magnificence of the swimming-pool, the sunshine glittering on Irene's fair hair.

Almost without realising what she was doing Taryna stiffened. Irene and Michael! Michael and Irene. The two were inseparably connected in her mind.

"I love you!"

The words were spoken; and Michael's voice was so deep, so moving that her heart leapt towards him at the sound of it.

"Oh, I love you!"

Words she had somehow never expected to hear any man, let alone Michael, say to her.

"Why?"

The question was hardly breathed and yet he heard it.

"Because, as I have already told you, you are so adorable. If I could only explain what you make me feel when you look at me with those dark eyes! When your mouth smiles and curves up a little at the corners; when I know you are shy and a little frightened. Ye gods! That's something strange to find these days, a woman who is shy and therefore utterly feminine."

Slowly Taryna drew herself a little away from him.

"I . . . rene," she faltered.

She knew then that the magic which had swept them

into each other's arms oblivious of everything else was passing. She almost cried out in pain to know that it must go, and yet already it was too late to hold it. Irene stood between them as clearly as if she had been there in person.

"What about Irene?"

Michael's voice was suddenly hard, the deep resonance of feeling had gone.

"You know what I mean?"

Taryna could hardly speak above a whisper and yet the words had to be said.

"She has nothing really to do with you and me. This is something that belongs only to ourselves, our own secret, Taryna."

She felt herself shiver. What were they talking about? Didn't he understand that secrets meant hidden things, things which were best left not only unknown but unsaid?

"I must go."

She had a sudden, urgent desire to get away.

"No, no, don't leave me."

He put out his arms to hold her again; and then, when she would have resisted him, he swept her masterfully close to him, holding her so tight that she could not struggle, could do nothing but try to move her head away as he sought her lips.

Even so he found them. He kissed her again, more passionately, more violently this time, almost as if he were half angry with her.

"No, no."

She tried to resist him, but it was too late. Already that ecstasy was creeping over her again, sapping her will, draining away her strength so that she could only cling to him and feel her mouth go soft beneath his. She was trembling, her whole body weak and pliant; and then suddenly she was free.

"I love you! Never forget that," he said.

Just for a moment she stood there trying to find the strength to go, and then she was running—running across the deck and down the companion-way into her own cabin.

She shut the door behind her and locked it, and then stood with her hands to her burning cheeks before throwing herself down on her bed, face first, trying to think, trying to calm the chaotic fever of her mind.

"I love you!"

She could hear his voice saying it; she could hear it echoing over and over again; and then her instinctive question:

"Why?"

Waves of feeling rippled over her body. She felt the warm fullness of her mouth, the tightness of her breasts. And yet she knew that nothing whatever mattered except her questioning thoughts. Why? Why? Why did he love her?

She had a sudden picture of him talking to Irene, sitting beside her by the swimming-pool, their faces very close together; smiling at Irene at the dinner-table; fetching her wrap; taking her hand in his. Irene and Michael!

And yet she was a married woman and . . . rich! Now, at last, the thought was there, the thought she had been avoiding, the thought she had been striving to keep away from herself. And yet it must be heard.

Michael thought that she was rich. She, Taryna Grazebrook, who hadn't got a penny to her name, was pretending to be the daughter of a very rich man, the girl with millions of dollars. She was the equal of Irene as far as wealth was concerned—and unmarried!

Taryna buried her face deeper in the pillow. It couldn't be true. Could any man act as well as that?

102

Could any man make her feel as Michael had done and yet be a hypocrite?

She felt the poison of her own suspicions sink deep inside her, sweeping away the last remnants of that magic which had held her so enthralled within his arms.

Michael thought she was rich—rich—rich!

She could see his picture looking up at her again from the *Tatler* lying on the table in her room at Cambridge. She could hear Kit's scratching words: "A waster! A hanger-on! Irene's lord-in-waiting! After all, they can live comfortably on Father's money!"

Kit's scornful voice ringing out and sounding at this moment like a death knell in Taryna's ears.

Rich! Rich! The fictitious money she was supposed to possess had become a trap and had ensnared her. And yet what did it matter? Taryna tried to ask herself. what did a kiss really amount to between two young people? Kit and her other friends had kissed dozens of men, sometimes without even knowing their names.

This had been different. This had not been anything like that, Taryna told herself. And then once again came the same question—why?

It was then she knew the answer and felt the tears rise slowly and painfully into her eyes; an answer which appalled her even while she must face it, even while she knew she could not escape it.

She loved him. She had loved him that very first moment when she had looked on his face and found it strangely arresting. She had loved him even as she had tried to hate him, when they met beside the swimming-pool at Earlywood. She had loved him when they talked together on the terrace; when she had been frightened because he had seen her come out of the call-box. She had loved him when tonight, knowing that he would be there, she had come up on deck.

103

It was her own fault that the situation had arisen. And yet, when all was said and done, nothing could really have affected the truth. Her love was already born inside her.

"I have got to hate him," Taryna said aloud. "I have got to see him for what he is and despise him. To face the fact that he is making love to me because of my money."

Yet even as she tried to whip up her anger, she knew it was hopeless. She loved him. She loved the dark strangeness of his face, the way his eyes were deep-set and the sudden little lines of humour which showed when he smiled. She loved the firmness of his mouth—a mouth that had kissed her, lips that had held her captive.

She felt herself quiver with a sudden delight at the very memory of his kisses and knew that it was hopeless. Whatever he did, whatever he said, she would still go on loving him.

Hours later it seemed to Taryna she dragged herself from the bed and began to undress. Her whole being seemed to be divided in two. On one side there was despair, distrust and humiliation; on the other was ecstasy, joy and a kind of blind optimism which said somehow things would come right.

"How stupid can you be?" she asked her reflection in the glass, and then felt the blood rise in her cheeks because she was remembering what he had said about the shyness in her eyes, the upturned corners of her mouth.

"I never want to see him again," Taryna said aloud, then went to bed praying that the night would pass quickly so that tomorrow would bring Michael to her again.

She thought she would be unable to sleep, but she must have been more tired than she knew.

She awoke to find it was nearly nine o'clock. The engines were silent and she had not even heard the yacht come into the harbour.

She jumped out of bed and pulled back the curtain over the port-hole. Outside she could see the quay, green trees with little red kiosks underneath them and people perambulating along—people who looked very different from those she had left on the other side of the Channel.

She was in France! She gave a little cry of sheer delight and snatching up her dressing-gown ran down the passage to Kit's cabin.

Kit was sitting up in bed with her breakfast on a tray in front of her.

"Hello! You're late," she exclaimed. "I thought you'd be up at dawn watching us come in."

"I'm so angry to have missed it," Taryna said. "Kit, we're in France, actually in France! I never believed somehow I would ever get here."

"Hush, hush," Kit said. "When the engines aren't running one can almost hear everything that's said on the ship. Don't forget you're a *blasé* traveller."

Her words brought back to Taryna the situation that she had fallen asleep to forget. A *blasé* traveller! She, the untravelled, ignorant daughter of an impoverished vicar. How could she keep up such a stupid pretence?

She was about to plead with Kit once again to let her tell the truth and then she remembered that Kit had her own troubles, and she knew that, if her friendship was worth anything at all, she must forget herself in helping her friend.

"Were you able to speak to Jock McDonald last night?" she asked, deliberately turning her back for the moment on all thoughts of Michael and her own emotions.

Kit nodded.

105

"It was wonderful," she said in a whisper. "I knew the watch he was taking and I slipped up on to the bridge. There was no one there except ourselves. We had a long talk. He loves me, Taryna."

The words were said soberly without the sparkle which had been there when Kit had spoken of Jock McDonald before.

"And you love him?" Taryna said gently.

Kit nodded.

"Of course," she said. And then with a little sob: "Jock says he won't marry me."

"But why not?" Taryna asked, going forward to grasp one of Kit's hands in hers.

"Because of my damned money!" Kit answered. "He says that he would never live on his wife. He wants me to choose whether I will give him up and never talk to him again or whether I will marry him and live on what he earns."

"What did you say?" Taryna asked.

"I was ready to say, of course, that money has never meant anything to me but unhappiness. He wouldn't listen. He said I had got to think about it seriously, not impulsively as I did everything else. He said, too, there was no question of our getting married until he was absolutely convinced that he could, in his own way, make me happy."

"That sounds all right to me," Taryna said. "Why are you so miserable about it?"

"Because I am afraid," Kit said. "I am afraid that I shan't be able to convince him that I really do love him. Besides ... Oh, Taryna, if I'm really honest, I'm half afraid that he doesn't love me enough. If he loves me as much as I love him, why can't we run away now, today?"

"I think he is being very sensible," Taryna said. "It's

no use making a mistake. Besides have you thought that you will have to have your father's permission?"

Kit nodded.

"I didn't think of it, but Jock did. That's why he says there's no question of running away. I have got to face the music, as he puts it, and tell Father that I am going to marry him and that I don't want any money. If I do that, you know as well as I do that Father and Irene will think of some plot to separate us; and because they are much more clever and ruthless than we are, they will succeed."

"I shouldn't be too sure of that," Taryna said. "Perhaps your father will respect you and Jock for wanting to stand on your own feet."

"You don't know Father," Kit said scornfully. "He is ambitious in his way just as Irene is. He is working his way up from the bottom, so he wants me to start at the top. Before I went to Cambridge he was always producing the sons of his friends, suggesting that we made up a party. It was only when I was so rude to them and he was ashamed of me that he stopped doing it. I knew what he was up to."

Taryna gave a little laugh.

"Oh, Kit, you must be a very uncomfortable daughter. Why can't you take things easily as they come and not fight about everything?"

"Because I know what I want," Kit answered. "I want Jock and I'm going to have him."

She looked strangely like her father for a moment and then the defiance crumpled up and tears brimmed over in her eyes as she said:

"First I have got to convince Jock. Oh, Taryna, help me."

"Of course I will," Taryna said soothingly.

"You will!" Kit sounded hopeful. "Will you have a talk with him? Will you tell him that you know I am in love with him and that you know I would never regret for a moment giving up everything in the world so long as I could be his wife?"

"I wonder if I could say that truthfully?" Taryna said.

Suddenly she thought of Michael. She would give up everything in the world for him, she thought, and yet she had nothing to give. How different it was for Kit!

She glanced round the luxurious cabin, at the gold toilet-set on the dressing-table, at the diamond bracelet and ruby and diamond ear-rings that Kit had worn last night and had flung carelessly down when she went to bed. Her dress was thrown untidily over a chair—a short dress of blue chiffon which had been made by a Paris *couturier* and had cost more than Jock would earn aboard the yacht in six months.

Kit might despise it now, Taryna thought, but the day might come when she would long for all this again, and much more besides.

"What are you thinking?" Kit asked.

"I was thinking of your life with Jock," Taryna answered.

Kit smiled.

"How wonderful it would be to be married to him!" she said.

"How can you be sure of that?" Taryna asked.

"I just know it," Kit answered. "I want to be close to him. I want to hear him talk to me. Do you know, Taryna, that he has never kissed me? I know it's because he won't aboard the yacht, and we have never had the chance to meet anywhere else. I've made him promise to meet me tonight. I'll get away somehow."

"Are we going to the hotel?" Taryna asked.

"I expect so, as soon as we are cleared by the Customs officers," Kit said.

There came a knock at the door.

"Come in," she called.

The door opened and Mr. Newbury, wearing a gold-buttoned yachting jacket entered the room.

"Good morning, girls!" he said. "As you see, we are in harbour. A very smooth passage; even Irene slept well."

"I am so annoyed that I slept so long," Taryna said. "I wanted to see the ship coming into the harbour."

"It's a compliment to the captain that he didn't wake you," Mr. Newbury replied.

"Are you going ashore, Father?" Kit enquired.

"The Customs officials are coming aboard now," Mr. Newbury answered. "I understand they want to make a pretty thorough search of the ship. It seems they suspect some of the sailors of bringing in contraband of some sort. Anyway, don't be surprised if they invade you."

"I'd better get up," Kit said. "I don't want a lot of men nosing around the room while I'm still in my nightgown."

"I will do the same," Taryna said and went back to her cabin.

She dressed quickly, feeling, now the moment had come, rather anxious about the package hidden in her sponge-bag. Supposing she failed Mr. Newbury after all? It was not such a very wrong thing and he was quite capable of paying the fine. At the same time, it was the only thing he had asked of her and she wanted to please him.

It was obviously going to be a hot day and she put on one of the crisp, full-skirted cotton dresses that Kit had lent her and picked up a short-sleeved cardigan to wear over it should the sea breezes become cool.

With a last glance round the cabin she opened the door. The sponge-bag looked innocent enough hanging on the chromium-plated rail, and yet she had a strong desire to take out the little package and put it in her handbag. Surely that would be better? Then she decided against it. Leave things as they were. Second thoughts were often wrong.

Kit came out of her cabin at that moment.

"We haven't been long, have we?" she said. "What's happening?"

"I haven't seen anyone or heard anything," Taryna replied.

"Let's go up and see what they are doing," Kit said. "I expect they're going through the sailor's quarters with a tooth comb."

"Has this happened before?" Taryna asked

"Oh yes! In Monte Carlo in the spring they made an awful fuss when we arrived. Father said then it was the sailors they were suspicious about, but they certainly turned everything upside down in my cabin."

"Surely that isn't usual?" Taryna said.

Kit shrugged her shoulders.

"Oh, I expect so. If they once get their teeth into you, they never let go."

They found Mr. Newbury on deck sitting in one of the chairs under the awning, a pile of papers on his knees.

"You can't go ashore," he said, "so you might as well make yourselves comfortable."

Kit and Taryna sat down. A moment later Taryna's heart gave a sudden leap. Michael came sauntering along the deck from the other end of the ship, his hands in his pockets, his shirt open at the neck. He looked relaxed and happy. As he turned towards her, she saw a sudden gleam in his eyes as if he had been thinking of her and the sight of her had merely fulfilled his dreams.

"Good morning!"

His voice was low and deep.

"You slept well?"

His questions seemed to be addressed to all three, but Taryna knew whose answer he wanted. She tried to steel her heart against him, tried to hate him, but found it impossible. He was too attractive, too irresistible—at any rate to her.

Despite herself she found herself smiling, the colour rising a little in her cheeks, her eyes flickering a little shyly before his gaze.

"Taryna slept until nine o'clock," Kit said accusingly.

"Then she's an experienced sailor. I woke the moment the engines slowed down. That was at six thirty-five precisely," Michael said.

"So you were awake," Kit said.

"Of course," he answered. "I am always very alert at sea."

"Afraid?" Kit asked a little scornfully.

"Not on the *Heron*," he answered quite seriously. "But at times in other sorts of ships I have been frankly terrified."

"Of what?" Kit asked.

But Michael had turned away from her and, taking up a newspaper from where they had been laid, seemed engrossed in the headlines.

"Quite the little mystery boy." Kit said in a lowered voice to Taryna.

Taryna said nothing. She was wondering if Michael had been in the Navy. She was wondering what ships he was talking about. She knew nothing about him, she thought; nothing about the man whom she had never met forty-eight hours ago and who had the power to magnetise her whole body so that it throbbed and quivered whenever he appeared.

"What is he thinking?" she wondered to herself. "Is

111

he remembering every moment of last night, every word that was spoken, every touch, every feeling?"

She felt that she longed to run to his side, to ask him if it was true, if he had really kissed her, if he had really told her that he loved her. She could not move, she could only sit there tense, remembering, thinking, feeling, until it was almost agony not to cry out loud with the pain of it.

One of the stewards came on deck. He said something to Mr. Newbury who went below.

"The Customs people are doing their stuff," Michael said. "Looks as if they've found something."

"What makes you think that?" Taryna asked sharply.

"The steward said the Chief Officer, or whatever he calls himself, wanted to see the boss," Michael said briefly.

"But what do you think they've found?"

He looked a little surprised.

"You sound worried," he said. "Don't tell me you're smuggling in a couple of bars of gold or anything like that?"

"No, no, of course not," Taryna answered.

"Perhaps they've found a case of rifles in the hold," Kit suggested. "In which case we shall all go to prison. The French are very hot on gun-running."

"Much more likely to have found diamonds," Michael answered. "They are nice cosy little things to take about. One can slip them anywhere—into one's toothpaste, shaving cream, or you can even put them in the sugar basin."

"Oh, you mean diamonds of that sort," Kit said. "I thought you were referring to Irene's Koh-i-noors."

"The French will never worry about the ornamentation of a pretty woman," Michael smiled.

112

"Do you mean they really look in one's toothpaste, the sugar basin and places like that?" Taryna asked.

"You sound worried," Michael said. "I really believe you are smuggling something."

There was a hint of seriousness in his voice that had not been there before.

"I . . . I'm not worried," Taryna said, thinking of her pink sponge-bag hanging on the rail.

Supposing, she thought, that it wasn't a present for Kit at all, but diamonds which Mr. Newbury was smuggling from one country to another? Supposing they were found and he repudiated any knowledge of them. It would only be her word against his. Would they take her to prison? she wondered.

She was suddenly aware that Michael was watching her; and then, at that moment, Irene came on deck. She was looking more elegant than usual in a dress of white jersey worn with heavy gold chunky jewellery which glittered and jingled as she moved.

"I have had to get up," she said crossly. "My cabin is crawling with men peeping under the bed and into the cupboards. I can't imagine what they are looking for."

"Come and sit down," Michael said soothingly.

He had sprung to his feet and brought forward a comfortable chair with a foot-rest. As Irene sat down, he arranged a cushion behind her. He seemed intent, chivalrous, and to Taryna's eyes almost subservient as he ministered to her.

"She's paying for him and so she's entitled to it," Taryna thought, and then hated herself because for the first time in her life she was being spiteful and unkind and thinking the sort of things she had always depre-cated when she had heard them expressed by Kit.

"We're all wondering what the excitement is," Michael said. "I have just been betting that it's

113

Taryna's fault for bringing a few gold bars across with her."

"We shall have to explain that she uses them as paper-weights," Irene said, then laughed at her own joke. "Really, all this fuss is absurd."

"When you come to think of it, it's only people like us who have the facilities for really big smuggling," Kit said. "The ordinary people who come across the Channel for a day trip wouldn't have much to smuggle, would they? And anyway, they wouldn't be able to afford to do it often. We are obviously much more likely to be suspects."

"Well, personally I wouldn't bother to smuggle anything," Irene said. "It's far too much trouble. Whenever I buy anything in Paris I always give a list to Corea and he declares it all—every drop of perfume and everything even down to a new pair of gloves. Walter is most insistent we should not try and cheat."

"So it's Daddy who's so honest, is it?" Kit said as though she inferred that Irene was not.

"An honesty which always pays!" Mr. Newbury exclaimed as he came up the companion-way. "You will be glad to hear that everything has now been found to be correct and we can proceed ashore whenever we wish."

"It's far too early," Irene said petulantly. "Why you couldn't have arranged for them to come and make all this commotion about midday I can't think."

"Don't let's quarrel with them," Mr. Newbury said in a voice that was quite gay for him. "The officers are now enjoying a glass of wine and I suggest we do the same thing. I have told the steward to bring up a bottle of champagne."

"Champagne!" Kit cried. "Are we celebrating?"

"Only our arrival in France, my dear," Mr. Newbury answered.

"As good an excuse as any other," Michael said. He looked up at Mr. Newbury who had not yet sat down and asked: "They found nothing?"

Mr. Newbury shook his head.

"Nothing," he replied. "And I, personally, am mystified as to what they expected to find."

"They didn't tell you?" Michael asked.

"Not a word," Mr. Newbury said. "Routine investigations was, of course, the phrase. Translated into French it sounded rather worse. But I am not a fool!"

"What do you mean, you are not a fool?" Irene asked. "Do you mean to say there was something behind all this fuss this morning?"

"No, no, my dear. It's just a rather over-zealous search on the part of the local officials. I am only sorry you have been in any way inconvenienced."

The steward brought the champagne and opened it carefully. Then he handed round the shallow glasses of golden wine. Mr. Newbury raised his glass.

"To three beautiful ladies on the *Heron!*" he said.

"I can't think why we're having Moet. You know I never like it," Irene complained, wrinkling her nose.

"I have got a different toast," Michael said. He lifted his glass, the sunshine glittering on it and making it seem as if he held a cup of liquid gold. "To the lights of England . . . and the lights of love."

Taryna felt as if she must choke. She could not meet his eyes, but Irene asked curiously:

"What does that mean? I've never heard that toast before."

"The lights of England, like the lights of love, mean different things to many different people," Michael replied quite seriously. "To me they mean dreams of what might be and what will be. They mean all the things that every man wants for himself and is quite

115

certain in his heart that, somehow, some day he will get them."

"It sounds lovely," Kit said. "I shall drink to the lights of England and of love, and may I find them both in France."

She drank quickly. Her father looked at her curiously but said nothing. Then after a moment Kit sprang to her feet.

"Come on, Taryna! Let's go ashore."

"We will lunch in the garden at the Normandie," Irene said. "You'd better meet us there about half-past one."

"Very well," Kit answered.

She walked down the deck and Taryna followed. As she reached the gangway which had been erected on to the quay, she could not help looking back to see if Michael was following. When she did so, she felt as if a cold hand had been laid upon her heart. Michael was not even watching them go, he was sitting close to Irene and talking to her intently.

Somehow the sunshine had gone from the day. But Kit did not realise how silent Taryna was. She was chatting gaily about the little town as they drove from the quay at Trouville the short mile to Deauville.

Here there were luxurious villas, impressive hotels, a small casino looking like an iced cake, and narrow streets filled with amusing, luxurious shops all arranged to tempt the rich visitor.

"Let's go and have some coffee in that café," Kit said, and rapped on the window of the taxi to tell the driver to stop.

She paid him and then they sat down at a little red table on the pavement, surmounted by a gaily striped parasol.

"*Deaux cafés noirs, s'il vous plaît,*" Kit said to the waiter, and then, putting her elbows on the table and

116

her head on her hands, she looked at Taryna and laughed.

"This is fun," she said. "I should have been lonely and miserable if you hadn't been here. Now I am going to show you Deauville."

They finished their coffee and slowly the gaiety came back into Taryna's eyes. She tried not to think of Michael, tried not to remember his face close to Irene's. They had toasted the lights of England and of love, which she had known had been a message for her alone, and yet somehow she could not trust him.

"What do you think of Michael?" she asked Kit as they walked from the shops along the road which led to the sea front.

"I like him better than I expected," Kit answered. "Of course, I hate all Irene's tame cats, but I must say he's the best of the bunch so far."

"Do you really think he's only that?" Taryna asked in a low voice.

"What else?" Kit replied. "Ask him what his plans are. Ask him if he's got a job. I bet you he'll be as evasive as all the others were."

Taryna said nothing. For a moment even the vivid blue of the sea seemed grey; and then she forced herself to concentrate on the wooden *plage* running along beside the sandy beach, on the brilliant crimson and blue tents, on the rows of bathing-huts, which Kit explained could be hired by the week or the month.

They looked at gay outdoor cocktail bars where women in glorious, elaborate swimming costumes which never saw the sea were sipping *apéritifs* beside sun-bronzed young men who looked as if they never did anything but lie in the sun.

It was all so exciting and exotic. The sun was shining and as they walked along the *plage* Taryna could hear

117

compliments being paid about herself and Kit by the people who sat in deck-chairs watching the passers-by.

"Les jolies Anglaises!"

It was somehow exciting to cause a number of Frenchmen to turn round and watch them go, to know that for once in her life she was not insignificant but was an object of interest and perhaps curiosity.

They sat for a while listening to a band play the very latest song hits, and then Kit glanced at her diamond watch.

"We'd better be walking back," she said. "I'm hungry; I don't know about you."

"I'm not," Taryna said. All the same, she jumped to her feet.

She felt a sudden urgency to get back, and knew there was only one reason for it—her desire to see Michael. Severely she tried to scold herself. What was the point of liking him? It was crazy even to imagine that she loved him. Surely she had enough self-respect, enough strength of will to fight against this thing that was consuming her, this love which could never be a true one because it was based on neither respect nor admiration?

But even as her mind denied her love, her body cried out against it. "I have got to be firm," she told herself. "I have got to hate him. I have got to cut this thing from out of my heart."

Deliberately she set herself to remember the moments when he had seemed particularly close or particularly attentive to Irene. Deliberately she made mind pictures of them and set them in front of her.

"Can you love a man like that?" she asked herself severely.

"What's the matter with you?" Kit enquired. "You are terribly quiet and you look unhappy. Don't tell me you're not enjoying yourself."

"But of course I am," Taryna replied. "I am enjoying every moment of it. I am so grateful to you for bringing me here, Kit. I never imagined it was anything like this."

"It is rather a surprise, isn't it?" Kit said. "Do look at those lovely blue-green roofs of the Normandie. That's where we're staying. Do you see something rather strange up there on one of the gables?"

"Yes, what is it?" Taryna asked. "Why, it's a cat!"

"A china cat! For luck I suppose," Kit said. "But it's a surprise, isn't it? Deauville is full of surprises. Perhaps there will be some for us too."

Her eyes were soft as she spoke and Taryna knew that she was thinking of Jock McDonald.

They entered the hotel and she saw Michael sitting with Irene in the lounge. "I have got to hate him," Taryna told herself.

He rose as they approached. Taryna glanced up and met his eyes. For a moment her resolution held, and then she knew it was quite impossible. Whatever he was like, however bad he might be, she loved him!

7

"When the others have gone to bed, come with me and I will show you some real amusements," a voice said softly.

Taryna looked round in astonishment. She had been watching the roulette table and felt for a moment almost hypnotised by the spinning of the ball, the croupiers' quiet voices and the click of the *plaques* as they were shovelled away towards the bank.

"Rien ne va plus."

There was a moment of silence in which Taryna felt it would be unwise to speak. Then there was the croupier's voice saying:

"Trente-six noir et pair."

And the chatter broke out again.

"What did you say?" Taryna asked.

"I said I would take you somewhere where it was really entertaining," Michael answered. "This is exceedingly dull unless you have the urge to throw your money away."

Taryna's eyes followed his across the table to where Irene was sitting with a great pile of *plaques* in front of her. She looked as if she was winning, although it was hard to tell because she had changed so many francs at the croupier's desk.

"Don't you play?" Taryna asked Michael.

Michael shook his head.

"I don't understand gambling," she said lamely. "I'm have a go."

120

Taryna flushed a little.

"I can't afford it," he said. "But I wonder you don't not even sure I approve of it."

"Would you like me to teach you?"

"No! No!"

The answer came quickly from between her lips—almost too quickly.

"Very well then. Do as I suggest. Irene will be going home soon and so will Mr. Newbury. When you have said good night, come down to the hall. I'll be waiting for you."

Taryna's instinct was to refuse. She knew that going out with Michael when her host and hostess thought that she was in bed was something that was not only wrong from the point of view of convention but was an action of which her father and mother would most decidedly disapprove.

"I think perhaps . . ." she began hesitantly, and then she felt the touch of Michael's hand.

"Please come," he pleaded.

Her opposition faded. Suddenly she wanted to go. She asked herself why she shouldn't take this opportunity of enjoying herself. Although the casino had been interesting, after two or three hours of it even the excitement of watching other people win or lose was beginning to pall.

Kit was walking from table to table putting on stakes at random.

"I don't take it too seriously," she said. At the same time, Taryna had discovered that Kit liked to gamble on her own; she didn't like to be watched. So there had been nothing for her to do but to stand about, and somehow Michael's suggestion had come at precisely the right moment.

"I ought to say no," Taryna said dutifully, speaking more to her own conscience than to Michael.

"But you won't," he replied. "I'll be waiting."

He gave her a smile which seemed to make her heart turn over again and then he left her and went back again to stand behind Irene's chair.

The wheel spun again two or three times, then Irene rose from the table.

"Collect my *plaques*, Michael," she said, in the tone that a Roman empress might have used to a slave.

Almost reluctantly Taryna went to Irene's side.

"Are you going home now, Mrs. Newbury?" she asked.

"Yes, I am tired," Irene replied. "Besides, I had much better leave when I am winning."

"Have you won much?" Taryna asked, feeling that an interest was expected of her.

Irene shrugged her bare shoulders.

"I'm not quite certain how much," she answered. "But enough to feel that I have earned my sleep."

She smiled at her own joke as Michael came up to them, the pockets of his dinner-jacket bulging with small *plaques* besides a number of the larger denominations which he held in his hand.

"Do you want them changed?" he asked.

"Yes, please."

He walked away towards the cashier. Irene looked round for Kit.

"We had better all go back together," she said. "I don't suppose my husband wants to stay on much longer."

"He's in the bar talking to the men who dined with us," Taryna said. "Shall I go and tell him?"

"Yes. Say I want to go home," Irene instructed her.

Two men, dark and rather swarthy-looking, were sitting with Mr. Newbury. They were all three smoking large cigars and they had a bottle of champagne on ice

122

beside them. Taryna stopped a little hesitantly by the table.

"Well, Taryna, what is it?" Mr. Newbury asked.

"Mrs. Newbury wants to go home."

"That suits me," he said, rising to his feet.

He shook hands with his friends, speaking to them in a language which Taryna did not understand. Then taking her by the arm he walked back across the casino to where Irene and Michael were standing by the desk.

As they drew near, Mr. Newbury stopped for a moment to speak to an acquaintance. Taryna walked on without him. Neither Irene nor Michael seemed to see her coming, and as Michael turned from the desk with a great sheaf of notes in his hands she heard Irene say:

"Oh, bother! Here's another *plaque* in my bag; one for ten thousand."

"I'll change it," Michael said.

"No, keep it," Irene answered. "You deserve it. I think you've brought me luck tonight."

For just a second it seemed to Taryna that Michael hesitated, and then he took the *plaque* from Irene and slipped it into his pocket.

"Thank you," he said.

For a moment Taryna could not believe that what she had seen and heard was correct. She paused, standing still where she was, waiting for Michael to continue. Surely, she thought wildly, he must finish the sentence. "Thank you, but I will change it for you; it won't take a moment." Or, "Thank you, but I really can't accept presents of that sort."

But he said nothing. With his hand deep in the pocket of his dinner-jacket, he looked up and saw Taryna watching.

"Here's Taryna," he said to Irene. "And she's brought Mr. Newbury."

"Now we can go," Irene said with a yawn.

"What about Kit?" Michael asked.

Irene turned to look back into the Casino.

"Really, the child is so tiresome. She always disappears just when one wants her."

"I can see her," Taryna managed to say. "I will go and fetch her."

She moved away, feeling for a moment as if she could not look at either Irene or Michael. "How shaming! How humiliating," she thought, "for any man to take presents and money from a woman, especially from a woman like Irene."

She did not know why, but that episode had shocked her more than anything had done for a long time. She knew now what Kit meant when she had called Michael a scrounger and a tame cat. She had expected him to accept presents of cars and race-horses, as apparently Billy and Eric had done, but to stoop to the acceptance of ten pounds, to be tipped like a schoolboy, or, indeed, like a servant, was something that Taryna had never believed possible.

And yet even before she had reached Kit's side she had begun to try and find excuses for him. There were doubtless lots of things he had to pay for when he came to a place like this, even though Mr. Newbury provided a roof over his head and the food that he ate.

What was the difference between taking a present in kind or in actual money? Taryna knew that there was a great and fundamental difference, and yet she could not put it into words. She only knew that she hated the thought of that ten-thousand-franc *plaque* in Michael's pocket.

"Are they going?" Kit asked as she reached her side. "Good! I've had a rotten run of luck and lost all my money."

"Oh, Kit, not really!" Taryna cried.

124

"Only the money I came here with, of course," Kit answered. "About twenty-five pounds, I suppose. But I always hate losing."

"Who doesn't?" Taryna asked.

She tried to prevent herself from thinking how much good twenty-five pounds spent in other ways could have done.

"Has Irene won?" Kit was asking.

"I think so," Taryna replied. "She says she doesn't bother to count it."

"That means she's won a packet," Kit said. "She thinks it's unlucky when she's winning to take too much interest in the money, on the principle of what you want you lose. Still, I'm glad she's won. It will put her in a good temper."

"You sound as if you particularly want her in a good mood," Taryna said.

Kit nodded.

"I'm going to meet Jock tonight," she whispered.

For a moment Taryna almost confided her own plans, and then she wondered if in actual fact she would go with Michael. How could they surreptitiously spend Irene's money in a way which she would, if she knew of it, most certainly disapprove.

"I won't go," Taryna told herself just as they reached the Newburys and Michael.

"Come on, Kit," Irene said crossly. "You always keep your father waiting."

Everyone knew it wasn't Mr. Newbury who minded waiting for Kit, but Irene; yet nothing was said, and Kit, instead of being on the defensive, more or less apologised.

"Well, let's go," Irene said.

She led the way from the *salle privée* through the dancing hall, where a cabaret was taking place, and

125

down the flight of stairs which led to the main door of the casino.

Outside Michael summoned one of the big cars which Mr. Newbury had hired for their private use. Without a word Irene stepped into the car, Kit followed her and Mr. Newbury went round to get in beside the chauffeur.

"In half an hour," Michael whispered to Taryna as she passed him.

"I'm not coming," she said.

There was no time for more. She got into the car and sat down beside Irene and Kit on the back seat. Michael sat on one of the smaller ones.

It was less than a minute's drive to the Normandie Hotel. When they got there, Irene swept in and said in her imperious manner that everyone was to go to bed at once.

"I won't have you hanging about downstairs in the lounge, Kit," she said. "It looks so bad for a young girl. Lady Heathcote was telling me only tonight that she never allows her daughter to sit about unchaperoned."

"Jane Heathcote would be quite safe if she was left alone naked in the middle of Piccadilly Circus," Kit replied.

"She's a very nice girl and knows a lot of nice people," Irene retorted.

Despite her resolution not to look at him, Taryna met Michael's eyes.

"Please come." There was no doubting the pleading in them, the message he was trying to convey. Almost imperceptibly she shook her head.

"Come along, come along."

Irene was making them follow her into the lift. There wasn't room for Michael and he waved to them as the gates shut.

"Good night."

"Good night, Michael. See you in the morning," Irene called.

The lift stopped at the third floor. They all got out and walked down the wide corridors to the doors of the big suite which was occupied by Irene and Mr. Newbury. Kit and Taryna had rooms in the same corridor adjoining each other.

"Good night, Kit. Good night, Taryna."

Irene wasted little time in making a pretence at kissing her stepdaughter. Then she went through the door of the suite.

"Good night, Father."

Kit kissed Mr. Newbury with more than the usual show of affection, and he shook hands with Taryna.

"I hope you haven't had too dull an evening," he said. "I noticed you didn't play."

"I enjoyed watching," Taryna replied quickly.

"Tomorrow we must persuade you to have a little flutter," Mr. Newbury said kindly. "I suppose my extravagant daughter will be wanting a cheque from me in the morning."

"That's right," Kit answered.

He smiled at them both and went into the suite. Kit came into Taryna's room.

"I am going now, at once," she said. "Jock is waiting for me outside the hotel."

"Suppose Irene wants to speak to you, or something like that?" Taryna enquired anxiously.

"She won't," Kit said cheerily. "She hates the sight of me. Besides, Jock has been waiting for nearly an hour. I hoped we'd get away earlier from the casino as it was the first night."

She dropped a light kiss on Taryna's cheek and slipping out of the room hurried away down the passage. Taryna shut the door and sat down at the dressing-table. She, too, might have been going downstairs. She

127

had a sudden yearning to see Michael, to talk to him. Then she remembered the ten-thousand-franc *plaque* and her heart hardened. She was ashamed for him, yet she knew that in her heart she longed to go to him.

At the thought of his kisses last night she felt herself suddenly thrill. Whatever he did, however he behaved, she could not deny the sudden quickened beating of her heart.

There was suddenly a knock at the door. She turned towards it, her eyes wide. Surely Michael would not come upstairs and argue with her with Irene in almost the next room? If they were found, it would put her in an intolerably false position.

She felt angry with him and crossing the room opened the door impetuously, ready to whisper angrily to him that he must go away at once. To her astonishment Mr. Newbury stood there.

"Oh, it's you!" Taryna exclaimed.

Mr. Newbury put his finger to his lips and almost tiptoed into the room, closing the door very softly behind him.

"I don't want Kit to hear us," he said. "I have come for her present which you so kindly concealed for me."

"Oh yes, of course," Taryna said.

She had almost forgotten about it in the busy events of the day, but now she went quickly into the bathroom adjoining her bedroom. Ella had unpacked her things again and, as she expected, the pink sponge-bag was hanging on a hook by the side of the wash-basin in the bathroom. It contained the sponge, flannel and soap which Taryna herself had packed into it before she left the yacht.

She pulled them out one by one. Underneath was the little package which Mr. Newbury had given her. She carried it into the next room.

"Here it is," she said. "I am afraid it is a little damp. You see, I put it in my sponge-bag."

Mr. Newbury smiled. She had the impression that he had been looking worried. Now he was smiling and at his ease.

"In your sponge-bag," he exclaimed. "A very clever place of concealment. It was hanging, I suppose, where anyone could see it, and yet it was the sort of place where no one would look."

"That's what I thought," Taryna said. "I remember reading a book once which said to conceal something well it should always be just under the very nose of the people who are looking for it."

"You are a very intelligent young lady, I can see that," Mr. Newbury complimented her. "You must let me buy you a little present to thank you for being able to outwit those very nosy Customs officials."

"Oh, but we don't know that they looked in my cabin," Taryna said. "In fact, I was never even asked if I had anything to declare."

"They looked at everything they wanted to look at," Mr. Newbury said. "And now Kit's present will be a big surprise, all thanks to you."

"It's her birthday the day after tomorrow, isn't it?" Taryna said.

"That's right."

"I must get her something," Taryna said.

"And you must let me get you a present as well," Mr. Newbury insisted.

"Oh no, please," Taryna said.

He patted her on the shoulder.

"We shall have to think of something really nice," he said. "And you won't mention to anyone how clever we've been about this? If it got back to the Customs officials, they would be even more stringent in their searchings another time."

"No, I won't tell anyone," Taryna said.

"Please don't," he said. "Women—even the best of them, like my wife and daughter—are so very inclined to talk, and talk gets round. You understand?"

"Yes, of course I do," Taryna answered.

He patted her shoulder again and went from the room, moving, Taryna thought, surprisingly quietly for a man of his size.

Alone, her thoughts flashed back again to Michael. How long would he wait? she wondered. She looked at her watch. It was only just after midnight.

Suddenly the telephone rang, startling her so much that almost instinctively she ran to it to stop its clamour. Even as she picked up the receiver she knew who was at the other end.

"Hello!"

"Is that you, Taryna?"

"Yes, Michael."

"I am waiting for you."

"I told you I wasn't coming."

"But, why?"

"Oh, I just think it's better not."

"But I want you to come, if only for a very short while. We will just go into Trouville. There are some small, unimportant places I know but which are very gay and amusing at this time of night."

Taryna felt she was being tempted.

"No, Michael."

"Why did you change your mind?"

"Because . . . Oh, not for any reason I can explain."

"Listen!" Michael's voice was suddenly serious. "I want to see you. It is important—important to both of us. Do you understand?"

"But, how . . . how can it be?"

"That is what I am going to tell you. Stop being

130

difficult and come downstairs. It will be all right, I promise you."

There was something in his voice that was irresistible. Taryna had been seated on the bed, but now she rose to her feet.

"All right," she said suddenly. "I'll come."

She picked up a wrap to throw over her shoulders. Her short evening dress of white organza appliqued with large bunches of coral flowers and embroidered with sequins flashed and shimmered as she moved across the room. Then the door was closed behind her, and she was running down the corridor as if she was afraid of being stopped.

She did not call the lift but went down the stairs. Michael was standing in the hall and because he had expected her to come the other way his back was towards her. She had a sudden glimpse of him, as it were, off his guard. His broad shoulders, his well-set head, the manner in which he stood, seemed suddenly utterly dependable, completely and absolutely secure. Whatever he did, however he behaved, somehow she felt she could trust him.

Her instinct told her that she could even while her brain cried out that it was not true, that she was being deceived. Yet she knew her heart was right. She reached his side and he turned round with an expression of absolute delight on his face.

"You have come. I knew you would."

He took both her hands and raised them to his lips, and then, guiding her with his hand under her elbow, he led her though the door and outside into the warm dark night. He called a taxi and helped her into it. He gave an address and got in beside her. As the taxi moved off, suddenly Taryna felt shy. She was alone with Michael and it was somehow an adventure to be driving off alone together.

"Thank you for coming."

His words were simple and utterly sincere.

"I ought not to have."

"Why not? You are your own mistress."

"I am the guest of Mr. and Mrs. Newbury."

"It still doesn't make them your guardians. If you want to go out, why shouldn't you? Besides, I shall take very great care of you."

"I am glad about that. I wouldn't want my body to be found washed up on the beach somewhere down the coast."

"Such things have happened before," Michael said. "But not when I am about."

Taryna smiled at the confidence in his tone.

"You sound like Sir Lancelot and Gary Cooper rolled into one," she teased.

"Perhaps I feel like them both because you look so lovely tonight."

"Nonsense."

"It isn't nonsense and you know it. Didn't you see all the men looking at you at the casino?"

"Of course I didn't," Taryna said. "Nobody gave me a glance. They were all far too intent on watching the wheel or the turn of a card. I am sure no woman has any hope of competing against the goddess of Chance."

"Not even when she looks like a goddess?"

Taryna felt Michael's hand come out to touch hers. She thought that he was about to kiss her and turned her face away.

"No, please," she murmured.

"Why?" he asked. "Have I done anything to offend you?"

She thought of the ten-thousand-franc *plaque* reposing in his pocket, and because she was unused to lying she could not bring herself to treat his question lightly.

"So there is something," he said after a moment.

132

"No, it's nothing. . . . I have . . . got no right," Taryna stammered.

"You have every right," he said softly.

He bent forward and pulling aside the glass which separated them from the driver said something in French. He spoke so quickly that Taryna did not quite understand or have time to translate, but she saw that the taxi altered its course, turning down a side street and going back a little way on their tracks.

For one moment she thought that Michael was taking her home, and then the taxi stopped and to her surprise she saw they were outside a church.

"What is it?" Taryna asked. "Why are we here?"

"This won't take a moment," Michael answered.

He opened the door and helped her out. She followed him wonderingly, wanting to ask questions and yet somehow finding them too difficult to formulate. She could say nothing.

They walked up the steps of the church. Michael pulled open a leather-covered door and they went in. There was a sweet, pungent smell of incense. There were no lights save the dozens of candles lit in front of statues of saints. The roof and the side aisles were in complete darkness. There were only flickering lights and the sweet, gentle faces of the saints above them.

Resolutely Michael walked up the aisle. Just before they reached the altar on the right-hand side there was a statue surrounded by more candles than any of the others. Tall, high candles; little thin ones; and many that were flickering on the verge of extinction like a prayer that had been said for a soul that was slipping away into eternity.

Michael stopped in front of them and Taryna saw that the statue towering above them was that of St. Thérèse of Lisieux. There was her dark robe, the sheaf of roses in her arms, and her sweet young face up-turned in ecstasy to Heaven.

For a moment they stood there in silence, then Michael drew something from his pocket. He said nothing. He only held it so that Taryna could see it very clearly—the ten-thousand-franc *plaque* which Irene had given to him.

For a moment she could only stare at it, and then she looked up and met his eyes in the light of the candles.

"For the saint who grants the little things that little people want," he said quietly.

His hand went out and he slipped the *plaque* into the alms box beneath the statue's feet. It fell with a little plop and then there was silence.

"Now that is disposed of," Michael said quietly, "we can feel free."

He took Taryna by the hand and led her down the aisle, past the other statues with their flickering lights, through the leather-covered door and out on to the steps of the church.

The taxi-driver was waiting. He bowed them into his cab, his cap in his hand, and then they were off again. The taxi turned once again into the direction of Trou-ville.

Taryna said nothing. Somehow there was no need for words. She could only wonder that Michael had understood her so clearly, that he had known what she was thinking and feeling, and had acted in a manner which had somehow swept away all her resentment, all the cruel and unkind things she had been thinking of him.

"Now we can be happy," he said quietly.

He did not attempt to kiss her and somehow Taryna knew that that, too, was part of his understanding. The atmosphere in the church, those lights before the statue, had somehow put her in a very different mood. What she felt for Michael at this moment did not need to be expressed by the touch of their hands or even of their lips. There was something deeper, something infinitely greater and therefore even more frightening.

They passed over the bridge and into Trouville before Michael spoke again. Then he said:

"We are going somewhere quite cheap, something I can afford myself."

"That's what I would like," Taryna said.

The taxi drew up at a small, lighted restaurant on the hill. As Taryna stepped out she saw that it was called La Caprice, and as the door was opened there was the sound of music and laughter and voices—a kind of gaiety which even at one's first taste of it was more intoxicating than wine.

There was a long, narrow room with a bar running down the length of it, and beyond it a terrace where there were little tables looking over the sea. Couples were dancing; but many more were just sitting holding hands, obviously entranced with their own company, forgetful of everything save the magic of themselves and the evening.

Michael and Taryna were shown a table on the edge of the terrace. As they sat down, Taryna realised for the first time that the whole place was quite inexpensively arranged. The terrace had at one time obviously been the back garden of a house which had been built up so that from it one could have a good view of the sea. The band consisted of three black men; the tables were only iron, but were covered with fresh, clean table-cloths; and the waitresses were smiling young women whose father served behind the bar.

Michael ordered a carafe of white wine and then turned towards Taryna.

"Later we will have something to eat," he said. "For the moment I want to talk."

"What about?" she asked a little dreamily.

"Ourselves," he answered. "Isn't that the most interesting subject in the world?"

"Tell me about yourself," Taryna said with sudden interest.

"Ladies first," he replied.

"No, that isn't fair," she answered. "I asked you the question."

"But I really want to know something about you," he said.

Taryna looked away from him. Far away below she could hear the sea lapping very gently against the beach. It had a beautiful, mysterious sound. Somehow it was inexplicably linked with the peace and serenity she had found in the church they had just left. She didn't want to lie to him and yet, somehow, she must answer his question.

"Very well," she said a little defiantly. "I will tell you about myself, but there is so little to tell. As you know, I am at Cambridge with Kit. I was going home for the vacation and she persuaded me, half against my will, to come to Earlywood with her. The rest you know."

"The rest I know," Michael repeated a little ironically. "And, of course, you are very, very rich."

"What does money matter one way or another?" Taryna asked.

"Oh, it matters a lot," Michael replied, "when you haven't got it."

"Well, why don't you get a job?" Taryna enquired.

"That's exactly what Kit asked me earlier this evening," Michael replied. "Only not so politely. In fact she was quite rude about it."

"That was wrong of Kit," Taryna said quickly. "But

136

she has a sort of unreasoning hate of all Irene's young men."

"Is that how you label me?" Michael enquired. "Irene's young man!"

"Well, aren't you?" Taryna asked.

He gave a little laugh.

"I would like you to think of me in a very different way."

"But I can't, can I?" Taryna said seriously.

He stared for a moment across the room although it was quite obvious that he was not watching the dancers moving in time to the gay rhythm of the band.

"No, I suppose not," he said. Then suddenly he turned and took Taryna's hands in his. "Let us forget it all. Just for tonight at any rate. Let us forget what you think about me or what I think about you. Let us pretend that we are just two people who have met and fallen in love and that there are no barriers to stop them loving each other just as much as they want. Let us not ask questions, let us not be inquisitive about anything, except what we feel in our hearts. Let us remember the lights of love. Is that a bargain?"

His enthusiasm was infectious. Taryna felt her fingers tighten on his; felt her breath coming a little quicker.

"I love you," Michael said in a voice that was suddenly deep and moved with emotion. "I love you. Let us forget everything else."

"Everything," Taryna answered, "except this."

"Come and dance."

Michael jumped to his feet and led Taryna on to the floor. The band was playing a soft, dreamy melody, but for a moment Taryna wondered wildly whether she would dance well enough. She had not had a great deal of practice—nothing like Kit, for instance, who was always at dances, night clubs or balls of one sort or another.

Even at Cambridge Kit would join up with other girls and several undergraduates and go dancing two or three times a week. But Taryna had stayed in her room and worked. Now she wished she had had more practice, but almost before the idea was formulated in her mind she knew she need not have worried.

From the moment that Michael's arms were round her, from the moment he held her close against him they moved as if they were one person, perfectly in tune with each other. And Taryna knew that whatever he did, however complicated his steps, she would instinctively and without question be able to follow him.

"I wanted to dance so that I could hold you in my arms," Michael said.

He put his cheek against hers, and as his arm tightened round her she felt herself quiver with sheer happiness because she was close to him.

"You are so light that I might be dancing with one of the wraiths that they tell me come inland with the sea mists."

"That sounds rather chilly somehow," Taryna laughed, even though her heart was beating quickly at the magic of his words.

"I will prevent you from being chilly," Michael answered. "Do you remember last night, how warm and alive we were? Oh, Taryna! I lay awake thinking of your lips and your face in the moonlight."

They went round the room once more and then Michael led Taryna back to their table.

"Now we are going to talk," he said. "I want to look at you. I want to tell you how lovely you are."

"I wonder if you would have thought so a week ago," Taryna answered.

"Why a week ago?" he enquired.

"Because I have altered since then," Taryna answered. "Kit made me have my hair cut and arranged in a new way. She lent me these clothes, as you know mine had gone home. I am really rather a dowd."

"You couldn't be anything but beautiful," Michael answered. "Your eyes are so expressive; they are also mysterious, dark and rather exciting. They make me wonder all the time what you are thinking. When you are angry with me I am afraid. I don't think I have ever been afraid in that sort of way before."

"You are being ridiculous," Taryna said, but she could not help the tremor of emotion in her voice.

"Darling, look at me," Michael commanded.

Despite a sudden shyness she turned her face towards him. The look in his eyes held her absolutely captive.

"I can only keep saying I love you," Michael said. "I want to make you love me, too. I want you to feel—feel, feel, feel all the things I am feeling for you. I want you with every inch of my body, with the smallest corner of my brain. I want to possess you; I want to keep you; I want to make you mine. This is love, Taryna. But a love so exciting and yet so overwhelming that I am almost afraid of it."

"I, too . . . am afraid," Taryna whispered.

"What's to become of us if we can't have each other?" Michael asked.

Taryna did not answer because she knew there was no answer for the moment. How, knowing that she was not what she seemed to him, could she say there was no reason why they shouldn't have each other?

Was he making love to her? she wondered suddenly with a little shiver, or was he making love to the rich Miss Grazebrook from Canada—beautifully dressed, exquisitely coiffeured, with a background of opulence

139

and luxury as good as, if not better than, the Newbury's?

"It is no use," she thought wearily. He didn't really love her. How could he? It was the rich and glamorous Miss Grazebrook he was in love with, not poor little Taryna from the Vicarage.

And then because she was in love, because she was young and because the fact of sitting next to Michael had some amazing magic about it, she said quickly:

"Let us go on pretending, pretending that only tonight matters."

"That is all that does matter," Michael said. "This moment when you and I are together, when we know that we love each other. It is true, isn't it, Taryna? You do love me a little bit?"

"Yes, I love you," Taryna answered, and as she said it her voice broke on a sob.

8

"We ought to go back."

"Yes, I know."

Neither of them moved. They were standing with their elbows on the sea-wall, looking to where the first glimmer of dawn was shimmering on the grey water.

This was the end, Taryna thought, of what had been the most perfect evening she could ever remember.

They had danced at La Caprice until even the smiling waitresses seemed weary and there was no one left but the band and themselves. Then they had gone gaily down the twisting, cobbled streets to find another place of amusement.

But it was no use looking for night spots because the night was over; and so they crossed the harbour where the *Heron* lay shrouded in darkness, and walked on to the wide, golden sands which joined Deauville with Trouville.

At first they ran, Michael trying to catch Taryna, and when he succeeded, lifting her up in his arms. But after a while they moved more quietly, hand in hand, arm in arm, until the Normandie Hotel came in sight.

The stars had disappeared from the sky and the first finger of dawn, golden and insistent, had appeared in the east.

"I must go."

Again Taryna said the words, but Michael turned and put his arms round her.

"I can't bear this night to end," he said.

"I wish it could go on for ever," Taryna answered. "But we have got to go back to reality."

Michael put his cheek against hers, but he did not kiss her.

"It may be difficult to do this again," he said. "You realise that?"

"Why?" she asked.

For a moment he hesitated and then said:

"Irene seldom goes to bed early. It is usually four or five in the morning before she'll leave the casino."

Taryna felt herself stiffen. It was the first time for hours that Irene's name had been mentioned between them. Now it seemed as if she stood between them—a golden barrier with her beauty, her jewels and her money.

"Must you always do what Irene wants?"

She had not meant to ask the question. It was said before she could stop it.

With what seemed to her almost a sigh Michael took his arms from her.

"For the moment," he answered.

"Why? Can't you explain? Or is there no need for an explanation?"

"Shall we say I am not going to give you one?"

His voice was suddenly rather sharp.

"I understand."

Taryna turned towards the hotel. There was only an occasional light in all the hundreds of windows. Its gables were silhouetted very clearly against the lightening sky.

"You don't understand," Michael said. "Taryna, don't go from me like that. You know I love you, but there are some things that I can't do."

"One of them being to offend Mrs. Newbury," Taryna said. "The other, presumably, is to get a job."

For a moment Michael did not speak and then he swept her into his arms.

"Think that," he said. "Think what you please. But you can't deny that you love me. I know it. It is there on your lips, it is in your eyes, it is in your very breath."

He bent as he finished speaking and sought her mouth. She did not resist him—indeed it would have been impossible for her to do so for he was at the moment driven by a wild passion that was half anger, half desire.

He kissed her lips, every kiss growing fiercer, more possessive; and then he was kissing her eyes, her neck, and once again her mouth until she cried out for mercy.

"Please, Michael! Please, you are hurting me."

It was as if he did not hear her. His kisses rained down on her, fiercer and more passionate, until she felt as if they drained every ounce of her strength away and left her limp and utterly helpless in his arms.

When at last he raised his face from hers, she was almost collapsing against him; and now as the sun rose higher he could see her face.

He looked down at her with what seemed to her almost an expression of cruelty in his eyes. He looked at the bruised softness of her mouth, the dark shadows under her eyes, the flush on her cheeks.

"You love me!" he said triumphantly. "Now would you deny it?"

"Please, Michael, no more."

She put up her hand as his lips drew nearer to hers again. Impatiently he brushed her fingers aside.

"Say you love me," he commanded. "Say it. I want to hear you say the words."

"I . . . love . . . you."

143

She had not the power to argue with him. She could only weakly obey his commands.

"Say it again, again," he ordered.

"Michael, we must go."

"Not until you have told me again that you love me. Whatever I am, however much you may despise me in some ways, you still love me because you cannot help it. Say it."

"No . . . I . . ."

"Say it," he commanded.

"I . . . love you."

"Just as I am?"

"Just as you are."

She felt him sigh with relief. Then he bent and kissed her once again, but more gently and with a tenderness that had not been there before.

"Poor darling. I made you tired. Come back to the hotel. You must go to bed."

With his arm round her shoulders they walked down the empty road.

"You, too, must get some sleep," Taryna said.

Michael shook his head.

"No, I couldn't sleep. I am too happy. I am going for a swim."

"Now?" she questioned.

"Now, this moment; as soon as I have sent you up to bed. It is the best time, when none of the fools are about."

"But mightn't it be dangerous? Supposing you got cramp or something like that?"

He smiled.

"You need not be afraid for me," he said. "I always turn up like a bad penny. Besides, I expect, if we but knew it, quite a lot of curious eyes are on the look-out for suicides or even lovers."

Taryna looked up apprehensively at the hotel.

144

"I hope nobody has seen us," she said.

"Nobody who matters, at any rate," Michael corrected.

They had reached the side road which led round to the front door. Michael stopped.

"Good night, my darling," he said. "Thank you for a perfect evening."

"I have been so happy," Taryna said wistfully.

She waited for a moment hoping he would say that he would try to see her alone during the day, or perhaps making an appointment to go out in the evening provided Irene went to bed early. But Michael said no more. He merely kissed her once again and then, without further words, led her round to the front of the hotel and in through the big, glass doorway.

The night porter bade them a sleepy "Good night."

"I expect he thinks we have been to the casino all this time," Taryna said.

"All he is thinking of is his breakfast and a comfortable bed," Michael answered.

They entered the big hall and Taryna went towards the stairs.

"Good night."

In the lights she glanced at Michael rather shyly. Somehow it seemed that they were both of them different now they were back to civilisation again.

For a moment Taryna thought he almost looked like a stranger. She ran up the stairs and he watched her go. When she got to the half-landing, she turned and waved. He made no response, merely watching her until she was out of sight.

She was out of breath when she reached her bedroom. The key was in the door. She turned it as quietly as possible, wondering if Kit had returned.

It took her only a few seconds to undress. She thought she must be tired; but when she got into the

145

big, comfortable bed she found instead her thoughts were racing and her heart beating quickly at the memory of all that had taken place that evening. Never had she believed it possible to be so happy.

"You are enchanting." She could hear Michael's deep voice saying it as he looked into her eyes. "There is something mysterious about you. I think perhaps you are a witch and ought to be burned at the stake."

"I wouldn't harm you even if I were."

She had not believed that her own voice could hold so much emotion in it.

"You have destroyed me already. Didn't you know that love is the most dangerous weapon anyone could use?"

Hours later she could hear herself ask:

"What is love?"

"It is being insanely, crazily happy like we are now. It is being desperately afraid that one will lose the person one loves. It is being supremely confident that one can, if one wishes, conquer the whole world. It is being utterly in despair that one may not be good enough to hold the love one has just won."

What wonderful things Michael managed to say, Taryna thought. The sun was coming through her window; she thought of him swimming out to sea, his head dark against the emerald waves, the bronze skin of his body as golden as the sun itself.

She loved him. She thought of his hands touching hers, of his shoulder against which she had hidden her face. She thought of his lips. She felt herself quiver a little and thrill again to the strength and passion of his kisses.

She put up her fingers to touch her mouth. It was tender and yet the very pain of it was somehow an exquisite pleasure.

"I love him." She must have said the words a dozen times before she fell asleep.

She awoke with a start to find Kit sitting on the end of her bed.

"I thought you must be dead," Kit laughed at her. "Do you know it's eleven o'clock? I've never known you sleep so late before."

"I'm not used to such late hours," Taryna said drowsily.

"Oh, do wake up," Kit begged. "I want to talk to you."

With an effort Taryna managed to open her eyes.

"Eleven o'clock isn't late," she said. "Not for Deauville."

"Look how sophisticated we're getting," Kit teased. "Why, a week ago you would have been shocked if I had suggested staying in bed until ten o'clock."

"A week ago you hadn't spoilt me," Taryna said.

She sat up, pushed her pillow behind her shoulders and put on a little dressing-jacket of satin and marabou which Kit threw at her.

"Now order your breakfast," Kit said, "and then I can talk to you."

Obediently Taryna pressed the little red button by her bedside and a few seconds later the waiter knocked at the door. When she had ordered coffee and rolls she said:

"Now I am all attention. What happened last night?"

"Jock and I went and sat on the sea front," Kit said. "And we talked and talked. It was heaven to be with him, but somehow we didn't seem to get any further."

"Why not?" Taryna enquired.

"Jock wants me to tell Father. I told him it was impossible. All that will happen is that I shall be sent home, or round the world, or something, and Jock will get the sack. I suggested running away with him. We

147

can go to Gretna Green and get a special licence by lying about my age. It can be managed. Or if it can't, I am prepared to go off with him and just force Father's hand to letting us get married."

"Supposing he won't be forced?" Taryna asked.

"That's exactly what Jock said. But I told him we have only got a year to wait until I am twenty-one."

"And what did Jock say to that?"

"He's just old-fashioned and stuffy," Kit said angrily. "There's something obstinate about the Scots and nothing you can say will budge them once they have made up their minds. Jock says he's got nothing of which to be ashamed. What he can't see is that Father and Irene will never allow it if they get the slightest suspicion of what's going on."

"But what is the alternative?" Taryna asked.

"To wait a year," Kit said tragically.

"Perhaps he is right," Taryna said. "After all, it will give you a chance to know your own mind."

"Don't I know it now?" Kit answered. "That's what I can't make him see. I know now that he is the person I want to marry, and nothing is going to stop my marrying him either."

"Then why not do as he suggests? Tell your father and see what happens."

Kit got down off the bed and walked towards the door. To Taryna's astonishment she opened it suddenly, looked outside and shut it again.

"I was just looking to see if anyone was listening," she said. "Taryna! The answer to your question is that I am scared."

"Scared of what?" Taryna enquired.

"Of Father," Kit answered. "Not for myself, but for Jock."

Taryna was just going to say, "what nonsense," and laugh at Kit when she checked the words. She was

148

remembering how she had heard her own voice coming through the secretaries' door.

"What do you mean?" she asked.

Kit lowered her voice.

"Father is utterly ruthless when he wants something," she said. "I haven't lived with him these past years since Mother died without knowing that he has altered in many ways. He has grown more ruthless, more autocratic. Sometimes I almost think he believes he's God."

"Oh, Kit, I'm sure you're exaggerating," Taryna said. "I wish I were," Kit answered. "It's just that things happen exactly the way he wants them. He forces people to do his wishes. Sometimes he bribes them, sometimes I know he threatens them. I don't want Jock threatened, or even worse things to happen to him."

"Kit, you're not suggesting. . . ?" Taryna said in a shocked tone.

Kit avoided looking at her.

"I'm not suggesting anything," she said. "I'm only saying that I'm frightened for Jock and for myself."

Taryna was silent.

"Help me, Taryna," Kit pleaded.

"But how?" Taryna asked. "What can I do?"

"I don't know," Kit answered. "I don't know what anyone can do, except perhaps if you talked to Jock he might see sense."

"I don't really see that anything you are suggesting is sense," Taryna answered. "If you try and get married without your father's permission, you will have to lie and he would go to the courts and get the marriage annulled. If you run away and live with Jock, even provided he will let you, your father can still force you to go back to him by law."

"He wouldn't stand for the publicity of that," Kit

said. "Think of the headlines: *Millionaire's daughter runs away with yacht hand*. Irene would never let him do that for the sake of what the newspapers would say."

"They will say the same sort of thing if you marry him," Taryna said. "Are you meeting again tonight?"

Kit nodded.

"Yes. He says he can get off at about nine o'clock. I shall tell Irene I've go a headache. After all, she had one last night."

"Supposing she comes to your room?"

"She won't if I put 'don't disturb' on the outside. Besides, one's got to take some sort of risk," Kit said philosophically.

She gave a little laugh.

"Irene gave me a lecture before we went down to dinner last night about being pleasant to Lord Quarry. Did you see him? A half-baked-looking man with a large adam's apple and glasses."

"I thought he was awful!" Taryna exclaimed.

"So do I," Kit answered. "But all that Irene worries about is that he's a lord. I believe he's completely impoverished with large, tumbledown estates somewhere in Dorset. She's mesmerised his mother into thinking that Father's money and a marriage dowry to me could do them up."

"Oh, Kit, I don't believe it," Taryna said.

"It's perfectly true," Kit answered. "I heard her saying to Lady Quarry: 'My stepdaughter is such an admirer of your son. She often tells me how clever he is.'"

"How could she say such a thing?" Taryna asked.

"Irene would say anything if it served a purpose," Kit answered. "She doesn't say much that doesn't. You don't understand, Taryna. You are so simple. When people want something, they use every method in their power to get it."

"Well, I suppose that's all right," Taryna said. "Daddy prays when he wants something very much."

"Prayers are a very different thing," Kit said impatiently. "That is relying on some power far greater than oneself. But Father and Irene, and people like them, rely entirely on themselves. They fight to the end—crookedly, dishonestly, by any method which happens to occur to them. They are determined to get what they want, and in nine cases out of ten they get it."

"We must be careful," Taryna said.

She had a sudden foreboding of the forces they would be up against. Once again she thought of that sinister tape-recorder under the dining-room table, of Mr. Newbury's eyes when he was listening to what his business associates were saying. Here was a man who could be dangerous if necessary.

She wondered wildly whether what they were saying now was being listened to. Might there not be a tape-recorder in this very bedroom? Or perhaps there were some other ways that Mr. Newbury had discovered of listening to what his daughter might be saying to her friend.

"What's the matter?" Kit asked. "Why are you looking round like that?"

"I was only thinking," Taryna said quickly. She felt she couldn't tell even Kit of what she had discovered at Earlywood. There was something so shaming about eavesdropping and a host sinking to recording without their permission what his guests had said.

There was a knock at the door which made both the girls start. When Taryna said, "Come in," it was Irene's maid who entered.

"I was looking for you, Miss Kit," she said. "Madam wants to see you immediately."

151

Kit glanced at Taryna enquiringly and followed the maid from the room.

She was gone a long time. Taryna got up and had her bath and was nearly dressed before Kit came bursting back into her room. She slammed the door behind her, then flung herself in the chair beside the dressing-table.

"I've had the most ghastly lecture from Irene," she said.

"What about?" Taryna enquired.

"Lord Quarry, of course! She said I wasn't pleasant enough to him. I said I was as pleasant as I was likely to be to a little squirt like that, and then she lost her temper and raved at me. She said I was a disappointment and a disgrace; I had done nothing but thwart her ever since she married Father, and she would wash her hands of me if she hadn't such a sense of responsibility.

"I told her I didn't want to be her responsibility, but, of course, it was no use. She raved on and on for hours, but it all came back to the same thing—she's got plans for me to marry this senseless idiot, and as far as I can make out Father is quite agreeable."

"He can't want you to marry somebody you don't love," Taryna said.

"I think Father's forgotten the meaning of the word," Kit answered. "Besides, from what Irene said I gather that he thinks Lord Quarry would be quite useful on some of his boards of directors. Some of his companies are pretty shady and a lord might make them sound better so long as they didn't see him in person."

Kit spoke with such bitterness that Taryna bent to kiss her cheek.

"Don't worry," she said. "Somehow we will find a way out of all this."

"The only pleasant thing Irene said was that it was a

pity I wasn't more like you," Kit went on. "And, incidentally, she asked your father's christian name. I gather she's going to send a puff to some of the newspapers to say what an important party we've got here, and she wants to include the rich Miss Grazebrook."

Trayna put her hands to her face.

"Oh, Kit, don't let her do that! Supposing Daddy or Mummy saw it?"

"Are they likely to?" Kit asked. "It will only be in the gossip columns."

"No, I suppose not," Taryna said doubtfully. "But it's rather dangerous, in case some inquisitive busybody took it to them. Daddy would be furious if he knew that I was acting a lie—in fact he would make me tell your father right away."

"Then the fat would be in the fire," Kit said cheerfully. "Irene, having approved of you, would think herself publicly defrauded if you weren't what you appear to be."

"I think I ought to slip away before the worst is discovered," Taryna said.

She did not, however, speak very positively. She wanted to stay here, to be near Michael, to see him even though she knew in her heart that it was making things worse.

Last night she had shied away from facing the truth. She loved him, but how unbearable that love was going to be when it must be concealed and hidden, when as far as she knew there was never any end to it.

Over and over again Michael had said that he loved her; and when he was not speaking, his eyes and lips had told her so even more eloquently. Never once had he said a word about marriage. Never had he suggested for one second that there might be anything permanent in their affection for each other.

For a moment she tried to buoy herself up with the

153

idea that it was too soon for Michael to have said anything of marriage, however much he cared for her. And then she knew that was only deceiving herself.

Michael had not mentioned marriage because he did not intend their love to be anything but a love affair—a beautiful, transitory thing which had flashed into their lives like a meteor and would doubtless flash out again just as quickly.

Taryna felt herself almost cry out at the thought. She could not lose him, she could not. And then she knew that this was the price she was paying for lying.

"Whenever you do something wrong, you get punished, however cleverly you may think to avoid it." She could hear her father telling her that when she was a little girl; and now, as never before, she knew the truth of what he said.

She had lied to please Kit, even while she knew it was wrong, and this was her punishment. Michael loved her, but he loved not herself but someone he believed her to be, and so the very foundation of what they felt for each other was false.

Was it because he thought she was rich that he did not ask her to marry him? Or was it because she was rich that he loved her? If he had seen her as she really was—Kit's poor, shabby, down-at-heel friend—would he have said all that he did last night? Or might he not have said it and added: "Will you marry me?"

These were impossible questions which she knew she could not answer, and yet they must ask themselves. The punishment was cruel but she knew she deserved it.

"Of course you can't leave me now," Kit was saying. "You know I can't do without you. And you are not to worry about anything Irene says. She won't find out if we are clever."

"We shall have to be very clever then," Taryna said,

"because there are such a lot of things that neither Irene nor your father must discover."

"Yes, I know," Kit said seriously. "But will you come and meet Jock with me tonight?"

"Will it be safe for us to do so?" Taryna asked.

Kit shrugged her shoulders.

"We have got to take some risks some time. I shall tell Irene I have got a headache as soon as we get to the casino. Once she's seated at the table she doesn't take much interest in anything else. You must say you'll come back with me."

"All right," Taryna said.

All through the day Kit's impatience for the evening to come somehow transmitted itself to Taryna. There was a huge party for lunch. Afterwards they went down to the beach where Mr. Newbury had engaged two brightly coloured tents, with chairs and cushions and every possible comfort.

They all bathed, a huge party of them, with the exception of Irene who lay about looking almost absurdly elegant in an exquisitely cut satin bathing-suit, with a wrap, bathing shoes and beach jewellery all to match.

Michael bathed too, but Taryna saw that long before the others left the water he had returned to sit by Irene's side, sun-bathing and talking to her. She felt her jealousy was almost a living pain in her breast as she watched them.

And later that evening, when they came down to dinner for another huge party, she felt herself almost choke as she heard Irene say:

"Michael, darling, you shall have a treat tonight and sit next to me. I did my duty at lunch. Tonight we will dispense with protocol and draw for places. But I have already drawn you, so there is no need for you to do anything but take the names round to the others."

155

"Isn't that cheating?" Michael asked.

His back was to Taryna and he had not seen her come in. She wondered if the expression in his eyes as he looked down at Irene was the same as it had been last night when he looked at her.

"Cheating is permissible under certain circumstances," Irene retorted. "I won't give you three guesses as to what those circumstances are."

Taryna felt as if she could bear no more. She was just about to slip forward and proclaim her presence when Kit came hurrying into the cocktail lounge.

"Am I late?" she asked, and Michael and Irene, who had been talking together in the corner where the tables were reserved for their party, turned round and saw both Kit and Taryna.

"Come along, girls," Irene said pleasantly. "I've just been telling Michael that tonight we are going to draw for partners. I've drawn already."

She gave Michael a little shy glance as she spoke and there was a pleased, possessive smile on her lips as he walked towards Kit with a little bowl containing a lot of folded names. Kit took one out.

"Damn!" she exclaimed. "It's Lord Quarry. I believe you put it on top on purpose. Can I have another turn?"

"Certainly not," Irene said. "We must play fair. Besides, I wanted you to sit next to Lord Quarry."

"That's obvious," Kit said. "Who have you got, Taryna?"

"Your father," Taryna answered.

"Well, I hope you will make him in a better temper than he has been all day," Irene said. "I really don't know what's the matter with Walter these days."

Taryna felt rather apprehensive and her fears were not allayed when Mr. Newbury was extremely late for dinner. All the rest of the party—about twenty of them—had finished their cocktails before he appeared.

"Where have you been, Walter?" Irene asked petulantly.

"I am sorry. I had some long-distance telephone calls," he replied. "Shall we go in to dinner? I've had a cocktail upstairs."

"Very well," Irene said rising to her feet, and beckoning her more distinguished guests, like Lady Quarry, to lead the way.

Taryna came last and most of the rest of the company were seated at the table before she reached her own seat. It was quite obvious that her host was preoccupied with his own thoughts. Twice the wine waiter had to speak to him before he realised that he must order the champagne, and then he sat tapping on the table with his fingers, his lower lip thrust forward a little as if in intense concentration.

Taryna did not like to interrupt his thoughts with some frivolous remark and so she sat silent, and it wasn't until the fish course had come and gone before, in passing her the salt, Mr. Newbury seemed suddenly to realise that she was there.

"Have you had a good day?" he asked perfunctorily.

"Yes, a lovely time, thank you," Taryna answered. "The sea was quite warm. I never realised that it got quite as warm as that."

She realised even as she said it that it was rather a giveaway remark for someone who was supposed to be much travelled. Mr. Newbury didn't seem to notice.

"I have got too much work," he said. "I can never get away from it. If you take my advice, you'll never mix your holidays with business. It doesn't pay."

"No, I can well believe that," Taryna said. "Can't you refuse to work for just a few days? Tell them they are not to telephone you; make your office take their own decisions instead of bothering you."

Mr. Newbury laughed.

"It sounds easy," he said. "I only wish it were possible. Perhaps I am inefficient. They always say that a man who works too hard doesn't delegate authority. But then, nobody wants to work for me as hard as I want to work for myself."

"What's the point of it if it doesn't make you happy?" Taryna asked.

Mr. Newbury looked for a moment as if her question was a surprise to him, and then he said:

"What is happiness except doing the things that you want to do? And I like working."

"But sometimes you must have a rest," Taryna insisted.

He shook his head, then added:

"You mustn't worry about me. I'm not a beautiful, leisured young lady like yourself, who can do what you want to do. My work is like an octopus, its tentacles twining around me, and I cannot escape it."

"It sounds frightening," Taryna said.

"It has its compensations," Mr. Newbury answered. "But let me give you this warning. Enjoy yourself while you can, while you are free, free to go where you like and do what you like. All too quickly, as you get older, do you become a slave to your own interests."

He smiled as he spoke and then his smile faded.

"Yes," he said, almost as though he was talking to himself. "You can go where you like and do what you like." He picked up his glass of wine and drank it. Then he said: "It's Kit's birthday tomorrow. You haven't forgotten that?"

"No, of course not," Taryna answered. "I bought her a present this afternoon. Only a small one," she added hastily. "Everything in the shop seemed . . ." She was going to say "so expensive," and turned it quickly into "so ordinary. I thought I would get her something when we get back to England."

"Yes, yes, I see."

Mr. Newbury was obviously preoccupied with his thoughts again. Then he said suddenly: "When are you thinking of leaving us?"

His question took Taryna by surprise.

"I ... I don't ... know," she stammered. "I haven't discussed it with Kit."

"You are in no hurry?"

"No ... no hurry."

"I mean a week or a fortnight, or perhaps longer, wouldn't make any difference to you."

"No ... I mean ... well, I have got to get back some time, of course," Taryna said.

"Yes, of course. But at the moment your time is your own. You are free, as we said before."

"Yes," Taryna agreed, feeling a little puzzled.

"You and I must have a little talk, Miss Grazebrook," he said. "I think you might be able to help me—in fact I'm sure you could."

"In what way?" Taryna asked.

"That's a secret," he said a little heavily. "But I shan't forget about it. There's something I want to ask you to do for me. Would you be prepared to do it?"

"It depends what it is," Taryna answered cautiously. "But, of course, I shall be very glad to help you if I can."

"Do you mean that?"

He turned to look at her and she realised for the first time how sharp and penetrating his eyes were. They seemed to bore into her.

"Yes ... naturally," she stammered.

"Good! That is what I hoped you'd say. You strike me, Taryna, as a very intelligent, sharp-witted girl. Am I mistaken?"

159

Taryna smiled.

"I hope you are right."

"I'm sure I am. I am seldom wrong when it comes to judging people. Very well. I'm going to trust you besides asking your help."

"What do you want me to do?" Taryna asked.

She wondered vaguely whether this was something to do with Kit. Was Mr. Newbury going to ask her to act as an efficient chaperon for Kit? In which case, knowing what she knew, what would be her answer?

It was at that moment that Irene rose at the head of the table.

"If we don't go to the casino soon," she said. "I shall find it difficult to get a seat at the big table, and I feel tonight as if I were in luck."

"I wish I could say the same thing," Lady Quarry drawled. "I have lost every night so far—not much, but enough to be annoying."

Taryna pushed back her chair. The others started to trail slowly across the restaurant towards the lounge. The men followed them and then, as Taryna went to join the last of the ladies, Mr. Newbury put out his hand and laid it on her arm.

"Wait a moment," he said.

She stopped and stared at him wonderingly. The last straggler of the party was out of earshot before he spoke.

"Would you be prepared," he said, "to go to the South of France for me? To carry a parcel which no one must know about?"

Taryna was so astonished she could only stare at him.

"Well, yes or no?" Mr. Newbury said. "It's not a big thing to ask, but for reasons of my own I do not wish to send anybody else whom I know. Will you do it for me?"

160

"But how? I mean . . ."

"All those details could be attended to," he said. "All I want you to do is to tell me now if you will do it."

"Yes . . . I suppose so . . . if you want me to," Taryna replied.

She felt somehow as if there was nothing else she could reply. It was all so unexpected, and yet, she thought swiftly, she was under an obligation to this man. He was her host; he had entertained her. Why shouldn't she do something for him?

"Thank you," Mr. Newbury said. "That is all I wanted to know. You will not say anything, to anybody, will you?"

"No, of course not," Taryna promised.

He stood by to let her pass. She walked across the restaurant only a very little way behind the last of the dinner guests who were just passing through the door. And then through the glass partition which divided the restaurant from the lounge she saw Michael. He was watching her.

9

Outside in the hall Irene and her guests were collecting their wraps.

"It's so hot we really don't want anything," Kit said to Taryna. "But I've brought you a shawl to put over your shoulders in case you need it."

She gave her a little wink as she spoke. Almost automatically Taryna took the shawl, which was an old-fashioned name for a piece of elaborate, bejewelled satin edged with mink, and slipped it over her shoulders.

"Don't forget, I've got a headache," Kit whispered as she moved away to help Lady Quarry with her fur cape.

Taryna was feeling stunned. Could Mr. Newbury really have asked her to go to the South of France for him? It somehow seemed incredible, and yet unless she was mad that was exactly what he had asked her to do.

She looked across the lounge and saw that Michael was still watching her. He was standing with several of the men who were talking as they lit their cigars, but he was not attending to their conversation. He was watching her.

She felt suddenly embarrassed, almost afraid; and yet she could not explain the feeling even to herself.

"The cars are waiting," Irene said a little impatiently.

"Let's walk," someone suggested. "It's such a lovely night it's almost a shame to be shut up in a car."

162

"I'll walk," Kit agreed. "I've got a headache. I can't think why."

"A touch of the sun perhaps," Lady Quarry said sympathetically. "I'm always warning my son to be careful when he's bathing. Sunstroke is so unpleasant and it's got far more easily than anyone thinks."

"Perhaps that's what it is," Kit said, rubbing her forehead.

"A dance with Lord Quarry will soon put it right," Irene said tartly. "Come along. We won't wait for the men. They are making every possible excuse to avoid our company."

She glanced in the direction of her male guests as she swept across the lounge leaving a trail of expensive perfume in her wake. The women followed her.

Outside, Irene got into the big limousine that was waiting. She never walked if she could possibly help it, and although the casino was literally only two minutes' walk away, she had every intention of arriving there in style.

Lady Quarry and another older woman got in beside her. The rest of the party moved off into the starlit street. It was without surprise that Taryna found Michael at her side.

"What was Mr. Newbury saying to you?" he asked in a low voice.

"Nothing," she said quickly, ashamed that she must lie, but knowing there was nothing else she could do.

"He must have been saying something," he insisted.

Taryna glanced up at him out of the corner of her eye. Was he jealous? she wondered. Somehow the idea seemed absurd. Mr. Newbury was old and never seemed to be interested in women. But it was obvious that Michael was curious and his voice was insistent.

"He was speaking of . . . Kit's birthday," Taryna said at last.

She had an idea that Michael looked relieved, but that must have been her imagination.

"Kit's birthday," he replied. "When is it?"

"Tomorrow," Taryna answered. "Mr. Newbury asked me . . ." She stopped suddenly. She realised with almost a sense of dismay that she was just about to tell how Mr. Newbury had asked her to bring a parcel over from England for Kit. With an effort she remembered that that, too, was a secret.

"You were saying?" Michael said.

"It was only . . ." Taryna answered, stammering a little, "that Mr. Newbury . . . told me he had a . . . present for her."

"She's twenty, isn't she?" Michael asked.

Taryna nodded.

"A year before she can get married," Michael said. "It's a good thing if you ask me."

Taryna looked at him in surprise. What had made him bring up the subject of marriage?

"What do you mean by that?" she asked.

"What I say," he answered. "Kit should wait. It would be a pity if she made a mistake."

Taryna stared at him, but at that moment Kit interrupted them.

"Oh, Michael, I've got such a headache," she exclaimed, slipping her arm into Taryna's.

"Have you?" he said. "I'm sorry."

His voice sounded sympathetic and unsuspicious, but Taryna was watching him with a puzzled expression on her face. What had he meant by what he said? A mistake! Did he know anything? Did he already suspect Jock McDonald or was it just by chance that he had spoken like that?

There was no time to say anything more. They had reached the casino, and Kit, still protesting volubly

164

about her headache, was walking beside Irene who had arrived just a little in advance of them in the car.

"If it gets worse I shall go home," Kit was saying.

"I'll come with you," Taryna interposed.

"Really, Kit! All you seem to worry about is your health," Irene said sharply. "It's very unbecoming in a girl. Men are bored with illness. If anyone must be ill they like it to be themselves."

It was Irene's usual cheap way of finding fault, but for once there was no sting in her words. Her thoughts were already preoccupied with the game of chance. She was pulling a great wad of *mille* notes from her bag. She handed them to Michael to change at the desk and there was in her eyes, Taryna could see, that little glitter of excitement which she never seemed to have at any other time.

The casino, with its big windows overlooking the sea, was packed with people. It was a fashionable night and film stars in their gorgeous dresses, were vying with maharanees in exquisite, glittering saris.

There were English dowagers wearing beautiful old family jewels which needed cleaning; and the wives of French industrialists, resplendent with the latest Cartier creations in bagettes. And, of course, there were the usual sprinkling of casino hangers-on, who wandered from table to table carrying about ten shillings' worth of chips in their hands and having no intention of risking it except on what almost seemed a certainty. They would sidle up behind a big banker or someone who seemed to be in luck and tentatively put their precious mite beside the more fortunate one's expensive *plaque*.

Irene was well known in the casino and an attendant hurried to find her a chair at the high table. She swept into her place, bowing curtly to one or two gambling acquaintances who bade her "good evening" and ingratiatingly to several more distinguished personages with whom she hoped to curry favour.

Michael took up his stand behind her chair to be there should she need him. The evening's play was in session.

"Now's our chance," Kit said as soon as she thought that Irene was firmly anchored to the green baize table.

She went up to Michael and touched his arm.

"My head is worse," she said in a voice of brave suffering. "I don't want to disturb Irene. Will you tell her I have gone home?"

"Are you taking Taryna with you?" he asked.

Kit nodded.

"Yes. I have told her to stay, but she refuses."

"I would rather go with Kit," Taryna said.

She tried to meet his eyes, but he did not look at her. She had hoped almost against hope that he would suggest that they should meet, if only for a few seconds. Perhaps he could have slipped out while Irene was playing. Perhaps they could have gone into another room and just talked together.

Taryna had a sudden yearning to say to him:

"Have you forgotten last night? Surely you want to be with me alone again? Surely you haven't forgotten?"

And yet she could do nothing. This was a different Michael from the one who had held her in his arms and rained wild kisses on her face. This was a man who managed to speak to her without a tremor in his voice—without, it seemed to her, even a flicker of the fire that had burned in his eyes.

She prayed for just some small recognition that she meant something to him, that the ache for him in her own breast was echoed in his. But she was disappointed.

"I will tell Irene," Michael said to Kit. "Have a good night. Good night, Taryna."

166

He smiled easily and charmingly, but to Taryna there was nothing secret, nothing special about it. Then he turned back to the table.

"Come on," Kit said, taking Taryna by the hand.

They wended their way through the crowds round the tables where the play was low and they were just going through the door of the *salle privée* when they ran into Mr. Newbury.

"Hello! Where are you going?" he asked.

"I have got such a bad headache, Father," Kit answered. "I am going back to the hotel. I think it must be a touch of the sun. I stayed in the water rather a long time today."

"It's very early to be leaving, isn't it?" Mr. Newbury enquired.

"I know. But what's the use of staying when one's feeling ill?" Kit asked.

"And Taryna is going with you?"

"She said she would like to come," Kit answered. "She's not used to late nights and, anyway, we will have a gossip before I settle down."

Kit smiled disarmingly at her father, but he was frowning. His eyes under his heavy eyebrows, Taryna noticed, looked more shrewd and penetrating than ever. It seemed to her that he hesitated as if he half decided to prevent them from going. And then he changed his mind.

"Very well then. I'll see you in the morning."

He was speaking to her, Taryna knew. Kit accepted it as permission to get away.

"Good night, Father," she said quickly. "Come on, Taryna."

They hurried past the *Boule* tables and round the dancing hall. Then they were out of the casino and into the warm, sweet, dusky air.

"Phew!" Kit drew a deep breath. "I feel as if I had been walking a tight-rope over Niagara Falls."

"Do you think we ought to go back to the hotel first?" Taryna asked as Kit turned in the opposite direction to the hotel.

"There's no point," Kit answered. "They're not likely to go and look for us. Besides, Jock will be waiting."

"Where have you arranged to meet him?"

"Down by the sea," Kit answered. "Where we went last night. There's nobody about at this hour. Oh, I'm longing for you to have a real talk with him. I'm sure you'll think of something, some way that we can get married."

"I'm certain I shan't think of anything that you haven't thought of already," Taryna said.

They hurried along, the high heels of their evening shoes making a curious little rhythm on the stone pavements. They reached the promenade. The tide was out and there was a long, flat expanse of muddy sand under a slightly overcast sky. There were no stars tonight and there was a curious oppression in the atmosphere as if later there was likely to be thunder.

Taryna felt suddenly depressed. She knew in her heart of hearts that she was being childish in expecting Michael to proclaim his love so that other people might be suspicious or suspect there was something between them. And yet because she loved him she wanted some demonstration of his affection, some sign that he still loved her.

Taryna felt curiously like tears and it was with an effort she forced herself to listen to Kit.

"We have got to think of something, Taryna—at least you have. You know how I rely on you. You're the only friend I can really trust . . ."

Kit suddenly broke off and gave a little cry of delight.

"There he is," she said, and started running down the promenade towards a man in the distance.

Jock McDonald had been sitting on a seat waiting for them. He got up as Kit approached and as she flung herself at him he put his arm round her and smiled down at her.

"I am sorry we are late," Kit was saying. "But it was nearly half-past nine before we finished dinner. You knew I would come?"

"I felt certain you'd turn up sooner or later," Jock McDonald said.

"And here is Taryna," Kit said. "I pretended to have a headache. She said she would come back to the hotel with me and keep me company."

Jock McDonald held out his hand.

"Pleased to meet you," he said to Taryna.

They sat down on the bench and Taryna looked at him. Had Michael's words, she wondered, made her more critical or were her impressions of him on this second meeting not so favourable as they had been at first?

She didn't know what it was, but somehow he looked different—coarser and by no means as attractive as she had thought him originally. Perhaps it was the rather familiar manner, she thought, in which he sat with his arm round Kit's waist which reminded her suddenly of the shop girls she had seen walking on a Saturday evening past the Vicarage windows. And Jock McDonald was certainly not very different from the young factory hands who squired them.

He had taken off his cap and without it he had lost a great deal of his good looks. His forehead was too low and his hair, cut rather short and rather badly, grew dark and course against his thick neck.

"I suppose Kit's been telling you about us?" Jock McDonald said to Taryna.

"Yes," Taryna answered.

"She's being obstinate. I hope you'll put a bit of sense into her," he went on. "I've told her that the one thing to do is to tell her Dad. No sense in running away and being hoicked back again. We've got to put our cards on the table and fight it out fair and square."

"But what's the use of doing that?" Kit said. "I've told you, they will only send me to the other end of the earth and you will get the sack."

"I don't know so much about that," Jock said. "It sometimes isn't wise to sack a man."

"What do you mean, wise?" Taryna said.

"When he knows too much," he said, and winked at her.

Taryna looked away from him out to sea. She knew unmistakably and instinctively in that moment that Jock McDonald was not the right man for Kit. Knowing what she did about Mr. Newbury, her mind leapt to the insinuation he had made.

Mr. Newbury had done things for which Jock McDonald was quite prepared to blackmail him. It might be a small thing like smuggling things past the Customs officials, it might be something worse. But whatever it was, this man who was employed on the yacht was quite prepared to use it to his own advantage.

Slowly Taryna felt a distrust and dislike creep over her as if it was a wave coming in from the sea. She began to see that there might be quite another reason for Jock McDonald's persistence in asking Kit to go to her father and say that they wished to get married.

Mr. Newbury was a very rich man. Jock McDonald might permit himself to be bought off.

"Perhaps I am being unfair. I mustn't jump to conclusions," Taryna thought. And yet the idea was there.

"I don't quite know what you mean," she said

slowly, simulating a wide-eyed innocence. "What has Mr. Newbury done that he would be afraid to dismiss you."

"Oh, that's telling," Jock replied with a false joviality.

"Tell us. Oh, do tell us," Kit said. "Has he been smuggling or something?"

"Perhaps," Jock McDonald said evasively. "And perhaps not. I'm not saying anything to get him into trouble. At the same time, I don't want no trouble either."

"No, of course not," Kit said. "But whatever you say. I know Father will be furious if I tell him we want to get married."

"You tell him and leave me to face the music," Jock McDonald said. "I know how to deal with him."

"There must be a better way," Kit said. "Think of one, Taryna. You're so much cleverer than I am."

"I think Mr. McDonald is right," Taryna said. "But I don't think you are the one to have to tell your father. I think he ought to do it."

She saw a sudden wariness in Jock McDonald's face and knew that the idea was distasteful to him.

"A bit awkward for me, isn't it?" he asked. "It's not as if I see the old man very often. If you were all on the yacht, for instance, it would be a different thing. Being up at the hotel—well, it's not so easy."

"You could send up a message in the morning."

"Besides, he'll have that Corea fellow with him," Jock said. "I never could stand him creeping about the place. Always gives you the impression he's going to pounce out at you. He fair gives me the creeps."

"You could ask to see Father alone," Kit said doubtfully.

"No! The right thing is for you to do it," Jock said.

"But why can't we just run away?" Kit asked.

171

"Well, for one very good reason—we haven't got any money," Jock replied.

"Well, I have got some," Kit said.

"How much?"

It seemed to Taryna there was something greedy in the question.

"I don't know what's in my account at the moment," Kit answered. "It's getting towards the end of the month. I suppose I have got a hundred or so left."

"A hundred!" Jock McDonald laughed. "That isn't going to last us long; not the way you like to live."

"But, Jock, I thought you said you didn't want to take my money; that you wanted me to live on what you earned."

Jock McDonald looked a little shamefaced.

"That's all very well romantically speaking," he said. "But when it comes down to a bit of common sense it just isn't practical and you know it. You've never done any cooking, or cleaned a house, or done the washing. No, if we get married we've got to live so that you're comfortable and happy. It wouldn't be fair otherwise."

Taryna clenched her fingers together. It was all quite obvious, she thought, what Jock McDonald was getting at. Either Mr. Newbury would have to pay him off altogether or else he would have to give them enough money so that Jock could live on Kit for the rest of his life.

She felt suddenly sick and disgusted, and at the same time terribly afraid for her friend. Kit couldn't be in love with this man, she thought. She was only in love with love—the love she had been seeking ever since her mother died.

Poor little Kit—lonely, unhappy, who would turn to anyone who would give her affection.

"But, Jock, I don't understand," Kit was saying.

"Don't try," Jock answered. "You leave it all to me.

And perhaps your friend will think of something clever. All you've got to do is to be sensible and listen to what I tell you."

"Yes, but, Jock . . ."

Taryna jumped to her feet. She felt she could bear it no longer.

"We have got to go now, Kit! You can meet Mr. McDonald another night. It's not safe; not at the moment. I'm sure of it."

"Better do what she says," Jock McDonald said quickly. "We don't want the thing to go off at half cock. It's best if it comes to your father just as a big surprise."

"Very well," Kit said grudgingly. "But I can't understand why Taryna feels like this. Good night, Jock."

She held up her face and Taryna looked the other way. She felt that all she wanted to do was to strike the man who was taking advantage of Kit's youth and vulnerability.

He was not so young, either, she thought. He must be over thirty, and she was certain, now, that he had deliberately gone out of his way to gain the love and confidence of a child whose only interest to him was that she had too much money.

She had no proof of this, nothing but her own intuition; and perhaps without meaning it Michael had signposted her in the right direction.

"Goodbye! See you soon," Jock was saying.

"I'll come down to the yacht tomorrow," Kit told him. "I'll make an excuse that I want to get something from my cabin, and then we can fix up to meet tomorrow night."

"O.K. Take care of yourself, Kit."

He waved to them as they walked away. Taryna merely hurried her footsteps.

"What's the matter with you?" Kit asked when they

173

were out of earshot. "You know as well as I do that Irene is not likely to come to the hotel."

"We must get back," Taryna said grimly.

"But why? Why?" Kit asked. "Last night I stayed out till about two and nobody worried."

"You don't want to take a chance," Taryna said. "Besides, the maids may be suspicious if Mrs. Newbury tells them we came back early."

"Yes, that's true," Kit said. "I never thought of that. Rosa always acts as a spy for Irene. I've caught her at it once or twice."

"Well, then, we must be careful," Taryna said.

They said little more as they hurried back from the beach and into the hotel. Up in Kit's bedroom everything was laid out and there was no one to be seen.

"There you are," Kit said. "Both the maids are down enjoying themselves. I'm quite certain they're not worrying about us."

She threw herself down on the bed.

"Really, Taryna! You are a fuss-pot. We could have stayed with Jock for much longer."

She clasped her hands behind her head and leant back against the pillow.

"Now, tell me what you think about him," she said.

"How old is he?" Taryna parried.

"I don't know," Kit replied. "I don't think I have ever asked him. About twenty-five or twenty-six, I should think. He's had lots of experience, going round the world and all sorts of things."

"What did he do in the war?" Taryna asked.

"He was in the Merchant Navy. That's why he got a job in the yacht."

Taryna was silent for a moment. She was trying to think of what else to ask. But whatever the answers, she knew they would not influence her decision. She

174

mistrusted Jock and the difficulty was how to convey it to Kit.

She knew it would be unwise to attack the man openly. That would do nothing but antagonise Kit from herself. The girl was infatuated with him, that was obvious. Apart from the life she led and her dislike of her stepmother and the very slender bond of sympathy between herself and her father, there was little to counterbalance any infatuation, however wild, however ill-judged.

"I've got an idea," Taryna said. "It's awfully early—not much past eleven. Let's go back to the casino. You can say you took a couple of aspirin and your head feels much better. If we stay here, you'll only feel depressed and worried and sometimes one's brain works quicker when other things are going on than when one tries to force an issue."

Kit sat up on the bed.

"I suppose we might as well," she said. "The casino did look rather gay tonight."

"I'm sure it would be amusing," Taryna said. "Before I tell you what I think about Jock I want to consider it. I want to try and get the whole thing into proper perspective."

Kit smiled at her.

"I know you will find a solution," she said confidently. "You're so clever, Taryna. Jock is wonderful, you can see that. I am determined to marry him whatever Father, or anyone else, may say about it. But I'm sure he's wrong. He just doesn't understand about Father and Irene. Who could if they didn't know them?"

"Yes, I think you are right over that and Jock is wrong," Taryna said slowly. "But I don't want to talk about it now."

"Then we won't," Kit said. "We will go back to the casino and see if Irene has made a fortune."

"How does she manage to have so much money to gamble with?" Taryna asked. "I thought everyone who went abroad was on an allowance."

"Oh, not Father," Kit said. "He's got property in practically every country in Europe. He's got some businesses in France, I know that. And one in Spain as well. It's useful, I can tell you. Wherever we go, we can spend as much as we like."

"That must be very useful," Taryna agreed, and wondered what the businesses were and what Jock McDonald knew about them.

All the way to the casino her brain was racing round and round and over and over Kit's problem, trying to see a way out. How could she make her look at Jock McDonald in a different light? Taryna wondered. How could she make her see his commonness, his lack of genuineness and, above all, the fact that the thing that really interested him was her money?

"I can't prove it. I can't prove it," she thought over and over to herself, and knew it would be fatal to accuse him of anything unless she had the actual proof of his perfidy in her hand.

The casino was much more crowded than when they left it. It took them some time to walk through the room to where they had left Irene.

She was still at the table, but Michael was not with her, and without saying a word they turned and went across the room in search of other members of the party.

Taryna saw Michael first. He was leaning against the bar talking to two men. He looked up as they approached, and then, nodding to the men to whom he had been speaking, walked towards them.

176

"You've come back!" he exclaimed. "Is anything wrong?"

Taryna shook her head.

"Kit's headache got better," she said. "And we thought it was a pity to go to bed so early when everything here is so gay."

"I see!"

Michael looked from one to the other as if he was in search of some other reason. Taryna suddenly had an idea.

"I think it would be fun to go and dance," she said. "What about those friends you were talking to. Wouldn't they like to join us?"

She felt as if the suggestion was outrageous even as it left her lips; but, as always when she had an idea, Kit acquiesced.

"Oh yes! Let's ask them," she said to Michael.

For a moment Michael seemed to hesitate, then he turned back towards the men who were still standing together at the bar.

"I would like to introduce you to Miss Kit Newbury and Miss Taryna Grazebrook," he said. "This is Ted Burlington and Jim Carson."

The men shook hands. They were both young, sunburnt and with that indefinable look of ease which is only attainable by an Englishman who has been at a public school.

"Have you been gambling?" Taryna asked, surprised at her own initiative in taking the lead and yet, at the same time, spurred on by a desire to take Kit's mind off the man she had left sitting on the sea front.

"We have lost all we can afford to," Ted Burlington answered.

He was a little the taller of the two, with fair hair and rather twinkling grey eyes.

177

"What about going and having a dance?" Michael suggested. "That's far cheaper."

"A good idea," Jim Carson said.

"You go and find a table," Michael said to Kit. "I'd better tell Irene what is happening."

"Yes, go and report," Kit said indifferently, and then smiled at Ted Burlington as they led the way to the dance hall, Taryna and Jim Carson following.

They found a table from which they could dance and listen to the cabaret. Taryna forced herself to chatter, to talk in the manner that she knew both the men would expect from a young Society girl. And yet every moment of it was an effort.

She tried not to look towards the door which led to the *salle privée*. She tried not to let the conversation flag as she waited and longed for Michael to join them. He never came!

Hours later, it seemed to Taryna, Ted Burlington suggested that they went to the night club.

"It's just across the road," he said, "and rather amusing."

"That will be fun," Kit said. "I'm enjoying myself, aren't you, Taryna?"

"Of course," Taryna answered, striving to make herself sound sincere and wondering why there was a heaviness like that of a stone inside her, and forcing herself once again not to turn her head to see if Michael was coming.

"Do you think we ought to tell Irene where we have gone?" she asked hopefully as the men paid the bill.

Kit shook her head.

"Why should we worry? She's obviously not worrying about us or she would have sent Michael with instructions as to what we were not to do."

"Perhaps he will wonder where we have gone," Taryna said.

178

"If he's interested he can come and find us," Kit answered.

It was the obvious reply and Taryna accepted it with a sinking feeling of unhappiness. Nevertheless she tried to enjoy the night club.

She had never been to one before and its long, luxurious dimness, with deep, comfortable sofa tables and band that seemed to make one's whole body vibrate, was an experience which she could not help finding exciting.

There was an exotic, rather daring cabaret, and after it the lights went even lower until there was only the little flickering candle lights on every table, and the music grew more seductive until one was caught up into the very rhythm of it.

"You are very lovely," Jim Carson said to Taryna.

He held her close and tried to press his cheek against hers. Somehow Taryna felt it would be rude or Victorian to refuse him. They moved together smoothly, cheek to cheek, for some time. Then Jim said:

"Why haven't I met you before? I have been to a lot of the dances in London this Season but I have never seen you."

"I haven't been in London," Taryna answered. "I am up at Cambridge."

"An undergraduate! Good lord! You don't look a blue-stocking."

"I am working very hard to try and get my degree," Taryna answered.

"What do you want a degree for?" he asked. "You'll get married and then what good will it be?"

"Perhaps I shan't get married," Taryna answered.

"Then it won't be for the want of asking," he said. "You're the prettiest girl I've seen for years."

"Thank you," she answered, laughing a little.

"It's a bit of luck having met you," Jim went on.

179

"Ted and I don't know many people over here. We've come for the Polo Week; it starts tomorrow. But actually neither of us have been to Deauville before."

"I believe it's very gay," Taryna said. "I've never been here either."

"Then we'll show each other around," he said, his hand tightening on hers. "Is that a promise?"

"I don't know," Taryna answered. "I'm staying with Mr. and Mrs. Newbury; Kit's my friend. I have to do what they want to do."

"I don't think we need worry about your friend," Jim answered. "Ted's a fast worker and when he's taken with anyone he doesn't take long to tell them so. If you ask me, he's fallen for Kit, as you call her, hook, line and sinker."

Taryna looked across the room. Kit and Ted were sitting at the table, their heads very close together, and it was quite obvious from the expression on Kit's face and the flickering of her eyelashes and the smile on her lips that whatever Ted was saying was entertaining her very much.

"There is no mistaking the look on a woman's face when she is being made love to," Taryna thought, and felt a sudden excitement because her plan might be working.

It had just been instinct that had made her ask Michael to introduce them to the two men to whom he had been talking. It had just been a blind desire to save Kit from herself which caused her to reach for the first life-belt she could think of—another man.

"There is only one antidote to love, and that is another lover." Taryna remembered reading that somewhere and had thought it cynical and quite unrelated to life as she knew it. Now she thought that it might prove to be the truth.

Surely, she thought, even without falling in love with

Ted Burlington she could see how different he and his friend were from Jock McDonald. There was not that roughness about them. There was not that kind of suspicion of something crafty and underhand in everything they said.

"Oh, please, God, make it work," Taryna found herself praying, then heard Jim's voice saying anxiously:

"You're looking very serious. Has something upset you?"

"No. I was really feeling happy," Taryna answered.

Even as she answered she thought that while she was happy for Kit her own unhappiness remained hidden deeply within her. Michael had gone away. He had introduced her to a man—two men for that matter—and left her without another thought.

She shut her eyes as she danced and tried to imagine she was back at La Caprice. It had been the nearest place to Heaven that she had ever known.

Could he have really said all those things and not have meant them? Could he have pretended the passion she had seen in his face and heard in his voice? Could the vibrations which had passed between her and him been only part of her imagination?

No, they were the truth. She was sure of that. Why? Then, why was he avoiding her? Why had he said nothing? Why had his only questions been of Mr. Newbury and of nothing else?

She turned impulsively to Jim Carson.

"Do you know Michael Tarrant well?" she asked.

"We were at school together," he answered. "But, even so, I don't know that I would say I knew him well. He's an odd sort of chap—always seems to turn up in the most unexpected places, and invariably broke. However, somebody was telling me today that

181

he's on to a good thing. He's got an heiress in tow. I only hope for his sake he brings it off."

Jim Carson finished speaking and then as Taryna said nothing he glanced at her face and gave a little exclamation.

"I say!" he said in embarrassed consternation. "Have I put my foot in it? You're not the heiress by any chance?"

10

Taryna was awoken by the telephone ringing shrilly in her ear. For a moment she thought she was at home, then realised where she was.

She sat up quickly in bed and took off the receiver. As she did so she glanced at the clock and saw in the light seeping through the curtains that it was only half past eight.

"Good morning, Miss Grazebrook."

To her astonishment it was Mr. Corea's voice. It was quite impossible not to recognise his precise, over-enunciated tones.

"Good morning, Mr. Corea. It's very early, isn't it?"

"I am sorry to wake you, Miss Grazebrook, but Mr. Newbury wants to see you. He suggests that you get up without waking Miss Kit and walk down to the beach. You will find Mr. Newbury in the tent that you all used yesterday."

"Very well, Mr. Corea. I will be there as soon as possible."

Taryna put down the telephone and then sat for a moment, yawning. They had not gone to bed until the early hours, and even then she had not been able to sleep. In fact for a long time she had lain crying, feeling the hot tears rolling down her cheeks and knowing a misery greater than she had ever known in her life before.

She had tried not to face the truth. Jim Carson, she told herself, had only been repeating a rumour, a bit of casino gossip. That Michael "had an heiress in tow" might have referred to Irene, without realising that she was married—or, as was much more likely, to Kit. She herself was unknown; and though the Newburys thought that she was a rich Canadian it was not likely that many other people in the social world would be the least bit interested in her.

Nevertheless, whatever explanations Taryna could try and make to herself, she knew that Jim Carson's words had struck deep and that they were all the more bitter to contemplate because they did not in any way affect her own love for Michael.

She loved him. That was only too real.

She had watched the door last night when they were dancing at the night club, hoping, as hour after hour passed, that still he would come. Surely, she thought, he would persuade Irene to join them; or, if they stayed up late enough, would come along after she had gone to bed.

It was obvious that Kit was enjoying herself, and she made no effort to go back to the hotel. Taryna was content to wait merely because she prayed that Michael would put in an appearance, even if only for a few moments.

Only when the night club emptied, when Kit at last reluctantly suggested they should leave, did she know that he was not coming.

"It has been fun," Kit said as, having taken them back to the hotel, the two men said good night and walked away.

"I thought Mr. Burlington seemed very nice," Taryna said.

"Oh, don't be so stuffy; do call him Ted," Kit said. "Nobody uses anything but christian names these days."

"Well, Ted then," Taryna smiled.

184

"He is really the tops," Kit said. "And he danced divinely."

There was no doubting her enthusiasm, and Taryna, unhappy though she was, could not help feeling glad that Kit, at least for the moment, seemed to have forgotten Jock McDonald.

"Ted suggested that we lunch with them tomorrow before the polo," Kit said as they reached their bedroom doors. "I said we would. Good night, Taryna. I expect you're tired, but it's been a heavenly evening."

"Yes, wonderful," Taryna managed to say, even though she knew in her heart it had been to her almost unbearable.

Only when she was alone in her own bedroom did she manage to relax. The smile that she felt was fixed to her lips faded and she sat for a moment with her face hidden in her hands before she began to undress . . .

Now, as she drew back the curtains and the sunlight came flooding in on her, its warmth caressing her naked shoulders, she wondered if her unhappiness had been exaggerated. For all she knew Irene might still have been at the casino when they left the night club. It might have been impossible for Michael to get away. After all, he had his obligations to his hostess—apart from any deeper or less conventional reasons he might have for doing what Irene wanted.

Outside the sun was shimmering on the sea which was as blue as the Mediterranean; the flags were flying along the *plage*. It was a riot of colour from the tents and umbrellas, from the flowers and the gardens below.

It was all so beautiful that Taryna told herself that she was exceedingly ungrateful to be miserable in such surroundings.

"He loves me! He loves me!" she whispered aloud,

185

and fought against the mocking voice in her brain which asked: "You or your money?"

With an effort she remembered that Mr. Newbury would be waiting. She pulled a bathing-dress out of the drawer and slipped into it. It was a new one which Kit had insisted on lending her, and was made of white sharkskin with red shoulder straps, a red belt and a red cap to match.

As Taryna powdered her nose and put a little lipstick on her lips she realised that there were dark lines under her eyes and she was very pale. Tears the night before were certainly not becoming.

Yet it was hard to feel that anything mattered except Michael, and it was unlikely that she would see him before lunch.

Taryna picked up her bathing-wrap and threw it over her shoulders. She opened her door and shut it again quietly. There was a 'Do Not Disturb' notice hanging outside Kit's bedroom. There was no one in the passage and at this time in the morning the hotel itself seemed shrouded and still.

Taryna hurried to the lift and waited until it came to fetch her. The lift boy was whistling until he opened the door and saw her.

"It's a nice day for a swim, *m'mselle*," he said as they descended to the ground floor.

"Yes, lovely!" Taryna agreed automatically.

The lounge was empty and she walked out through the door which led towards the sea. It was quite a little way to the promenade and Taryna moved slowly, her head bent.

There were very few people about on the *plage*—only a few sunburned youths playing with a huge rubber ball and one or two hardy swimmers who were already in the sea.

Taryna threaded her way through the brilliantly

coloured tents to the one they had occupied the day before. As she reached it she saw that Mr. Newbury was there. He was lying in a deck-chair, wearing a towelling dressing-gown which somehow on him seemed incongruous. He was reading a newspaper and there was a pile of others on his lap. Between his fingers was a big cigar.

"Good morning, Mr. Newbury!"

He looked up as Taryna spoke to him and put down the newspaper.

"Good morning, Taryna," he said gravely. "Forgive me if I don't get up. I have always found it difficult to get in and out of a deck-chair."

"No, of course, don't move," Taryna said.

She fetched a comfortable rubber mattress from inside the tent and put it down beside Mr. Newbury's chair.

"Have I woken you too early?" he asked. "I suppose you young things were very late last night."

"We were rather," Taryna confessed. "But we had a very nice evening at the night club."

"I heard you had not gone to bed," Mr. Newbury said.

Taryna could not help glancing at him sharply. Was there anything that he didn't know? she wondered. Did Mr. Corea and his espionage system work even in the casino?

"I thought this was a good opportunity," Mr. Newbury went on, "to talk over what I mentioned to you last night."

"About going to the South of France?" Taryna said. "I . . . I don't think I can."

"You promised me that you would help me," Mr. Newbury said. "And I must hold you to that promise. It won't be a very hard thing to do. Shall I explain?"

"Yes, please do," Taryna said, wondering wildly

now the moment was upon her how she could refuse to do what he asked of her.

"I am, as of course you know, concerned in a great many kinds of business," Mr. Newbury said. "It is my job to promote trade wherever it is possible. Occasionally in business we come across revolutionary ideas. Usually the inventions—because that is what they are—are quite impracticable, or else in some other part of the world other people have evolved exactly the same thing at almost identically the same time."

He paused for a moment and puffed his cigar.

"This is not so strange as it may sound," he said "because scientists and technicians are working all the time on more or less the same lines of thought. It is only a question of one striking lucky, as one might say, before the others discover exactly the same crock of gold."

Mr. Newbury chuckled.

"I sound rather obtuse," he said, "so I will be more precise. What has happened at this moment is that someone has discovered something really different from the others—in fact he is not one step ahead but half a dozen. Do you understand?"

"Yes, I think so," Taryna replied. "What do you want me to do about it?"

"I want you to help me by taking the plans of this new invention to someone who can utilise it in the best possible way," Mr. Newbury answered.

"Why me?" Taryna asked.

"Because my competitors and rivals are on my track," Mr. Newbury replied. "They think—though they are not sure—that I have something which will beat them at their own game. They are determined, if possible, to get hold of this secret and to use it to their own advantage."

"But surely," Taryna asked, "they can't prevent your

188

sending the plans by post if they are registered or insured?

Mr. Newbury smiled.

"Let me show you something."

He picked up the papers and took one from the bottom of the pile. He opened it up and turned over several pages, then handed it to Taryna, pointing with his finger at a certain small paragraph low down on the page.

"You can read French, I suppose?" he said.

"I think so," Taryna answered.

She read the paragraph he had pointed out, translating it slowly:

Henri Bierot, postman, who has recently celebrated twenty-five years in the postal service, was attacked on Thursday morning while delivering the letters in the neighbourhood of Cannes. The contents of his mailbag were scattered all over the road before the thieves made off. Henri Bierot, who is suffering from concussion in Cannes Hospital, said that he had no chance to get a look at his assailants. It is thought that the outrage might have been caused by practical jokers because when the mail was collected it was found that nothing was known to be missing and that several registered parcels were left undamaged.

Taryna finished reading the paragraph and then looked up enquiringly at Mr. Newbury. His cold, dark eyes met hers.

"Henri Bierot," he said quietly, "was delivering letters to the villa of a friend of mine."

"The friend to whom you wish to send the plans?" Taryna asked.

"Exactly," he said. "There was a letter in that mailbag which failed to be discovered when the rest of the contents were collected together. Fortunately it contained nothing of the least importance. It had been

189

sent, in fact, for the sole purpose of seeing if it was likely to arrive safely."

"But, that's . . . incredible," Taryna said.

Mr. Newbury nodded his head.

"That is what most people would say. People who have a trusting faith in the law and in the civilised behaviour of human beings. Unfortunately, greed is a very strong incentive to lawlessness, and this invention of which I am speaking is worth millions to whoever can use it first."

"I see," Taryna said slowly.

"And that is why I want you to help me," Mr. Newbury continued. "I and my family are suspect. I never leave the hotel without wondering whether my room will have been searched before I get back. Corea is an able watch-dog, but even he has to rest sometimes and there are not many people I can trust."

"And you think you can trust me?" Taryna asked.

"I am sure of it," he replied positively. "Besides, you are the perfect person for my plans. You know few people and no one would be surprised if you suddenly go to the South of France for a day or so."

"But . . . how can I?" Taryna asked.

"Everything will be arranged," Mr. Newbury answered. "I expect, like most young ladies, you are on an allowance. Even the richest of fathers try to make their children have some responsibility towards money. I do the same with Kit, although I must admit it isn't very successful."

"It isn't exactly that," Taryna said.

"You are also thinking of what excuse you can give," Mr. Newbury said. "Has your father or mother got any near relations—a brother or sister?"

He shot the words at her so sharply that Taryna answered almost without thinking.

190

"My mother has a sister," she said. "But she's very retiring and doesn't go about much."

"Splendid. What's her name?"

"Jane Woodruff," Taryna answered. "But . . ."

"She will do," Mr. Newbury said. "Now, listen, for we haven't much time. Later this morning a letter will be pushed under your door in the usual way. It will come from your aunt, Jane Woodruff, and will be written to you from the Carlton Hotel, Cannes. She will ask you to go and stay for a few days—only a few because she is going on to Italy. You will send her a telegram and tell her that you are arriving tomorrow. I shall arrange for the car to motor you to Paris to catch the *wagon-lit* which leaves tonight at about eight-thirty."

"But . . . I . . . can't . . ." Taryna began, only to be silenced by an imperious wave of Mr. Newbury's hand.

"You will tell my wife and Kit that you feel it only right that you should see your aunt. You will leave the letter that you have received from her lying about in your room. That is important. Leave the envelope too. It will have the correct date-stamp on it because it was despatched from Cannes yesterday."

Mr. Newbury drew on his cigar.

"You will go, as I have said, to Cannes," he went on. "You will arrive there tomorrow morning at approximately eleven o'clock. Your aunt will meet you at the station. She will recognise you, so you have got nothing to do but kiss and be charming to the woman who meets you and go back with her to the hotel. You will spend tomorrow and the next day in her company and then you will return here to us."

Taryna sat fascinated. She could hardly believe she was listening to instructions for herself. It sounded more like a fairy story, a tale out of some magazine which must inevitably, sooner or later, be concerned with murder.

"But this . . . this woman who is supposed to be my aunt," she said.

"She will be an ordinary, respectable, middle-aged Canadian," Mr. Newbury answered.

The word "Canadian" seemed to bring Taryna to her senses. This was ridiculous, she thought. She must do something; she must say something to stop him. How could he possibly go on with this absurd pretence? A woman in Cannes pretending to be Aunt Jane!

If Mr. Newbury could only see Jane Woodruff, she thought—a rather crushed little spinster who lived a quiet life in Devonshire, sometimes making a little extra money by knitting jumpers and shooting-stockings for her friends. Aunt Jane would hardly have heard of Cannes, let alone ever have dreamt of going there.

"I must tell him who I really am," Taryna thought, taking a deep breath. Then suddenly she thought of Kit. Kit who was afraid of her father; Kit who was involved in what was obviously a very unsavoury love affair; Kit who must be protected because she needed love so much and had had so little of it in her life.

And there was Michael too. But here Taryna thrust the thought of him away from her.

"I shall not speak to you again," Mr. Newbury was saying, "except, of course, in public and to say goodbye. But here are your instructions."

He glanced over his shoulder as he spoke. There was no one within fifty yards of them and as she watched him Taryna suddenly felt a sense almost of horror because even Mr. Newbury, a frightening and imperious business man, was showing signs of fear.

"What you have to do," Mr. Newbury went on, is to talk quite naturally of your aunt and make quite certain that everybody realises that you think it rather a nuisance but your sense of duty compels you to go to her. It is not a question of pleasure, you understand?"

"Yes . . . yes," Taryna murmured.

"Kit will doubtless try to prevent you from leaving," Mr. Newbury said. "You must promise her to hurry back as quickly as possible. I shall say how sorry I am that Kit is losing her friend. Just as you are stepping into the car to leave for Paris, Corea will present you with a spray of orchids with my compliments. You will pin them on your coat and leave them there. On no account must you remove them."

He lowered his voice before he continued:

"When you arrive in Cannes, and not before, you must unpin the orchids and then when you change your dress you will throw them into the waste-paper basket in your bedroom. Is that quite clear?"

"Yes, quite clear," Taryna replied in a bewildered voice. "But, I . . ."

"That is all you have to do," Mr. Newbury said sharply. "I have been very frank with you, Taryna, because I felt you were a sensible girl and I would not insult you by asking you to do something unless you knew exactly what you were about. Now I am going to ask you to give me your word of honour to swear on anything that you hold really holy and sacred, that you will not tell anyone what I have told you. Will you give me that promise?"

He held out his hand and almost automatically Taryna laid hers in it. She felt his fingers, strong, hard and somehow extraordinarily repellent, press hers.

"Promise me," Mr. Newbury said insistently. "I know I can trust you, and I certainly would not say that to most women."

"I . . . I promise," Taryna murmured.

She felt as if the words were wrenched from her, and

yet there was somehow nothing she could do but give him the promise because he asked it.

"Will you swear to me?" he repeated.

"I . . . swear."

He released her hand and sat up.

"Thank you, Taryna," he said. "You will not regret this. When you return I shall make an excuse to give you the loveliest present which I hope you have ever had. With your colouring it ought to be in rubies—a stone of which I am very fond."

He stood up, pulled his dressing-gown around himself, nodded to her, then started to walk away.

"But, Mr. Newbury . . ." Taryna said faintly, putting out her hand as if to stop him.

"Go and bathe, Taryna," he commanded. "That was why you came down here, you remember—because you woke early and felt that you wanted a swim."

He looked down at her face, worried and anxious, and added:

"Thank you, my dear. You are doing me a real kindness. I only hope someone will do the same for you if you ever need it."

He could not have made an appeal which went more directly to Taryna's heart. It swept away a lot of her worries, a lot of her anxiety. She was helping someone. That at least was something she understood, something she knew was right.

At the same time she could not help feeling that the whole plan was too fantastic to be anything but a figment of her imagination. Aunt Jane! Cannes! *Wagon-lit!* Orchids! Could anything be more utterly divorced from the vicarage in Bermondsey or Aunt Jane living in No. 2 Lower Chine Cottages in a tiny, unknown Devonshire village?

"It's mad! Mad!" Taryna told herself, and at the same time realised that it was only because she had lived such a quiet uneventful life that the whole thing seemed fantastic. To Mr. Newbury and Kit, and people like them, jumping on an aeroplane, tearing down to the South of France, driving half across Europe to see a friend, meant no more than when she and her mother took a fourpenny bus ride or came up to the West End for a day's shopping.

"If only they knew how strange it is to me," Taryna thought, and wondered once again whether she ought to have told the truth.

"This is what comes of lying," she admonished herself severely. "You are getting more involved and sinking deeper and deeper into the mire."

She wondered if Mr. Newbury realised how utterly inadequate she was to carry out his instructions. She had never been to Paris before, never travelled in a *wagon-lit*. Cannes to her was a place on the map. And though he had spoken of making all the necessary arrangements, she hoped he would not forget to give her enough money. She did not possess even enough to tip the sleeping-car attendant.

She had spent the last francs she had with her on buying a birthday present for Kit. It was only a prettily embroidered belt, but it had cost nearly two *mille* and now she was absolutely broke until Kit paid her her next week's wages—and that, Taryna thought with a little smile—was something Kit was quite likely to forget to do.

With a little sigh she realised that time was passing; and taking off her bathing-wrap and shoes, she ran down to the sea. The water was cold but invigorating. She swam out a little way and then back to the shore.

That would be long enough, she thought, to give authenticity to her story. Pulling off her bathing-cap and running her fingers through her hair, she walked slowly back to the tent. She had reached it before she

195

saw that someone was lying in the deck-chair that had recently been occupied by Mr. Newbury. Taryna had almost bumped against it before she realised who it was, and then her heart seemed to turn over in her breast.

"Michael!"

She felt her lips part on his name although no sound came.

"Good morning, darling."

He got up from the chair and picking up her wrap placed it over her shoulders.

"How did you know I was here?" Taryna asked.

"I didn't," he answered. "I came down for a bathe and saw your wrap. You're very early."

"Yes, I am," Taryna answered.

She went into the tent, slipping off her wet bathing-dress and then, fastening the towelling wrap tightly around her, came back into the sunshine.

"You look very sweet," Michael said softly.

Taryna turned her head away.

"Don't," she said involuntarily.

He looked at her averted profile for a moment. Then he sat down beside her on the rubber mattress.

"Are you angry with me?" he asked.

"Yes," she answered, but her answer seemed to break on a sob.

He took her hand in his. It was cold from the seawater and he warmed it with his fingers.

"My sweet, you mustn't be cross," he said. "Things are difficult for me—more difficult than I can possibly explain. But I love you. Can you try and be sure of that?"

"How can I?" Taryna asked.

"Because what is between us doesn't need words," he answered. "Taryna, look at me."

She shook her head because there were tears in her eyes, and then he put up his hand and taking her chin turned her face round. She struggled against him for a moment and then capitulated suddenly.

She found herself looking up into his eyes, and what she saw there held her spellbound.

"My poor little love," he said gently. "Don't be unhappy. I'm not worth it. Only be sure of one thing. That I adore you. I do, really. Whatever I do, or whatever I say to the contrary. I love you, Taryna."

"But yesterday . . ." Taryna began.

"Yes, yes, I know," he said. "Don't let's talk about it. Let's go back to where we left off the other night. We were pretending, do you remember? There was nobody else in the world, no problems, no difficulties. There was only us alone—you and I."

There was something in his voice, deep and resonant, that made her forget her unhappiness of the night before, the misery she had endured as she had waited hour after hour, hoping he would come to the night club. He had the power to magic her into another world—a world of pretence in which, as he had said, they were alone and nothing else mattered.

"You look very young, almost like a child, with your hair untidy and that white bathing-wrap," he said. "Or is it because you have an extraordinary look of innocence, almost like some small and tousled chorus-boy or perhaps a little angel who has fallen out of Heaven by mistake?"

Taryna laughed.

"Now you are teasing me again," she said.

"I'm not," he answered. "That's what first made me love you—that look you have of being untouched, of being so absurdly innocent that the world is half bewildering and half an exciting adventure. Most women are *blasé*, they've done everything and been everywhere; there's nothing a man can tell them that is new, nothing they haven't heard before."

197

Taryna's eyes fell before his. How could she tell him, she thought, that what he sensed was only too true? She had been nowhere and seen nothing. Everything he was saying, everything he did was new and thrilling to her.

"You are so sweet," Michael said. "I want to kiss your toes, those ridiculous tiny feet of yours. I want to kiss your fingers, too, and most of all, darling, your lips."

Taryna felt herself quiver and a sudden leaping flame of excitement shot through her.

"Tell me something," Michael said. "Something that I have wanted to know ever since the other night."

"What is it?" Taryna asked.

"Am I the first man who has ever kissed you?"

He asked the question as if he were half afraid of the answer. With a little feeling of delight Taryna knew that this at least she could answer truthfully, about this there was no need for pretence.

"The only one," she told him.

"Oh, my sweet!"

He bent his head and opening her hand pressed his lips long and lingeringly in the palm. Then he kissed her wrists, his mouth making the pulse beat wildly.

"You drive me mad," he said, and now his voice was deeper and she saw the sudden fire of passion in his eyes.

"I want to kiss you properly," he said. "I want to hold you as I held you the other night. I want to feel you kiss me in return."

"Don't," Taryna said again. This time it was a very different plea.

"Don't do what?" he asked gently as if he already knew the answer.

"Don't make me love you so much," Taryna pleaded. "It frightens me. I've never felt like this before; I've never known one could feel so . . ."

198

"So what?" Michael prompted.

"So ... wild, so ... unrestrained," Taryna stammered.

He laughed at that, but tenderly, as if every word she said was a delight.

"Do you know what I would like to do?" he said. "I would like to take one of those boats at the edge of the sea and carry you away in it. I would like to row and row until we found an island that was completely uninhabited except for ourselves. I would like to lie there with you all day and know that we were alone and no one would come and interrupt us.

"I want the chance to tell you how much I love you and what you mean to me. I want to touch you and kiss you. I want to bury my face in your hair. I want you to say, 'don't', in just that voice which makes me thrill as nothing has ever made me thrill before."

Taryna's fingers tightened on his and then she looked up into his eyes. It seemed to her as if he did, indeed, kiss her, as if they were joined one to each other, until they were utterly indivisible.

"Darling! Darling!" Michael said, and his voice broke on the words.

The big rubber ball from the sunburned young men, who were still playing, came bowling past them and broke the spell. A man came darting after it. He picked it up, his bare feet scattering the sand behind him.

"I must go back," Taryna said suddenly.

"What made you come down alone?" Michael asked. "Why didn't you bring Kit with you?"

"She was asleep," Taryna answered, "and I didn't want to wake her."

"Was anyone here when you came?" Michael asked.

She did not know why but she felt as if the question had a special significance. There was something in the way Michael said it, something that was almost studiedly casual, and yet it was not such a very different voice to the one in which he had been speaking to her.

Just for a moment she felt inclined to say no one. That, she felt, was what Mr. Newbury would have wanted. And then suddenly, out of the corner of her eye, she saw something. It was half hidden in the sand and yet it was obvious that it had not been there all night. It was the butt of a cigar which Mr. Newbury had been smoking.

"Oh, Mr. Newbury was here," Taryna said. "I was surprised to see him. I never thought he bathed."

"Nor did I," Michael answered.

She knew then that he had seen the cigar, but, if so, she asked herself, why had he asked her the question? Had he deliberately tried to trap her? She shook the idea away.

This intrigue was beginning to play on her nerves, she thought. She was suspecting everyone and everything. There was no reason why, even if Michael had seen the cigar or met Mr. Newbury walking back to the hotel, he should think that they had met. They might have come by different routes. It would have been quite easy to do so, and she could have arrived even a few seconds after Mr. Newbury had gone and not even realised that he had been there.

"He is a strange man," Michael said reflectively. "What did he talk to you about?"

"Oh, he asked me if I was late last night," Taryna answered truthfully.

"How did you like Jim and Ted?" Michael enquired.

"Very much," Taryna answered.

She felt somehow her words were stiff and the unhappiness she had experienced at the night club was vividly in her mind again.

Slowly she got to her feet.

"I must go," she said, and yet she still hesitated.

Michael rose too.

"I am going to stay and swim," he smiled. "So forgive me if I don't walk back to the hotel with you."

She had a feeling that that was not the reason he was not accompanying her, and then once again she told herself that she was being absurd. Irene would still not be awake or be likely to be looking out of the window. And yet there would be other people who would be only too ready to tell her that Michael and Taryna had been down to the beach together should they see them walking back to the hotel side by side.

"The water is rather cold," Taryna said, for something to say.

"Oh, my darling, forgive me," Michael whispered. "I know I am failing you. I know I am making you unhappy. But there is nothing I can do about it. Just go on trusting me; just go on pretending, will you?"

There was so much appeal in the question that she could not refuse it.

"I will try," she said unsteadily.

"Trust me. Just trust me," he begged.

He bent his head and kissed her hand, and then, because she knew there was nothing more she could say, she turned away from him.

She knew he was watching her and yet she forced herself not to look back. She walked slowly, carrying her wet bathing-dress and her cap in her hand, up the sand and on to the wooden *plage*.

She crossed the road and started back towards the hotel. Only when she had gone quite a long way did she feel that she could bear it no longer. She turned and looked back. Michael was running down to the sea. She saw him reach the water and strike out, his dark head silhouetted against the blue.

With a little sigh she turned and walked on. She had

201

an absurd idea that Michael was swimming out towards the island that he had spoken of while she was moving away from it.

Why couldn't she have told him that she was leaving? That she was going to Cannes tonight? She thought of the promise that she had made to Mr. Newbury, and almost hated him for having extracted it from her.

The largeness of the hotel looming up ahead of her suddenly frightened her. There were things waiting for her which would set a whole chain of new events in progress.

She wished suddenly more than anything else that she could confide in Michael. Somehow, despite everything that he did to her, despite the uncertainty and the strangeness of him, he seemed more sure and more protective than anyone or anything else.

Her bedroom was just as she had left it. She turned on her bath and sat down at her dressing-table to comb her hair. As she did so she heard a slight rustling sound at the outer door. She got up. As she had expected, there was the *Daily Mail* and a letter.

For a moment she stared at it, almost afraid to pick it up from the floor. It was almost uncanny, she thought. Then she forced herself to take it in her hands. There was her name neatly addressed in a round, feminine hand; the postmark was from Cannes the day before.

She turned the letter over and looked at the flap intently. It had been very carefully done, but she could see that the envelope had been opened. She slit it herself, roughly, with fingers that trembled. The letter inside was headed in print, *The Splendide Hotel, Cannes.* "My dearest Taryna . . ."

She had a sudden desire to laugh—an almost hysterical laugh. This could not be happening. It couldn't be true. And yet she was quite certain that whatever Mr. Newbury had said was as inevitable as the fact that the night would come.

There was the sound of a key turning in the door and then Kit came bursting in.

"Are you awake?" she asked. "I thought I should sleep much later, but I'm not the least tired, are you?"

"No," Taryna answered.

"Have you got a letter?" Kit enquired.

Taryna put it down on the dressing-table.

"Kit, I'm in such trouble," she said.

"Good Heavens! What's happened?" Kit asked, seating herself on the bed.

"It's about your father," Taryna answered. "And I think that we shall have to tell him the truth. There's nothing else for it."

"We can't do that," Kit said quickly. "I was thinking last night how wonderful it was to have you here. It would never have happened if we hadn't pretended that you were important. Irene would never have allowed me to bring you otherwise."

"But much more serious things have happened than that," Taryna said. "Your father wishes me to go to Cannes for him. He asked me last night and this letter is supposed to come from my aunt whom I am to meet there."

"What on earth does he want you to do that for?" Kit asked.

"I don't know," Taryna lied, knowing that this was where she had to be very careful, for she must not let Kit for a moment suspect that she knew more than she was prepared to tell her.

"He asked me if I would go and, somehow, because I had so much to hide, I didn't like to ask too many questions. I really wanted to see you and ask you what I had better do."

203

"He wants you to go to Cannes!" Kit repeated incredulously.

"Yes," Taryna answered. "To meet an aunt of mine who is to be, of course, a Canadian. She's to have my real aunt's name and, oh, Kit, when he suggested it I just somehow felt I couldn't tell him what we had been doing. It seemed so awful to have lied so much and so often."

"Of course you mustn't tell him," Kit said hesitantly. "For how long does he want you to go?"

"Oh, only two nights," Taryna answered.

"That's all right then," Kit said, her face clearing. "Just do as he wants. I suppose he has some good reason for it. I'm only surprised that he's sending you and not Corea."

"He seems to think that I'm the right person," Taryna said humbly.

"Well, that's splendid then," Kit approved. "If Daddy's taken a fancy to you it will make things so much easier."

"But, don't you see," Taryna pleaded, "it's all so difficult because I'm not supposed to tell you. This letter," she picked it up, "is to persuade you and your stepmother that I am being called away to see a relative."

"I can't see that it matters," Kit answered. "It's infuriating that you've got to go at all, I quite agree, and I shall miss you frightfully, even though it's only for two nights. But it's something to keep Daddy in a good temper. And, besides, Irene was talking of going down to Biarritz after this and, of course, I want you to come with us."

"But, Kit, I can't . . ."

"Now, listen, Taryna," Kit interrupted. "You've seen my family now, you know what they are like. You're doing the kindest and most unselfish action that anyone

204

could do in helping me, in making things so much easier and better than I ever imagined they could be."

She paused and added obviously as an afterthought.

"We're going to send the money, as I promised, to your father and mother. If I asked them, I believe they would much rather you were with me than working in some dirty café or getting mixed up with some very undesirable people just because they were ready to pay you—as I am."

Taryna repressed a desire to say that she thought she was getting mixed up in some very undesirable things where she was, but she knew that in some rather twisted manner Kit was speaking the truth. Her mother would much rather she was at Deauville or Biarritz—what mother wouldn't?—than trailing round the back streets of London in search of a job. And, of course, she would want her to have good food and wonderful clothes to wear; and entertainments of all the most luxurious type.

It was no use pretending for a moment that her father wouldn't have been shocked at the lies and pretence. But her mother, who Taryna had discovered had at times quite a worldly streak behind her sweetness and her self-sacrificing character, would undoubtedly have said that the means justified the ends.

"I don't know what to think or what to do," Taryna said.

"But, it's simple," Kit answered. "Do what Father wants and everything will be perfect until the end of the vacation. If you go blundering in and telling them we've lied to them and that you're an imposter, they will be absolutely furious; you'll be sent home and I shall have the most terrible and miserable time."

She watched Taryna's face and added:

"Well, if you do tell them I shall force Jock to run

away with me, whether he wants to or not, I promise you that."

"Oh, Kit, don't do anything desperate," Taryna said instantly.

"Well, I shall if you're stupid," Kit retorted. "That may sound like blackmail, but I mean it. It's been such fun having you here and we can do things together that I should never have been able to do without you. Look at last night, for instance. If it hadn't been for you I should never have met those two nice men. Anyone Irene introduces me to is always poisonous."

"I expect you're prejudiced before you even meet them," Taryna said. "That's the truth, isn't it?"

Kit laughed.

"I suppose it is," she agreed. "I hate Irene so much that instinctively I hate anyone who she says is nice. I must have got a complex about her just as you said."

"You don't want to have a complex about everyone else as well," Taryna said.

"Well, anyway, Ted's untainted as far as Irene is concerned," Kit replied. "And we're meeting them for lunch. What time have you got to go?"

"I've got to catch the *wagon-lit* from Paris tonight," Taryna said. "We're not supposed to know it yet, but your father is going to send me to Paris in the car."

"I see," Kit answered. "Well, you needn't leave until bout three o'clock. That will give time for us all to have lunch together."

"And while I am away," Taryna said, "you promise me you won't do anything stupid about Jock. Promise me, Kit."

"I promise," Kit replied.

Taryna felt suddenly relieved, and yet she knew that it was Ted who had made Kit answer so lightly and with no reservations. She wished she wasn't going away tonight.

It would be so much easier to promote this friendship if she were here. She was determined, secretly, to ask Ted to look after Kit until she came back. She thought with sudden subtlety that if she could make him feel that Kit was in need of protection there was every chance of his making a real effort to see her and take her mind off Jock McDonald.

She looked down at the letter with a sudden distaste. How much easier it would be if there weren't so many complications in life—and, yet, how much duller?

"What you want to do," Kit was saying, "is to go to the telephone and get on to Mr. Corea, tell him your story and then everything will be *en train* immediately."

"For goodness' sake be careful," Taryna said. "The one person who should be surprised and upset at my going is you."

"I know, and I am," Kit said.

"Your father . . ." Taryna began, and then she gave a sudden cry. "Oh, Kit! I'd forgotten it was your birthday. Many happy returns of the day, darling. Here's my present for you."

She got it out of the drawer and put it into Kit's hands.

"It's lovely," Kit exclaimed. "You shouldn't have spent your money on it. But it's exactly what I wanted."

She tried it on over her dressing-gown, pirouetting in front of the mirror. Taryna walked to the telephone and picked it up. She asked to be put through to Mr. Corea and when he answered the telephone she said:

"Oh, Mr. Corea, I've had a letter from my aunt in Cannes. She wants me to go down there at once and see her for a couple of nights. I wonder if you could possibly arrange it for me?"

"Certainly, Miss Grazebrook. I think you will have

to catch the eight forty-five from Paris. I will ask Mr. Newbury if he could send you through in the car. It would be a much easier journey that way."

"Thank you very much," Taryna said solemnly.

She put the receiver down and made a grimace at Kit.

"I rather agree with you, he's a horrid little man."

"And now we will go and tell Irene," Kit said. "I hope your aunt is rich and important."

"She must be," Taryna said. "She's staying at the Splendide at Cannes."

Quite suddenly she began to laugh. There was something so ridiculous to think of Aunt Jane with her knitting, her glasses, and her untidy grey hair being impersonated by someone who would look the part to stay at any smart hotel.

Kit began to laugh too, and they both collapsed in helpless giggles.

"You know," Kit said when she could get her breath. "This is the first time in my life that I've ever been able to put anything over on Father and Irene. It's giving me more pleasure than anything I've ever done, just to be one up on them. And, of course, on Michael, too."

There was a moment's pause and then Taryna said in a very different voice:

"Yes, of course, we are deceiving Michael as well."

11

"I must get dressed," Kit said. "And you had better do the same. As soon as Irene is awake you will have to tell her you are off."

"I will come in when I am ready," Taryna said, knowing that she was likely to be far quicker than Kit.

As soon as she was alone she dressed quickly and methodically, choosing from the wardrobe a pretty, fresh cotton dress, the simplicity of which deceived the on-looker into thinking it had been cheap when actually it came from one of the most expensive houses in Paris.

Taryna looked at herself in the glass and could not help wondering if Michael would think she was pretty. At the mere thought of him a frown came between her eyes and then, resolutely, she walked towards the door, determined not to give herself time to think.

Kit, as she expected, was only half dressed.

"How quick you've been!" she exclaimed.

"Do you think your stepmother has been called yet?" Taryna asked.

"I should think so," Kit answered. "Ring her maid Rosa. If she isn't in her room it will mean that she's with Irene."

Taryna turned towards the telephone and as she did so it rang.

"Shall I answer it?" she asked Kit.

"Yes, do," was the answer.

Taryna picked up the receiver.

"Can I speak to Miss Newbury?" a deep and rather charming voice said.

"Will you hold on a moment?" Taryna said formally. She put her hand over the receiver.

"I think it's Ted," she whispered.

Kit's eyes seemed to light up. She ran across the room and took the receiver from Taryna's hand.

Taryna watched Kit's face. There was no mistaking
"Hello!"
that she was interested and amused by the man to whom she was speaking. If only he could be serious about her, Taryna thought suddenly; and she breathed a little prayer that Ted Burlington would fall in love with Kit.

"All she wants is love," Taryna thought. "Just to be wanted, to feel that she is of paramount importance in somebody's eyes."

"That will be lovely," Kit was saying. "Yes, I'll tell Taryna, but she may not be able to come for a little while. Anyway, I'll be down in ten minutes. Meet you in the hall."

She put down the receiver.

"It was Ted," she murmured unnecessarily. "He wants us to play tennis with him and Jim. I said you might not be able to come along quickly, but it won't matter because Jim's got something to do first. Ted and I are going to have a single."

"That's splendid," Taryna said.

"And then we'll bathe afterwards," Kit went on. "Before we go to lunch. They are going to take us to an amusing little place they know of down by the polo ground. They say it's not fashionable, but I said we couldn't care less about that."

"No, of course not," Taryna agreed.

"I'll take my bathing-dress down with me," Kit said, rummaging in a drawer and throwing everything in

210

every direction. "I've got a new one somewhere and a cap I've never worn."

"Here, let me do up your dress," Taryna said.

"Yes, please do," Kit answered. "If I ring for Ella she'll take half an hour coming along and I don't want to keep Ted waiting."

"No, you mustn't do that," Taryna smiled.

Kit ran a comb through her hair and put on a little extra lipstick.

"Do I look all right?" she asked.

"You look lovely," Taryna said seriously.

And it was true. Kit, when she was animated and happy looked like an impersonation of spring.

Kit picked up her bathing-dress and cap and flung them over her arm.

"Now my tennis racket," she said.

"Here it is in the corner," Taryna cried, fetching it for her.

"Don't be long," Kit said. "When Jim arrives it will be more fun to have a foursome."

"I'll be as quick as I can," Taryna promised, thinking that things couldn't have planned out better than that Kit and Ted should have a little time alone before she and Jim joined them.

"Ring for Ella and tell her to tidy up, will you?" Kit said as she opened the door.

She didn't wait for Taryna's answer but hurried away down the passage. Taryna looked round the room and gave a little laugh. It looked rather as if a bomb had hit it. Ella would certainly be needed to get things straight and to put away all the things that Kit had thrown out of the drawers in her search for the bathing-dress.

She was just about to pick up the telephone receiver when once again the bell rang.

"Hello!" Taryna said.

"Is that you, Kit?"

There was no mistaking who was speaking. Taryna recognised the Scottish accent and the rather harsh voice immediately.

"No, Mr. McDonald," she said. "It's Taryna Grazebrook. Kit's gone out."

"Well, I've got to speak to her, and quickly."

"I am afraid that is impossible," Taryna said, determined that Jock McDonald should not spoil Kit's time with Ted Burlington if she could help it.

"It's important. Can't you get hold of her?"

"I don't think I can at the moment," Taryna said. "Can't you give me a message?"

There was a moment's hesitation and then Jock McDonald said grudgingly:

"Well, I suppose I shall have to. It's like this. I'm in trouble."

"What sort of trouble?" Taryna asked.

"Serious trouble."

Taryna waited and then after a moment she said:

"Hadn't you better tell me exactly what you mean by that?"

"It's like this," Jock McDonald answered. "I went out last night and got into a fight. It was in one of these low dives round here and one of the swines who owns it got abusive. I clipped him one and . . . well, I suppose I hit him harder than I meant."

There was a moment's pause.

"Is he dead?" Taryna asked.

"No, I don't think so. But he's pretty bad. They've taken him to hospital and I've been arrested."

"Where are you speaking from?" Taryna asked.

"From the police station. They've let me telephone when I said who I wanted to speak to. Kit's got to help me, and quickly."

"What do you expect her to do?" Taryna asked.

212

"Tell the old man, of course. It's what I've been telling her for a long time, and now this is where she comes across with the truth. Tell him what's happened and say he's got to bail me out and get a really good lawyer—or whatever they do in France. I'm in a spot."

"What was the row about?" Taryna asked.

She didn't know why but she felt the answer to this was important. It was obvious that Jock McDonald was hesitating before he answered.

"Well, I suppose you're bound to know sooner or later," he said. "It was over a woman. Not that she was of any importance—just someone I'd taken out for a bit of supper."

"I see." Taryna's voice was icy. "And you want me to tell Kit that?"

"Oh, hell! It doesn't matter if she does know the truth. It was just a question of passing the evening somehow. Anyway, that's not the point. The old man's got to pay up for me. Is that clear?"

Jock McDonald's voice had toughened and Taryna felt herself shiver. Could Kit really have thought that she loved this man? She could hear the fear and the coarseness in his voice, his bullying determination to get his own way. And something else, some sort of confidence which made him think that whatever he said or did Kit was bound to support him.

"Supposing Mr. Newbury doesn't believe Kit's tale?" Taryna said suddenly. "Supposing he refuses to help you?"

"He won't refuse," Jock McDonald replied hastily. "I've got letters from Kit—letters which wouldn't make at all pleasant reading if the newspapers got hold of them. They'd like that sort of stuff, wouldn't they? 'Heiress in love with yacht hand!' Mr. Newbury wouldn't stand for that."

"You've got it all worked out, haven't you?" Taryna

213

accused him. "I suppose you expected all along that Mr. Newbury would buy you off when he knew that Kit thought herself in love with you?"

"Now you keep out of this," Jock McDonald said menacingly. "It's nothing to do with you what I thought or what I didn't think. All I'm asking you is to tell Kit what's happened and tell her to hurry up and get the money down here. I don't want to be kept in their stinking prison longer than I can help."

"If the man dies, I imagine you'll be there for some time," Taryna retorted.

"If he dies or lives, old man Newbury can get me out if he wants to," Jock McDonald answered. "I know enough about him to know that he can get away with murder, or worse, if it suits him. Well, it can just jolly well suit him to save me, you understand?"

"Yes, I understand," Taryna said.

"Well, get cracking," Jock McDonald commanded. "Kit won't want to see someone she's as fond of as she is of me mouldering in a French prison. And if there's any difficulty you might mention the letters."

"Have you got them with you?" Taryna asked.

"No, they're in the . . ." He stopped suddenly. "They're safe enough. You don't want to worry your head about them. You get on and do what I have told you."

"Very well," Taryna forced herself to say meekly.

She put down the receiver and stood staring across the room wondering what she should do, feeling an almost vitriolic hatred for this common, rough man who was besmirching Kit's youth and sweetness.

What had she done to deserve this? Taryna thought. She was quite certain now that Jock McDonald had deliberately made Kit fall in love with him. No doubt Kit had been only too pleased to have a friend all her own, to think that someone cared for her; and it would have given spice to her infatuation to know how angry Irene would have been if she'd known about it.

But what had happened now was horrible. Taryna could not bear to think of Kit's feelings when she heard about it. The man she'd trusted, the man she'd thought she had loved, going out at night with some low woman he had picked up in the streets, taking her to a disreputable bar and then getting involved in a brawl. Taryna could imagine it all too clearly; and she could imagine, too, Kit's humiliation when her father learned that this was the man to whom she had given her first love.

What would Irene say? Taryna could almost hear the sarcastic, snarling remarks which would fall from Irene's lips. Nothing could be worse for Kit at this moment than to feel that they were all against her and that Jock McDonald had only one use for her—her money.

"How can I save her? What can I do?" Taryna asked wildly. For a moment she forgot her own problems. She thought only of Kit—Kit so sweet and so vulnerable, so lonely, already hating society and all that it stood for. This would only give her a worse complex, so that she might feel that all men were bad and there was no decency or genuine feeling in the whole world.

Perhaps money really was cursed, Taryna thought to herself. It had certainly brought no happiness to poor Kit, and this would only confirm her conviction that she was different from other people, tainted and tarnished because of the great wealth that surrounded her.

"I must do something, but what?" Taryna whispered the words to herself and then almost automatically walked across the room to the door.

She opened it to go to her own room and saw Mr. Corea standing just outside in the very act of knocking on her bedroom door.

"Oh, there you are, Miss Grazebrook!" he exclaimed.

215

"I have here your tickets. Can I come in and give them to you?"

"Yes, of course," Taryna said, opening her bedroom door.

"This is your ticket for the *wagon-lit*," Mr. Corea said in his precise tones, "and another for your return journey. And here is some money which Mr. Newbury thought you would need."

He put a fat envelope down beside the tickets on the table.

Taryna suddenly made up her mind.

"Mr. Corea, I want your help."

He looked up at her and there was undoubtedly surprise in his eyes behind his thick glasses.

"If I can be of any assistance, Miss Grazebrook . . ." he began formally.

"It's about Miss Newbury," Taryna began, then went on impulsively: "Mr. Corea. Can I trust you to do something without making trouble?"

Mr. Corea seemed to hesitate.

"It depends what it is, Miss Grazebrook. Mr. Newbury is my employer; my loyalty is to him."

"Yes, yes, I know," Taryna said. "And I also want to save him from being hurt or unhappy."

"Won't you tell me what it is?" Mr. Corea asked.

His voice was still dry and curiously devoid of emotion and yet somehow Taryna felt that he was sympathetic, that there was a spark of human feeling in him somewhere.

She chose her words carefully.

"There is a man on the yacht—the mate in fact—who has got into trouble," Taryna said. "He telephoned just now and asked me to give a message to Miss Newbury. He . . . sounded rather unpleasant, almost as if he were trying to . . . blackmail her."

Mr. Corea's eyebrows went up. There was no doubt that this was not what he had expected.

"Blackmail!" he repeated.

Taryna nodded.

"Yes. He is trying to force her to ask Mr. Newbury for help. He's got embroiled in a brawl and he's hit a man so hard that he's been taken to hospital. The police are holding him."

"This is serious," Mr. Corea said. "I wonder the captain has not reported it."

"I expect he will do so," Taryna replied. "Please, Mr. Corea, when he does, will you keep Kit's name out of it?"

"I see no reason why Miss Newbury should be mentioned at all," Mr. Corea said primly. "After all, she can hardly know this man."

"That's just the point," Taryna told him a little breathlessly. "He says he has letters from her and threatens to give them to the Press if Mr. Newbury does not bail him out, or at least assist him in every way at his trial."

Mr. Corea did not move, but Taryna felt sure that his agile, intelligent brain was taking in every detail.

"Have you any ideas where these letters are?" he asked after a moment's pause.

"I am almost certain they are in the yacht," Taryna answered.

Mr. Corea nodded.

"That will be easy," he said briefly.

"There's one thing more," Taryna said. "I don't want Miss Newbury to know of this, you understand? No one must tell her. If the man writes to her from prison, the letters mustn't reach her. If there is anything in the newspapers, she mustn't see it. Can you somehow ensure that?"

"That will be quite easy," Mr. Corea answered. "As

far as Miss Newbury is concerned, the man will disappear. He will not be heard of again. What Mr. Newbury will do when he hears that one of the crew of his yacht has been behaving in this manner I do not know. But I don't think he will be pleased. As a matter of fact the man was never very satisfactory. We got him at a moment's notice when the mate who had been with us some time fell ill. I don't think that anyone will miss him very much."

It was as if he wrote an epitaph on Jock McDonald.

"I suppose that he will get a fair trial?" she asked.

"I shouldn't worry your head about that," Mr. Corea answered. "He will undoubtedly get what he deserves, and as far as the other matter is concerned, please don't give it another thought. Miss Kit will know nothing."

"Thank you," Taryna said with a little sigh.

"And now, if you will excuse me . . ."

Mr. Corea gave a little bow and went from the room.

When he had gone, Taryna breathed a little sigh of relief. Horrid though he might be with his dried-up manner and the way in which, according to Kit, he spied on other members of the household, there was no doubt that in an emergency like this one could rely on him.

Taryna was quite certain that those indiscreet letters of Kit's would never be heard of again. No one would ever see them. She knew, too, that unless something very unforeseen happened Kit would never hear from Jock McDonald again either.

For one wild moment Taryna wondered if she had done right. It was frightening to play about with other people's lives, to interfere with their affections and their emotions. But here, surely, she had a special excuse. Jock McDonald could do nothing but harm to Kit.

Taryna's eyes fell on her ticket lying on the table.

218

Time was passing. She must hurry with the preparations for her own journey. Resolutely she walked across the room, went into the passage and knocked on the door of Irene's suite. The door was opened almost immediately by Rosa.

"Is Mrs. Newbury awake?" Taryna asked.

"Madam is having her breakfast."

Taryna crossed the *entresol* and opened the door into the sitting-room. It was a big room bathed in sunshine. Everywhere there were huge bowls of flowers and the fragrance of them, mixed with the exotic perfume which Irene habitually used, was almost overpowering.

Irene was seated in the window. She was wearing a lacy négligeé which made her look like a fashion plate. And seated opposite her on the other side of the table, was Michael.

Both of them looked up as Taryna entered and she had the impression that she had interrupted a very private conversation.

"Good morning, Taryna! What do you want?"

It was quite obvious from Irene's voice that she was not pleased at the interruption.

"I came to tell you," Taryna said, "that I have got to leave this afternoon for the South of France."

"Indeed!"

Irene's voice was obviously not particularly interested, but without looking at him Taryna heard Michael push his chair back. She knew that he was standing staring at her, and it was difficult for her to keep her eyes fixed on Irene and not even to glance in his direction.

"Yes, my aunt has written to ask me to stay with her in Cannes," Taryna went on. "I have to leave at once as she is going on to Italy. I shall therefore be able to come back—that is, if you will have me—on Monday."

"Of course, we shall be delighted to have you with us

again," Irene said perfunctorily. "It is so nice for Kit to have a friend with her. It is a pity you must leave us even for so short a time. But you had better see Corea. He will make all arrangements."

"Thank you very much," Taryna said. "It is so kind of you."

"Not at all," Irene answered.

"But surely it can't be so important as all that for you to visit your aunt?" Michael asked suddenly.

Taryna turned towards him. She was instantly conscious of what seemed to be anger in his eyes.

"She ... she is my only aunt," she managed to stammer.

"Really, Michael!" Irene broke in. "If Taryna wishes to see her aunt I see no reason why you should interfere."

Irene's voice was sharp and there was no mistaking that she was annoyed at Michael's protest.

"No, no, of course not," Michael said in quite a different tone. "I was only thinking that it is a long way to go for such a short visit."

"I expect Taryna likes travelling," Irene said. There was a moment's silence and then she added: "Well, I expect you will want to be with Kit. Run along."

"Thank you very much and goodbye," Taryna said, feeling like a schoolgirl who was being dismissed by the headmistress.

She stole just one more look at Michael and then went from the room. Well, that was over, she thought as she got outside the door; and then found that she was shaking, not from fear, but from the tension of knowing what Michael was thinking and not being able to explain to him.

And yet why should he question her right to go away, when he was quite obviously playing a part with Irene? Was his love yet another pretence?

220

Once again she could hear Jim Carson's voice saying: "He has an heiress in tow. I hope he brings it off."

Was she the heiress? Was Kit? Or was it Irene? Michael thought that all three of them were rich.

Taryna put her hands to her face. Always when she thought of Michael her thoughts must go round and round in a circle so that she could not escape from them.

With an effort she collected her bathing-suit, borrowed one of Kit's tennis rackets and went down to the courts.

Jim was already there sitting watching Ted and Kit play a spirited and quite high-class single. He jumped up as Taryna came and held out his hand with a smile.

"I thought you were never coming," he said.

"I am sorry, I got delayed," Taryna answered.

"I believe really you were lying in bed being lazy," he teased.

She shook her head.

"I promise you I have been up for hours."

"So have I," he answered. "You ought to have been with me this morning. I had a wonderful gallop all along the sands on one of my polo ponies."

"I bathed quite early," Taryna answered.

She sat down beside him on the seat and they talked until the single was finished. Then they played a strenuous doubles until Kit protested she was so hot that she must have a bathe to cool herself down. Taryna agreed with her immediately and they ran to the tent, Kit and Taryna changing inside it while Ted and Jim went to a bathing-hut which they said they owned on the *plage*.

"Did you tell Irene?" Kit asked as she slipped off her dress.

"Yes," Taryna answered.

She had a curious reluctance to say more in case Kit

221

should ask if Michael was there. For the moment Taryna shrank from even mentioning his name. The mere thought of how he had looked hurt her so much that it was almost a physical pain.

"Was she curious?" Kit asked.

"No, not very," Taryna replied.

"That's a good thing. If she had an idea that Father had sent you, she might begin to nose around to find out why."

"I don't think she's interested," Taryna answered. "And do be careful, Kit. Somebody might be listening outside the tent."

"I hope not," Kit said quickly. She glanced outside and seeing no one there said in a lowered voice: "I say, Taryna, Ted's asked me to have dinner alone with him tonight. He wants to take me to a place about eleven kilometres away. How am I to go without Irene finding out what I'm doing?"

"Does it matter if she does?" Taryna answered.

"Not really, except that she'll make nauseating remarks, ask who Ted is and how much money he's got. You know that awful manner she has of assessing everyone by what they are worth. I don't want her pawing my friends."

Taryna could not help feeling pleased that Kit was thinking of Ted as her friend and was ready to be truculent in defence of him.

"Why don't you say you are going out with Jim?" she said. "That will side-track her enquiries. And if you go off fairly early while she's still dressing for dinner, she won't see him when he comes to fetch you."

"Taryna, you're too clever for words," Kit exclaimed.

Taryna shook her head.

"I think I am getting very deceitful," she said mournfully. "I don't know why but since I have been

222

here I seem to look at things from a different angle. I should never have behaved like this at home."

"Behaved like what?" Kit said. "Being helpful to me? Or have you got some other hidden secrets I don't know about?"

"Lots," Taryna answered truthfully, but she knew Kit didn't believe her.

"I wish you weren't going away," Kit said. "But you'll be back on Monday. I shall have such loads to tell you. I like Ted, don't you?"

"I think he's charming," Taryna said warmly, "and such a genuine person."

"He's very rich too," Kit said. "So I don't have to feel that he's impressed by my money."

"I don't think people care about money half as much as you think," Taryna said.

"Not people like Ted, at any rate," Kit answered happily.

She opened the tent and went out on to the sand.

"I'll race you into the sea," Taryna heard her say to Ted, and then she went out more slowly to join Jim.

The morning passed quickly. They had luncheon at the little restaurant where Jim and Ted said the *moules marinières* were better than anywhere else along the coast. It was certainly gay and amusing. There were tables with check cloths set outside in a tiny garden, and strange musicians who wandered in from the street to sing a song, to play an instrument and collect a few centimes.

"It's a very unusual cabaret," Kit laughed.

"These people go from restaurant to restaurant," Jim said. "I sometimes think of doing it myself. I'm sure they make a fortune one way or another."

"But it's a short season," Ted laughed. "In the winter you would only have the fishermen's bars to do, and I don't suppose they part easily."

The two men talked nonsense the whole way through lunch, while Kit and Taryna laughed and egged them on to further extravagances.

"This is fun," Taryna thought, and felt how different it was from the formal, heavy luncheons and dinners they had to endure when Mr. Newbury and Irene were there.

She had a sudden longing for Michael. She knew he would fit in. Then as the coffee was brought to the table Taryna glanced at her watch.

"I must be getting back," she said. "I've got to leave at three-thirty."

"Isn't it sickening that she's got to go at all?" Kit asked.

"Can't you get out of it?" Jim asked.

There was a look in his eyes which told Taryna only too clearly that he wanted her to stay.

"I wish I could," she answered. "I shall be back by Monday."

"We'll have a party for you when you return," Jim said. "Is that a date?"

"Of course it is," Kit cried before Taryna could speak. "We will do something really gay and exciting. Don't tell her we'll plan it while she's gone."

"We'll talk about it tonight," Ted said in a quiet aside that only Kit heard.

"That will be fine," Kit answered, her eyes meeting his.

"I must go," Taryna said. "Please don't come with me."

"I'll drive you in my car," Jim answered.

"Are you quite sure you wouldn't like me to come?" Kit asked.

"Quite sure," Taryna replied.

She kissed Kit and held out her hand to Ted.

"Look after her for me," she pleaded.

"You needn't be afraid," he answered. "I'm not going to leave her side for a moment if I can help it."

Kit was walking away from them down the garden towards the car with Jim. Ted turned to look after her and Taryna saw in his eyes something she had longed to see there.

"She hasn't had an easy life," she said gently.

"Whatever it's been like," he answered, "it's made her into the sweetest person I've ever met."

"That's exactly what she is," Taryna answered.

She hurried after Kit and Jim.

"Goodbye, darling!" Kit said again. "Do hurry back. I can't bear to think of you having to go all that long way in this heat."

"Goodbye!" Taryna answered.

She got into the car and Jim drove her quickly back to the hotel. The big car which Mr. Newbury habitually used was standing outside the door.

Taryna hurried up to her room. Ella had packed her things and the suitcase had already gone downstairs. Taryna put the tickets and the money, still in their sealed envelopes, into her handbag. Then she changed into a neat tussore suit which Kit had suggested several days ago would be useful for travelling. There was a little pink hat to match it and a coat of the same colour but in a thicker material in case it should turn cold in the evening.

"I suppose I've got everything," Taryna said to herself.

Somehow it didn't seem to matter what she took or what was left behind. She was hating this moment of leaving, not only because of Kit but because of her own feelings at leaving Michael. And yet she was not sure that she did not hate him.

She picked up her handbag and went down in the lift. She had not expected to see Mr. Newbury or Irene again and it was with some consternation that she saw them both, followed by a party of friends, coming into the lounge.

They had been lunching outside in the garden and Taryna thought resentfully that if she had been only two minutes sooner she would have just missed them.

Mr. Newbury saw her first.

"Ah, Taryna!" he exclaimed, walking across to her. "I hear that you are to leave us for two nights. I am sorry about that. Kit will miss you. I hope you have a good journey."

"Thank you very much," Taryna replied. "And thank you, too, for the lovely time I've had here."

She turned to Irene.

"Goodbye, Mrs. Newbury! Thank you so much."

"Goodbye, Taryna."

Irene's farewell was perfunctory. She was busily engaged in talking to a rather distinguished-looking man with grey hair and an eye-glass, who was obviously someone of importance.

"I will see you to the car," Mr. Newbury said to Taryna.

"Let me do it, sir."

Michael had detached himself from the other guests. Taryna tried not to look at him as they all three walked through the outer hall to where the car was waiting.

"Goodbye, my dear!" Mr. Newbury said again.

"Goodbye!" Taryna said, shaking him by the hand, and then turning to Michael she put her hand into his. She felt the hard, quick pressure of his fingers, and she felt something else too, something in the palm of his hand he was pressing into hers.

"Goodbye, Taryna! *Bon voyage,*" he smiled. "Give my love to the Côte d'Azur."

Almost automatically her fingers clutched what he had passed to her. She turned towards the car. It was at this moment that she saw Mr. Corea come from the hall carrying something in his hands.

"What's that, Corea?" she heard Mr. Newbury ask. "Oh, yes! Flowers. Of course! I'd forgotten."

He took the flowers from Mr. Corea's hand and pulled off the silver wrapping.

"A little present from Kit and myself," Mr. Newbury said.

"Oh, how kind!" Taryna managed to appear surprised.

"Pin them on your coat. They are just the right colour," Mr. Newbury said.

Mr. Corea hurried forward with a pin.

"Oh, thank you," Taryna smiled. "They are lovely. It was kind of you to think of it."

"You must thank Kit for that," Mr. Newbury said.

Taryna pinned the orchids on her shoulder and got into the car. She waved her hand as they moved away and looked back. She thought there was an expression of anxiety on Mr. Newbury's face, but Michael was not waving. He was watching her go. It seemed to her that his face was unusually serious.

She gave a little sigh and sat back. Then, surreptitiously, so that not even the chauffeur could see, she opened the tiny piece of paper that she held in the palm of her hand. She spread it out.

Tell the chauffeur to stop at the hotel in Brionne, she read.

That was all. No signature—just rather neat and yet somehow characteristic writing.

Why should Michael want her to stop? she wondered. Was he going to send her a message? And then she guessed the reason. He was going to telephone her there.

She felt a sudden joy lift her spirits to the skies. Afer all he had not let her go without saying goodbye.

Stop at the hotel in Brionne. Strange that those few words should transform the whole world so that it was golden with glory and she was filled with an almost wild happiness.

They were driving quickly through the hedge-bordered roads, twisting and turning until finally they came to the main road leading to Paris. Now they were speeding along and there was little traffic to slow them down, through village after village, while Taryna watched the signposts.

At last she saw the words she was waiting for: *Brionne 10 kilometres.*

She bent forward and said to the chauffeur:

"Will you stop, please, at the hotel in Brionne."

He did not seem surprised although she wondered what he thought.

"Very well, *m'mselle.*"

That was all he said, and now she was counting the kilometres one by one—five, four, three, two. They were in Brionne. It was only a small village. There was one hotel, an attractive one standing a little way back from the road.

The car drew up to the door. The hotel looked fairly deserted at this time of the afternoon. There were only two cars outside—a big Renault and a small, dusty Fiat.

A little shyly, frightened as to how good her French might prove now she was on her own, Taryna walked into the hotel. There was nobody at the reception desk in the hall. She passed it and went into a lounge with a low ceiling, oak beamed, and comfortable chairs round an ancient fireplace.

There was no one here and she was about to turn back to the reception desk when through a french window leading to the garden there came a man. For a moment Taryna could only stare at him in stupefaction

228

and then she gave a little cry of surprise and joy mingled together. It was Michael!

"Are you glad to see me?" he asked.

"But how did you get here?" she questioned.

"I came in a very small and very fast Fiat," he said. "I passed you about twenty minutes ago. You were looking rather wistful, I thought. As I didn't want the chauffeur to see me, I couldn't stop."

"Oh, Michael, why didn't you tell me?"

"I wasn't certain I could manage it," he said. "I thought I might have to telephone you."

"That's what I thought you meant to do."

"Come and sit down."

He took her by the hand and led her on to the verandah. It had obviously been built as a protection from the winter winds. It looked out over a small flower-filled garden beyond which a small stream wound its way through wooded banks. They sat down on a cushion-covered seat.

"Darling, you didn't really think I would let you go away without saying goodbye, did you?" Michael asked.

"I didn't know what to think," Taryna answered.

"I told you to trust me," Michael replied. "But why didn't you tell me this morning you were going to Cannes?"

"I didn't know myself," Taryna answered quickly. "I only got the letter when I got back to the hotel."

"I thought that was what must have happened," Michael said. "I couldn't believe that you would deceive me."

Taryna's eyes fell before his.

"Why should I want to?" she murmured.

Michael reached out and put his arms round her.

"I love you so much," he said simply. "If only things were easier; if only I could explain. But I can't.

229

I can only go on saying that you have got to trust me. But don't try me too hard, my darling."

"What do you mean by that?" Taryna asked.

"Must you go away tonight?" he asked.

"I have to go," she replied.

"I hate to think of you taking that long journey by yourself. I wish I could come with you. You're so small to travel about alone. You always seem to me to be in need of protection."

"I shall be all right," Taryna said.

"And you will be back on Monday? Well, that's something at any rate. But all the same, I have an absurd feeling that I ought to stop you."

"That is absurd, isn't it?" Taryna said with a little quiver in her voice.

"I suppose it's because I grudge every moment that I can't be with you," Michael said.

He looked down at her face and then, putting his hand under her chin, slowly tipped back her head so that it was against his shoulder.

"Oh, my darling!" he said. His voice broke on the words and then he kissed her.

For a moment Taryna tried to withstand him, tried not to let the wonder and thrill of his kiss sweep her completely off her feet. And then because she could not help it her whole being surrendered itself and she felt herself cling to him, her lips giving him back kiss for kiss, her body trembling and quivering within his arms.

"I love you!"

The words seemed to be wrenched from him, almost as if they were a vow, not a statement. And then, almost unsteadily, he rose to his feet.

"You have got to go, my sweet, and I have got to get back."

The shadow of Irene seemed to come between them.

"Will . . . they . . . miss you?" Taryna asked.

230

"I hope not," he answered. "I said I was going to get a haircut."

He kissed her again and somehow the passion had gone from it. For a moment she thought it was only the ghost of the kiss he had given her before.

"Goodbye!"

She put her hands in his and looked up at him.

"You are so lovely," he said. "I wish I had thought to give you those."

He touched the orchids as he spoke and then, because she longed so much to stay, Taryna almost brusquely moved away from him.

She walked through the little lounge without looking back, and as she reached the reception desk she could not help turning. He was standing on the verandah where she had left him, just watching her go.

She hesitated. She wanted to run back to him; she wanted to cling to him, to beg him to go with her. Then, with what seemed to her almost a superhuman effort, she forced herself to walk out to the car sedately and with her head held high.

12

Taryna could not sleep in the *wagon-lit*. For a long time she sat with the blind up, watching the dark night rushing past. Then at length she undressed and got into the soft, comfortable bed, but sleep escaped her.

Round and round in her mind the events of the past forty-eight hours seemed to chase themselves, until it seemed to her that it was difficult to know where fact ended and fantasy began.

The whole story was so incredible, so utterly fantastic in many ways that she felt, were she to tell it to some impartial outside person, not a word of it would be believed. Everything seemed so unnecessarily dramatic that over and over again she asked herself whether she were not, in fact, imagining things.

And yet she knew she had not imagined Mr. Newbury's suggestion that she should come to the South of France; or that she should wear a spray of orchids on her shoulder—orchids which she could see swinging on her coat as the train gathered speed.

She had not been able to resist looking at them closely when she was alone in the *wagon-lit*. They had seemed to her like any other orchids. She had not had the chance before of examining many such sprays. Only rich women could afford to wear such exotic blooms. There were two large purple blossoms—Cattleya, she thought they were called—and their stems were welded together by a purple ribbon of exactly the same colour which was rolled round and round so tightly that it was quite impossible to guess whether or not something lay concealed underneath.

And yet she knew that, of course, was where the plans must be hidden. The roll of purple ribbon was certainly thicker than was necessary and what could be a better or more cleverly thought out place?

But apart from the orchids and Mr. Newbury's strange story of the plans and espionage there were so many other problems to keep her awake.

What, by now, had happened about Kit? If only she had not had to come away; if only she could have stayed to protect her. Yet, somehow, strange though it was, she had complete trust in Mr. Corea. He was so efficient and at the same time so unscrupulous in his methods that Taryna could not help feeling quite certain that no message would get through to Kit, no letter would reach her, and that if anything was reported in the French papers there was no chance of their being found in the Newbury suite.

By tomorrow, if not today, Kit would begin to wonder what had happened to Jock McDonald. If she just wrote to the yacht that would be safe enough—the letter would be intercepted. But if she went down to look for him, if she questioned the rest of the crew—what then?

Taryna could only pray that Kit's new-found interest in Ted Burlington would, for the moment, make her forget that she had ever imagined herself in love with a member of her father's crew.

Supposing she had married Jock? Supposing she had run away with him? Taryna felt herself shudder at the thought of the disillusionment, the unhappiness, which would have been the inevitable consequence of such an action.

Kit had been saved from that—at least Taryna prayed she had saved her. And then, because she knew

233

it was the one thing that she was trying to avoid, eventually her thoughts were of Michael.

She felt her lips burning as they had burned when he kissed her; she felt her eyes grow heavy at the thought of the fire in his; she felt a little flame flicker and rise within her as she remembered the touch of his mouth on her neck, the feel of his hands holding her.

"I love him! I love him!"

The train seemed to be repeating it over and over again.

"I love him! I love him!"

On, on, endlessly, just one refrain which throbbed and beat in every nerve of her body.

She must have slept a little because suddenly she awoke with a jerk to hear the French porters shouting. She jumped up and looked out of the window. It was all so beautiful that for a moment she could only draw in her breath and feel as if even speech and thought had gone, leaving only an intensified feeling at the loveliness of what she saw.

The sea was so blue that there was nothing to which one could compare it—except, perhaps, the glass in the windows of King's College, Cambridge. The sun, early though it was, was blazing, and everywhere, it seemed to Taryna, there were flowers—great purple and crimson patches of them, growing over the walls and in the gardens and right down to the water's edge.

There were flat, white villas and golden sands, and a sky that seemed translucent in its shimmering heat. And over everything a kind of enchantment which made Taryna feel almost as if she had stepped out of this world into the next.

She sat entranced at the window like a child with its nose against the plate-glass of a sweet shop, until the attendant knocked at the door and brought her a cup of tea. Then she realised it was time she should get dressed.

Quickly she put on her things, hardly for a moment taking her eyes from the beauty outside. And as the train travelled slowly along the coast, she saw the bathers splashing into the water, the small waves rippling against the red rocks, the boats with their coloured sails coming out slowly from the harbours.

"This is what I dreamed it would be like," Taryna said to herself, and for a moment she forgot everything that lay ahead of her, all her apprehensions of what would happen when she got to Cannes; instead she drank in the beauty that she had never believed she would be privileged to see.

"Cannes! Cannes!"

The porters were chanting the name and giving it a lilt. Taryna quickly put her hat on her head and shut her suitcase. She picked up her bag and gloves and glanced at herself in the mirror. Despite her sleepless night she did not look tired—in fact her face was alight with excitement, her eyes shining.

"I look as if I were going to meet my lover," she told herself whimsically, and had a sudden pang as she thought of Michael so far away in the North of France. The orchids on her shoulder looked little the worse for their night in the train. Perhaps they had lost some of their crispness, but they still gave her an expensive, almost exotic appearance as she stepped down slowly on to the platform.

For a moment she stood there, indecisive.

"Does *m'mselle* require a taxi?" a porter asked in French.

"I think I am being met, thank you," Taryna said.

He led her along the platform and then suddenly Taryna saw, bearing down on her, a middle-aged woman, a smile of welcome on her face. A second later

235

she had no doubt that this was the fictitious Jane Woodruff.

"Darling Taryna!" the woman said, flinging her arms round Taryna and kissing her on both cheeks. "How sweet of you to come all this way to see me! I can't tell you how glad I am to see you."

She spoke in a loud voice with an obvious Canadian accent. Then she linked her arm through Taryna's and told the porter, in rather bad French, that she had a car outside.

"I do hope you had a good journey," she said as they walked along. "I thought of you travelling all this way and felt it was almost cruel to invite you while it's so hot."

"I was very comfortable, thank you," Taryna said in a rather stiff little voice.

She could not help feeling embarrassed, and at the same time almost afraid. The whole thing was so unreal; and when she stole a glance at her companion, it seemed even more unbelievable that this smart, well-dressed woman should pass herself off as poor, dowdy Aunt Jane.

"I had great difficulty getting you a room," the impostor was saying. "The Splendide is so full at this time of year and, of course, I knew you would want to be on the front. They tried to give me a back room, but I soon put a stop to that. 'My niece is used to the best wherever she goes,' I told the reception manager. And, of course, after I had made enough fuss they suddenly found there was a room vacant—and on the fourth floor so that you have your own balcony."

"That will be lovely," Taryna managed to enthuse with difficulty.

"Now I want to hear all the family news," her companion went on. "You must tell me all about your dear mother. I was so worried about her last winter."

236

Taryna was just about to ejaculate "Why?", then she realised that would be an indiscreet question. Fortunately, by this time they had reached the entrance to the station. The porter was putting Taryna's suitcase into a very smart-looking limousine that was waiting outside.

She would have tipped him, but her supposed aunt waved him aside.

"Here you are," she said.

She offered what looked to Taryna a quite abnormal number of notes. The man was obviously delighted and his *"Merci beaucoup, madame"* followed them long after the car had driven off.

It was only when they were away from the station and the woman had leaned forward to see that the glass compartment between them and the chauffeur was tightly shut that she seemed able to relax.

"That was fiendish," she said. "I was half afraid that you wouldn't come."

Taryna said nothing. Somehow she didn't know what to say. She had her instructions, she thought, and she would carry them out to the letter. She would make no mention to the woman of the plans or anything else.

"You're not at all what I expected," the middle-aged woman was saying. "I thought it would be somebody older and pretty hard-boiled, if you know what I mean. Why, you're only a child."

"I'm nearly twenty-one," Taryna said.

"And that, to me, is an infant in arms," the woman answered. "Goodness, I wish I could say I was nearly twenty-one. I wish, too, I could have my time over again."

It was obvious she did not expect Taryna to ask why, so again there was a little pause as they drove down towards the sea.

"It's so beautiful," Taryna said in an awed voice as

237

they turned on to the *plage* and she saw the long line of palm trees, the brilliantly laid out flower-beds and the crowd of vividly coloured pleasure-seekers playing on the sands.

"Haven't you been here before?" the woman asked.

Taryna shook her head.

"Oh, well, it'll be an experience then. Though I expect you've travelled a lot."

Taryna said nothing. Somehow she saw no reason why she should lie to this woman, but she supposed that she, too, had been told that she was the rich Miss Grazebrook.

"It's not always to this sort of place that one gets sent," the woman said, with what seemed to Taryna something wistful in her voice. "It's usually to dirty little cafés in back alleys, or to assignations in East Germany which fair give one the creeps."

"In Germany?" Taryna asked.

The woman looked uncomfortable.

"Don't say I've said anything, will you?" she said. "We're not supposed, as you know, to say where we've been."

"I'm afraid I don't know," Taryna said.

"Oh, well, in that case please forget I ever said anything," the woman pleaded.

She seemed suddenly to shrink and not be so over-powering.

"You don't want to get me into trouble, do you?" she asked. "So be a sport."

"I won't say anything," Taryna answered. "Of course I won't."

This is getting fantastic, she thought to herself. Who is this woman? And what sort of people employ her? Somehow she felt there was more than Mr. Newbury behind all this. Or perhaps he was capable of being more ruthless than she had imagined.

She remembered the tape-recorded conversation at Earlywood and felt herself shiver.

"Look," she said suddenly. "I want to go back tonight. Will that be all right?"

"Not unless those are your instructions," the woman answered with almost a harsh note in her voice.

"I would much rather do it if it can be managed," Taryna said.

She did not know why, but she felt she could not stand very long of this woman's companionship. She was curious about the mystery that surrounded her, and yet, at the same time, she did not wish to know what it was all about. It was all too unsavoury, too unpleasant.

"I can't see any reason why I shouldn't go," she insisted a little obstinately. "Once I've done what I came to do."

"That's up to you, of course," the woman answered. "But if you take my advice you won't do anything that's not expected. There's usually awful trouble if you do."

"Trouble with whom?"

The woman turned her eyes away.

"You know the answer to that," she said.

"Is there an evening train?" Taryna enquired.

"Of course there is," the woman snapped. "There are trains, aeroplanes and ships if you want to take them. But if you've been told to stay here until tomorrow, then you'd better do as you're told. You'll find they can make it very unpleasant for you if you don't."

Again Taryna felt herself shiver. This was all so nameless, so incomprehensible. Privately she made up her mind she would telephone Mr. Newbury. She would be able to get him about six o'clock. And if he didn't like it—well, what could he do?

She suddenly felt she wanted to laugh out loud. How absurd she was, being frightened of anything or any-

239

body. After all, she was Taryna Grazebrook; and at home there were her father and mother, Edwina and Donald. There was the shabby Vicarage to go to and all of them waiting for her.

They might be angry with her for having told a lot of lies. But at the same time, whatever she had done, or however stupid she had been, they would stand by her. She belonged to them and they belonged to her and that was all there was to it.

The woman beside her looked at her in surprise.

"Have you thought of something pleasant?" she asked.

"I was thinking of my family," Taryna answered.

"They must be something special to make you look like that," the woman said sourly.

"They are as a matter of fact," Taryna answered.

"Well, here's the Splendide," the woman said as they turned off the road up a small, very short drive to a porticoed door.

Porters came running and Taryna got out slowly. They were bowed in while her companion talked loudly.

"Here's my niece arrived safely," she said. "The train was on time for once. I quite expected I should have to wait half an hour at the station. Will somebody take her up to her room and send up the luggage?"

She turned to Taryna.

"I expect you will want to change, dear, won't you? Put on something really cool and you'll find me sitting out in the sun just outside the bar. I'll have a nice cool drink waiting for you. Don't be long."

"No, I won't be long," Taryna said almost automatically.

She got into the lift, her pretended aunt waving her hand; and as she turned, Taryna could hear her talking volubly to the man at the desk.

Her room on the fourth floor was large and even more luxurious than her one at Deauville had been. The sun canopy was drawn low over the little balcony and yet the room seemed full of sunshine, and there was a big bunch of pink carnations on a table by the window.

The porter put Taryna's suitcase down on the little stand provided for it, waited while she tipped him, then thanking her went from the room, shutting the door quietly behind him.

Taryna stood for a moment looking round her. How strange it was that she should be here! And yet, at the same time, she could not help running to the window to look out at the sea below.

She was in Cannes! Well, whatever happened, however angry anybody was with her about this escapade, at least she had seen two places she had never expected to see in the whole of her life.

Almost soberly she remembered the woman who was waiting for her downstairs. She supposed she must change and go down to her. It was a nuisance that she had to be here with anyone. She would have enjoyed it more if she had been on her own—and then she thought of the expense and gave a little grimace.

She opened her suitcase and took out her dress. She had only brought two with her—one in pink trimmed with little touches of white; the other in a cool leaf-green. There was an evening dress, of course, sandals, and bathing dresses, and all sorts of odd things that Ella had put in at the last moment and which Taryna thought it was unlikely that she would use on such a short visit.

Anyway, it was something to know that she need not be ashamed of her appearance, thanks to Kit. Slowly she unbuttoned the pink suit she had worn to travel in, and then she unfastened the orchids on her shoulder. She turned them over in her hands. She had an almost

241

irresistible impulse to undo the purple ribbon which bound them, to see what was there, to try if she could decipher or understand this important secret with which she had been entrusted.

And then she knew that would be a betrayal of Mr. Newbury's trust. Whatever she felt about him, she had given him her word; and however suspicious she might be of him or his confederates, at least he had shown her nothing but kindness and generosity.

For a moment she held the flowers in her hands, and then, as if she did something irrevocable, she dropped them, as she had been commanded, into the waste-paper basket.

After that she began to hurry. She wanted to get out of the room, wanted the flowers to be removed before she returned to it again. She hung up the suit in the cupboard and slipped into the full-skirted green dress. It fitted her tightly at the waist, the neck was low and her arms were bare. It was a very simple dress and it made her look very young.

If only Michael was here! She almost said the words aloud.

Then she stamped her foot. She could almost hear her own voice scolding her own stupidity. "Go downstairs and enjoy yourself, Taryna. You'll never have this opportunity again. Here you have for years been longing to go abroad, and now you are here you do nothing but moan after some stupid man you've only met a few times. Go down and look at the sea and be happy. And if it does last only twenty-four hours, what does it matter? At least you've had those hours and the joy of them can never be taken away from you again."

She turned from the dressing-table and almost ran from the room. She would take her own good advice. She would forget all those doubts and suspicions and miseries and enjoy Cannes just because it was Cannes.

242

She rang the bell for the lift. She had to wait for it for a little while, and when it came the man apologized, saying that he had been taking a lady in a wheel-chair to the top floor.

"*Quel beau temps, m'mselle!*" he added, and Taryna found herself smiling at him.

"Yes, it's wonderful weather, isn't it?" she said, and felt her spirits rising. It was going to be fun after all.

They reached the ground floor and as the lift stopped Taryna gave an exclamation.

"How silly of me," she said. "I have left my bag behind. I am sorry but would you mind taking me up again?"

The lift-man shut the doors and they went up again. Up, up, to the fourth floor.

"I won't be a moment," Taryna said.

She had the key of her door in her hand and she ran down the passage to her room. She fitted the key quickly into the lock and opened the door. She walked in.

For a moment she didn't see him. He was standing to the left of the door looking in the wardrobe. And then, as she realised that a man was there, she gave a gasp, half of anger, half of fear.

"What are you doing?" she asked, forgetting for a moment she should have spoken in French.

The man shut the wardrobe door and turned to face her. It was Michael!

For a second Taryna thought she must have gone mad. She could only stare at him and everything in the whole world seemed to stand still. Then, as he just looked at her, she moved back a pace to reach out an almost unsteady hand towards the foot of the bed.

"Michael! Why are you here?"

"I think perhaps you had better tell me that," he answered.

243

"I don't know what you mean."

"I think you do," he said.

She stared at him. It seemed to her that he looked older and more responsible, or perhaps it was only the change in his voice.

"Michael, I don't understand," Taryna said.

"You told me you were coming down here to meet your aunt," Michael said. "That was a lie."

"How do you know?" Taryna asked.

"Because I have seen her," he answered. "She's nobody's aunt—or, if she is, her nieces are certainly not in the least like you."

"Oh!"

Taryna felt for a moment as if she had nothing to say. She sat down on the end of the bed.

"You had better hand them over to me right away," Michael said.

"Hand what over?"

"Taryna, don't play with me," he said. "You have been very clever. I was completely deceived by you. But I want them and I intend to have them."

"I don't know what you are talking about."

Taryna did not look at him as she spoke. Somehow she felt that she must fight, however much a losing battle it might be, for the pretence which till now had seemed so unimportant but now appeared menacing and infinitely frightening.

Michael came to the end of the bed and put his hands on the polished board.

"How did you get mixed up in this?" he said.

"I don't think you have any right to question me," Taryna said a little wildly. "Who are you to burst into my bedroom, to search my things, to confront me with questions? Why should I tell you anything?"

"You are going to tell me everything," Michael said, and there was a steely note of determination in his voice which seemed to Taryna infinitely more menacing than anything she had ever heard before.

"Who are you?" Taryna asked. "Who gave you the authority to question me?"

"That I might tell you later," Michael answered. "In the meantime, let's get down to brass tacks. What have you done with them?"

"I don't know what you mean by 'them.' "

"Very well then. If you want it in plain English—the plans."

Taryna got up off the bed and walked towards the window. It seemed to her that a jigsaw puzzle was falling into place. Mr. Newbury had spoken of his rivals and competitors. He had used her as a cover for his plans, and his rivals, whoever they might be, were using Michael. He was on the other side. He was, therefore, an enemy of Mr. Newbury, and whatever her heart felt about it she must be loyal to the man she had promised to serve.

She turned round to face him.

"I am afraid you are making a terrible mistake," she said. "I came to Cannes because I wanted to. It was not, as you have been clever enough to find out, to see my aunt, but to see someone I particularly wanted to see."

She thought, though she was not certain, that Michael's mouth tightened a little.

"A man?" he asked.

Taryna smiled and dropped her eyes.

"That's entirely my business," she said.

"I don't believe you. If that is true what were you doing with Kitty Marlowe?"

"Kitty Marlowe!"

Taryna's eyes were wide and innocent.

"The woman who had obligingly registered herself as Miss Jane Woodruff."

"Oh, well, she was just an excuse so that I could get away from Deauville and come down here."

Michael suddenly walked across to Taryna and put his hands on her shoulders.

"Stop lying," he said. "You are the worst liar I've ever seen. And, somehow, though I must be a fool to let you take me in, I don't believe you're really involved in this. Tell me the truth, Taryna. Tell me!"

At the touch of his hands she felt herself quiver. Now she looked up at him and for a moment she was almost lost. She wanted, more than anything she had ever wanted in her life, to put her arms round his neck, to tell him the whole story, to tell him who she was and how she had become involved in all this.

Then she knew she couldn't. For her own sake she couldn't say anything. She could only stare at him, and then she tried to turn away her head.

"Well?" Michael said.

"I can't," she said simply. "I can't tell you anything."

"You prefer me to think what I am thinking?"

"I can answer that completely and absolutely truthfully," Taryna said with a little break in her voice. "I have not the slightest idea what you are thinking."

He dropped his hands.

"You are being exasperating," he said. "I have got to get to the bottom of this; I have got to."

There was silence between them and then impulsively Michael said:

"Listen, Taryna! I will come clean and tell you what I know. When you left Deauville last night you carried with you some plans. They were very important plans—so important that somehow I have got to persuade you to tell me where they are or what you have done with them. Please don't make it difficult for me. You see, I love you."

His words were a surprise but Taryna drew in her breath quickly.

"How can I believe that," she asked, "when you come here unexpectedly, bullying me, trying to make me tell you something which I can't?"

"Are you afraid?"

"No, not afraid," Taryna answered.

"Then tell me," he said. "We can settle this so easily together."

"Settle it for whom?"

He looked at her for a moment and then he said quietly:

"For those most concerned. For those who should matter to you as much as they matter to me—Great Britain and France."

Taryna was suddenly still.

"What do you mean?" she asked.

"I mean," Michael answered, "that those are the two countries vitally concerned in what you are so cleverly hiding."

"What are they then?" Taryna asked. "Are they plans which concern weapons or rockets?"

"As if you didn't know," Michael said a little scornfully. "Well, if you want it in plain English, no! You know as well as I do that it is entirely a commercial invention."

Taryna felt her tenseness subside a little. For one awful moment she had thought that she had been playing traitor to her own country. Thrillers, in which the plans of some nuclear weapon factory had been taken half across the Continent, had rushed through her mind.

But now she knew that her fears had been groundless. Mr. Newbury had spoken the truth. It was, as he said, only something which concerned business and there was no reason at all why Michael, representing the rival company, should have what belonged to Mr. Newbury.

"I am sorry, Michael," she said quietly. "I think I do understand what you are speaking about now and I think I know what you are. You belong to the rival company and they have no right to the plans, and therefore if they can't get them by fair methods they will get them by foul."

"That is wrong. It is so much more important than that," Michael said. "Listen, darling! I still don't understand how you are concerned in this, but you do know what I am talking about. Therefore use your own common sense and you must see."

"No, I don't," Taryna said swiftly. "And I think it is wrong and despicable of you to try to wheedle me into giving you something which you know, as well as I do, is not mine to give or yours to take. Go away, Michael. I thought I loved you. I see I was wrong."

"And I thought I loved you," he answered. "And I still do—even though I don't understand, even though it terrifies me to think who you are or what you are."

"If you think those things about me I don't want you to love me," Taryna said hotly.

Michael took a step towards her and almost instinctively she moved away from him.

"Don't touch me," she said. "You are being unfair and I despise you for it. Go away from my room. I will talk to you about this downstairs."

Michael still advanced towards her.

"I am not going away until you have told me where those plans are," he said. "I will take them if I have to shake them out of you."

"So that's how much you love me," she said, throwing up her head and looking him straight in the eyes.

"That's how much I love you," he answered grimly.

"I am not going to let you do anything that you will regret for the rest of your life."

Taryna met his eyes. She knew then that both of them were angry. Her hands were clenched. She could feel her anger rising in her, ready to defy him even if he should, as he had said, try and shake it out of her. She knew he was angry by the steely glint in his eyes, by the squareness of his jaw, the tight line of his lips.

"Damn you! You're driving me mad!"

He came towards her and she opened her mouth to scream. Even as she did so there came a sudden knock and the door opened.

Almost instinctively they both stood still, their faces turned towards the man who had entered. It was only the *valet de chambre* wearing the familiar uniform of a sleeveless grey waistcoat and a dark apron.

"*Pardon, madame! Pardon, monsieur!*" he said.

He walked across the room and as he did so Taryna knew why he was there. He had come for the orchids in the wastepaper basket. He picked it up, flicked an imaginary piece of dust off the dressing-table into the basket, and turned towards the door.

"*Bonjour, madame! Bonjour, monsieur!*" he said and went towards the door.

Perhaps there was something in Taryna's face; perhaps it was some instinct which made Michael know that this was something unusual. Whatever it was he suddenly moved.

"Wait!"

His voice rang out like a pistol shot, and then in two strides he was across the room. He had taken the wastepaper basket from the valet.

For a moment the man seemed to struggle. He pulled with all his might on the basket and then, as Michael pulled too, he suddenly turned and ran from the room. The door slammed behind him.

Michael stood with the basket in his hands peering down into it. Then with a little sound he dropped it and pulled out the orchids. For a moment he stood with them in his hands, and then swiftly he began to unwind the purple ribbon which covered their stalks.

"So that's how you did it," he said. "Clever! Very clever!"

The purple ribbon grew longer and longer. Taryna watched his fingers, almost fascinated. The film was coiled very tightly round the stems. It was only about two inches wide and as Michael held it up to the light it was about a foot long.

He looked at it for a moment and there was an expression of great satisfaction on his face. Then he slipped it into the pocket of his coat.

"Thank you," he said.

She knew that he was being sarcastic. Somehow he no longer made her angry. She could only stand, feeling limp and deflated, a little girl who had failed in an errand on which she had been sent, a child who expected to be punished because she hadn't been clever enough to obey a somewhat complicated command.

She was suddenly aware that Michael was looking at her with a strange expression on his face. Then he said softly:

"Why did you do it, Taryna?"

"Because Mr. Newbury asked me to," Taryna answered. "How could I refuse? I was his guest. There was no earthly reason why I shouldn't come down to the South of France, and it seemed so ungrateful, somehow, to say no."

Michael walked swiftly to her side.

"Is that the truth? The whole truth?" he said.

He put his hand under her chin and turned her face up to his.

"Of course it's the truth," Taryna answered. "And I

am tired of your suspicions, your insinuations and the way you have been behaving. I think you are a thief and a brute and I hate you."

So suddenly that it surprised herself, the tears ran down her cheeks. Michael put his arms round her.

"My stupid, idiotic darling," he said. "I believe you really are telling the truth about what happened."

"But of course I am," Taryna sobbed. "But he trusted me and I'd done exactly what he told me to do, and now you've come along and spoilt it all. Oh, poor Mr. Newbury! Michael, won't you give them back to him?"

"Poor Mr. Newbury, indeed!" Michael laughed.

It was not a very pleasant sound.

"Would you like to know the truth about him?"

"If it is the truth," Taryna said, her breath catching on a sob.

"Well, the truth is that our Mr. Newbury is a very greedy man," Michael said. "He only cares for one thing in his life, and that is money. He doesn't care how he gets it or from whom he gets it. As he has apparently told you . . ."

He paused a moment and taking a handkerchief from his breast pocket wiped Taryna's tears away. "As he has apparently told you," he repeated, "these plans are an industrial project. Actually they are the plans for revolutionising machinery and the safety of coal-mines. They have been invented by a very clever young Czech who has been working in England since the war.

"Now, we knew what he was doing and he has, at certain times, had grants of money from various industrial bodies. But what we didn't know was that his plans were completely successful and finished.

"How Mr. Newbury got in touch with him I don't now, but, anyway, I suppose men like that smell out money wherever it may be. Anyway, the first thing that

251

gave us an inkling as to what was happening was that Mr. Newbury started asking questions of the Coal Board as to how much they would be prepared to pay for this new design. He then asked the same question in France. The two countries got together and decided that we would share the plans because it would be of advantage to everyone in Europe and in England that this new invention should be put into our mines."

"Was Mr. Newbury told this?" Taryna asked.

"Oh, he knew it was wanted," Michael said, "but he was just holding out on the price. The Czech had handed the whole business arrangements over to him. I think actually they were to share out on a fifty-fifty basis."

"And then what happened?" Taryna asked.

"Another country got interested," Michael answered. "You can guess what country, but Mr. Newbury played them off very cleverly. He asked them for three times the amount of money he was asking from England and France, knowing that he had reached the limit as far as we were prepared to go."

"But surely he was quite entitled to do that?" Taryna said.

Michael nodded.

"Yes, ethically and theoretically, of course he was. Morally, no. This invention had been made by a man whom Britain had sheltered. Experiments had been done with British money and though we were prepared to allow France to come in we were not prepared to allow everyone else in Europe to have the first advantages of it. But we were being held up for blackmail, which is another thing they don't take very kindly to in Whitehall."

"So what happened?" Taryna asked.

"Well, we learned that Newbury could not be certain of the money from the other country unless they could

252

first of all have a look at the plans, and they arranged, after some correspondence, which was luckily intercepted, to meet somewhere in France.

"The difficulty was, where? Someone, I should imagine it was Newbury, had the bright idea of it being in Cannes. There were always foreign aeroplanes arriving; one more or less would not cause any particular comment, especially if it came here via Vienna or Yugoslavia.

"The difficulty was, then, as far as Newbury was concerned, to get the plans here. He knew we were watching for him, knew we were determined that somehow these plans should not be seen by the rival power, and he should not be offered these tremendous sums for something to which he had contributed absolutely nothing."

Taryna gave a little sigh.

"I am beginning to understand."

"I thought you would," Michael said gently.

He walked across to the bedside and picked up the telephone.

"*Donnez-moi la Sûreté, s'il vous plaît,*" he said.

Taryna sank down in the chair and put her hands up to her cheeks. Had this really happened? Was this really a true story? She looked at Michael, intent on talking into the telephone in very fluent and very fast French, and knew that it was the truth.

Then who was Michael? And how did he find out about her? She had a sudden panic in case he discovered without her telling him how deep her deception had been.

Michael put down the receiver.

"They are sending a police car for this," he said, "and they are going to fly it back to England in a special aeroplane this afternoon."

He walked across to her and put his hand in hers.

253

"And now that the job is finished we can think about ourselves."

Her fingers instinctively tightened on his.

"In what way?" she asked a little nervously.

"I can tell you, for one thing, that I love you," he said. "Darling, you must forgive me for the hard things I thought about you. It was only for a moment that the circumstantial evidence seemed so overwhelming that I thought you might really be involved in this, that you might have been taking money from Newbury, or only pretending to be what you seem to be. Then, when I looked into your eyes just now I knew what a fool I was. The only pretending you could ever do was our pretence, ours, darling, that there was no reason why we shouldn't love each other.

He suddenly drew her into his arms, holding her very tight.

"That's all over," he said. "Our pretence is no longer necessary. We can love each other, you and I, just as we've always meant to do."

Taryna felt herself to begin to tremble. His lips were drawing nearer to hers. She wanted to tell him the truth, and this was the moment, she felt, when, as he had said, there could no longer be any pretense between them.

But somehow she could not bring herself to speak the words. She must do it. She must! She must! And yet Michael's mouth was almost touching hers and she wanted his kiss more than she had ever wanted anything in her life before.

"I love you! Oh, my darling, I love you!"

He was kissing her. It was too late. She was drowning in his love, going deep, deep down into the waters of deception and knowing only that the whole world was well lost for the sake of his kiss.

13

There was a ring at the front-door bell. Taryna put down what she was doing, wiped her hands and went to see who was there.

A small, breathless boy was waiting in the porch.

"Please, miss, will the Vicar come to twenty-two Bull Lane. Ma says to tell 'im that grandad won't last the night."

"The Vicar isn't in at the moment," Taryna said. "But I will tell him as soon as he gets back. Twenty-two Bull Lane. You're Jimmie Hawkins, aren't you?"

"That's right, miss."

The small boy gave an impish grin, then shot away like a streak of lightning, obviously relieved to be finished with his errand.

Taryna shut the front door, wrote the message on a pad that was kept specially in the hall, and went back to the kitchen.

She was making a cake, but as she beat the butter and added the eggs her thoughts were far away. She was thinking of the sunshine on a blue sea, the flowers and the palm trees around her, and she was hearing Michael's voice saying: "Now we can talk about ourselves. When are you going to marry me?"

She knew then, after the whole world had seemed to turn a somersault and whirl about her, that she couldn't tell him the truth. She couldn't spoil the glamour and the glory of that moment by confessing that she had lied—not once but a thousand times.

She felt she couldn't bear to see disillusionment in his face, to know that his eyes were no longer tender, but were looking at her with contempt.

She had not forgotten the grimness in his face when she had first found him in her bedroom. He had been suspicious of her then, but somehow she had convinced him. But now there was no get-out for her, no way of proving that she was innocent—because she wasn't.

She had lied and lied, and she felt her face burn at the thought of it. How degrading, how sordid to have to say, "I am not what I seem. I don't own even the clothes I am wearing. I haven't a penny in my pocket except what belongs to Mr. Newbury."

It was that, more than anything else, that decided her that she could not tell him. Instead, with an effort, she had forced herself to control the trembling of her fingers, the quivering of her lips, to say:

"Please, we can't talk about that here."

"Why not?" Michael asked with a smile on his lips.

And it seemed to her that there was, indeed, no reason. All the people at the adjoining tables were intent on their own conversation. She and Michael were, to all intents and purposes, alone, isolated on their soft, cushioned seats with a little white table in front of them, and oblivious of everyone else in the world.

"I love you, you know that, don't you?" he said.

She did not dare look at him lest he should see the torture in her eyes. What could she say, what could she do without admitting that she was an impostor?

"I am so thankful this job is over," Michael went on. "I didn't really want to take it. I have been out abroad, in Africa—in the Sudan as it happens—and when I got back I was due for a long spell of leave. But the

256

Foreign Office asked me to do this for them and I couldn't very well refuse."

"The Foreign Office?" Taryna asked, her eyes widening.

"Not officially, of course," Michael said. "If I failed or got myself into trouble, they would have disowned me. But actually they were desperately anxious that this invention should not get into the wrong hands."

"Will they be very grateful to you now?" Taryna asked.

"They won't give me a medal or anything of that sort," Michael replied jokingly. "They will just say— 'Not too bad, old boy. I daresay we shall have something else for you in six months' time.' "

"What sort of thing?" Taryna asked.

"That rather depends on you now," Michael answered.

Again she felt panic overtaking her. Did everything they could say have only one ending? She wondered whether by that last remark he meant that he might get a better job if he had a rich wife, and then despised herself for the thought. And yet combined with her misery at her own imposture was also the memory of Jim Carson's words which had haunted her ever since: "He's on to a good thing now."

If only Michael knew, she thought; and she had an almost hysterical desire to laugh because it was so bitter, so utterly unfunny.

"Why couldn't he have fallen in love with Kit?" she asked herself. That would have been perfect for him. And yet even at the thought of his loving another woman she felt jealousy creep at her heart so that she almost winced at the pain of it.

"Have another drink," Michael was saying, and she had not realised that she had drunk a champagne cocktail without even tasting it.

"No, thank you."

"Then let's go and lunch together somewhere in the sunshine."

They strolled along under the palm trees to where they could eat under gaily-striped umbrellas, with the sea almost lapping at their feet. It was all an enchantment, a magic dream from which Taryna knew that sooner or later she must awake.

The afternoon seemed to slip by almost before she realised it was passing. There was Michael making love to her; Michael saying sweet and tender things which made her drop her eyes and feel the blood rising in her cheeks; Michael whispering words of passion which kindled a fire within herself in answer to the one in his eyes.

And then suddenly it was late afternoon.

"I am going to leave you for an hour or two," Michael said. "I have got to go down to the Sûreté, telephone to London to learn if the aeroplane has got there safely, and make a few plans for tomorrow. I suppose you will be going on the morning train?"

"To where?" Taryna asked almost helplessly.

"Back to Deauville, to Kit, I suppose," Michael answered. "Unless, of course, you feel you can't face the old man. Then, I suppose, you will go home."

Home! That was really the word she had been waiting to hear, Taryna thought. Now she knew what she must do—and quickly.

"There is no need to make up your mind in a hurry," Michael went on. "I will take you back to the hotel now and you can lie down for a bit. And then, if you will be ready about nine, we will dine somewhere quiet and perhaps dance afterwards."

Taryna was not quite certain what she said or how she answered him. She only knew, as they drove back to the hotel in an open taxi, that this was goodbye.

He held her hand, and as they reached the imposing entrance to the Splendide he raised it to his lips and kissed her fingers.

"Till nine o'clock," he said. "Don't keep me waiting."

She felt his lips, warm and hard, she saw his eyes looking into hers, and then, with a little incoherent murmur of goodbye, she turned away from him.

She waited until his taxi had driven away and then she went to the desk.

"I have to leave at once," she said. "Please send a porter up for my luggage in five minutes and get me a taxi."

She deliberately did not say where she was going because she knew that Michael would make enquiries later. She hurried up to her bedroom, packed her suitcase and wrote Michael a very short note.

I have gone home, she said. *Please don't try to find me, just forget it has ever happened. It was so wonderful while it lasted. Taryna.*

She slipped it into an envelope and when she went downstairs gave it to the hall porter

"A gentleman will be calling for me at nine o'clock," she said. "Will you tell him I have been called away unexpectedly and give him this note?"

"Very good, *m'mselle.*"

She got into the taxi and told the driver to drive along the *plage.* Only when they were out of earshot of the Splendide did she direct him to the airport.

She was thankful to find that she still had enough money left from what Mr. Newbury had given her for the journey to pay for her air ticket. "I will pay it all back every penny," she vowed, and with a sinking of her heart knew that it was going to take her a long time.

The hotel bill and tips had seemed prodigious for

such a short stay, and the fare to London by air made her think of the dozens of journeys she could have done in a less expensive manner.

But she had no time to think, no time to consider ways and means of saving money. All she wanted to do was to get away from Michael, from Cannes, from everything that would ever remind her of him and his life.

And yet once she was flying high in the sky over France she knew that she never could escape her memories. All the way home she could think only of his voice saying, "I love you!", only of his eyes looking into hers, of his lips near her mouth.

"I love you! I love you!"

She found herself whispering the words aloud until the air hostess stopped and said:

"Do you want anything, madam?"

She blushed as she replied quickly:

"No, thank you."

The aeroplane was full and she was lucky that there had been a cancellation.

"We don't usually have empty seats at this time of the year," the official told her.

But somehow Taryna felt that nothing and nobody could stop her at this moment in her escape from Michael. Because she longed so terribly to be with him, she knew that fate must inevitably force them apart . . .

"I love you!"

She could hear the words still echoing in her mind and heart as she mixed a cake in the dark, old-fashioned kitchen at the Vicarage. She put the mixture into the tin, covered it with a piece of greaseproof paper, and put it in the oven. As she did so she heard the front-door bell ring again.

"Oh, brother!" she said aloud, pushing her hair back

from her forehead with a floury hand and hurrying to the door across the depressing little hall with its worn linoleum.

She opened it. It was Michael who stood there!

"Oh!"

Taryna could only stand and look at him. The sound which came from her lips was neither an exclamation nor a sigh, but a mixture of both.

"May I come in?"

Michael had swept off his hat and was standing there, his eyes in his sunburnt face dark, attractive and somehow inexplicably appealing.

"Yes, I suppose so," Taryna said, and there was a hint of tears in her voice.

He moved into the hall and she shut the door behind him.

"Will you come into the sitting-room?" she asked.

She led the way, wiping her hands, as she did so, on the little gingham apron she wore. Then taking it off she laid it on a chair just inside the door.

She was wearing an old cotton frock. It was faded with frequent washings, and yet, badly cut though it was, it could not entirely disguise the slimness of her waist or the sweet swellings of her breasts, which had been so obvious in the expensive and beautifully tailored dresses that Kit had lent her.

The sitting-room looked worn and shabby. Her mother's work-box stood by the sofa with a pile of socks on it that needed darning. Edwina had left a half-painted picture surrounded by her paint-box, brushes and painting rags on one table, and there was the usual clutter of parish magazines, half-made objects for the old people's sale-of-work, and some reference books for her father, scattered over the chairs and the furniture.

"I am sorry everything is so untidy . . ." Taryna said

almost automatically, and then her voice died away and she stood looking at Michael.

He was standing with his back to the empty fire-place. There was something in his expression she did not understand.

"How did you find me?" she asked suddenly.

"I telephoned Kit and made her tell me where you lived. I was sure you had gone home."

"And why have you come here?" she enquired.

"To see you," he answered. "Because I felt I was entitled to an explanation."

She was afraid this was what he would say and she felt herself tremble as she turned her face away from him and stood holding on to a chair, wishing miserably that the house would crash about her ears or the earth open and swallow her up.

"Don't you think you owe me that?" Michael asked gently.

"I . . . suppose so."

"Why didn't you trust me?"

"How could I? Things had gone too far."

"All the more reason, I should have thought, why you should have told me the truth."

"I couldn't," Taryna said passionately. "I couldn't."

"Well, won't you tell me now?"

Some pride, which showed itself in a spurt of anger, raised itself from Taryna's misery.

"Can't you see for yourself?" she asked. "Can't you see that I'm not the rich heiress I pretended to be. I'm Taryna Grazebrook, the daughter of a Bermondsey vicar. This is my home—and everything you thought about me, everything I have told you, was untrue."

She spoke wildly, and then, after a moment, Michael said:

"Everything?"

"Everything that is of any importance," Taryna answered.

He didn't move, but somehow she felt he had come closer to her. She held on to the chair until her knuckles gleamed white, and then at last she said:

"Now you know the truth. I haven't a penny. Why don't you go?"

She shut her eyes as she spoke, half expecting to hear him pass her and his footsteps going away down the hall.

"So you really think I am interested in your money?" Michael said with a hint of laughter in his voice.

"You thought I was rich, and you needed the money," Taryna said a little incoherently.

"Who told you that?"

"Jim Carson, for one person."

"I'll wring his neck when I see him," Michael said cheerfully. "Jim always was an incorrigible gossip. So you thought I was a fortune-hunter?"

"But of course. Kit thought so too. That was why you were with Irene."

"Yes, there's logic in that," Michael conceded. "It happened to be the only way I could get myself into the Newbury household. But you and I were different—at least I thought so."

There was a silence and then he added:

"And if I tell you that money was not in my mind, what then?"

"It was in a way," Taryna answered. "Even though you perhaps didn't want it for yourself. You saw me as a person surrounded by money, dressed by money, educated by money, with a rich, luxurious background. That is the person you thought you were in love with—and I am none of those things. I am somebody

263

quite different, somebody whom really you have never met."

"Then it will be all the more exciting to get to know you," Michael said.

"No, it won't," Taryna contradicted.

She turned away from him at length and walked across the room to stand at the writing-desk.

"You don't understand," she said. "I've got nothing in common with the people you know or in whom you are interested. I don't understand that world; and though it's been exciting to be in it for a little while, I couldn't live up to it. I couldn't take part in it for long. It would find me out."

There was silence as her voice died away, and then Michael said very gently:

"We could pretend to like it together."

There was something in his voice that made her long to run to him, to hold out her arms, to tell him that she would be anything and everything if only he would go on loving her. And yet she knew she mustn't; she must save him, not from himself but from her, from what he imagined her to be like.

"Please go away," she said. "You don't understand what you are saying or what you are doing. We can be nothing to each other, you and I. You are in love with someone who doesn't exist."

"What about you?" Michael asked. "Who are you in love with?"

Despite every resolution Taryna felt the tears come into her eyes.

"I shall have my work," she said a little unsteadily.

"Will that be enough?" Michael asked. "Will you really be content to forget that night on the yacht when I first kissed you? That night when we danced together in those strange places in Trouville, when we walked back along the shore and I kissed you in the shadow of the hotel? Have you forgotten all that, Taryna?"

"Stop!"

Taryna turned round and faced him.

"You are torturing me," she said. "You are doing it deliberately. You are trying to make me weaken, trying to make me . . ." Her voice broke. "I don't know what you are trying to do, but please go away, quickly, now."

The tears were running down her face and suddenly Michael was by her side.

"Oh, my darling!" he said. "How blind and stupid and idiotic you are being. Don't you realise that I love you."

"But you don't," Taryna sobbed. "Not me, not the real me."

He held her so close that she could hardly breathe.

"I love someone called Taryna," he said, "who's got dark hair and troubled, honest eyes; who's got a dimple in her cheek when she laughs and a mouth which simply invites my kisses. I don't know that I care for them mixed with salt tears, but I'll risk it."

He bent his head and his mouth was on Taryna's before she could stop him. She tried to push him away, but her hands fluttered weakly against him and then suddenly were still.

He strained her to him, his mouth taking complete possession of her so that she could only lie in his arms, weak and helpless and utterly at his mercy.

After a long, long time he raised his head and looked at her face, flushed and tremulous against his shoulder.

"Why do you fight against the inevitable?" he asked.

"Oh, Michael."

Her voice was barely above a whisper. Somehow she had nothing more to say. It had all been said in a kiss.

"I love you and I am going to marry you," Michael

said, and then he was kissing her again, wildly and passionately so that the room whirled around Taryna and seemed full of sunshine and stars and all the glory of the Mediterranean, and she knew that nothing mattered except that she was close to Michael and Michael loved her.

Ages later, it seemed to her, they were sitting hand in hand on the sofa and she asked:

"What made you suspicious of me? Why did you come to Cannes?"

"I wondered when you would ask that," Michael replied. "I will tell you what happened. After I left you at Brionne I went back to Deauville and when I got to the hotel went up to Corea's room to find out where everyone was. I knew that if Irene had gone out she would have left a message with the secretary.

"Corea wasn't there and there was only Miss Harris—I don't know whether you met her, she is a rather junior secretary and not very bright. 'Has Mrs. Newbury left a message for me?' I enquired. 'She's gone to the Royal for a cocktail party, Mr. Tarrant,' Miss Harris told me, 'and wants you to join her there as soon as possible.'

" 'I will go along right away,' I said; and then, as I reached the door, a sudden thought struck me. 'Did Miss Grazebrook remember to take her passport with her?' I asked. 'She went off in such a hurry it might have been forgotten.' 'Oh, I'm sure Mr. Corea would have remembered it,' " Miss Harris replied.

"She got up and opened a drawer in the desk. 'It will be a Canadian passport,' I said, in case she didn't know what she was looking for. 'Oh, no! Miss Grazebrook had an ordinary British one,' Miss Harris replied. 'There were only two foreign passports when we arrived in the yacht. One belonged to Mrs. Newbury's

266

maid Rosa, and the other to one of the footmen who's a Pole.'

"I didn't argue with her because I realised she was speaking the truth. It was suddenly absolutely clear to me that you were not a Canadian and never had been. I remembered how reluctant you had been to talk about Montreal, the little things you had said at Southampton that showed you hadn't travelled much; and quite suddenly I was kicking myself for being a gullible fool at having let you and the plans slip through my fingers.

"I went to my room and packed my bag, then walked back to the office and told Miss Harris that I had had a call to say my uncle was extremely ill and I had to go to him at once. I then went to the airport and took a plane to Cannes."

"So you arrived long before me," Taryna said.

"Oh, yes," Michael replied. "And that was how I found out who the supposed Miss Jane Woodruff was. I'd known her before, when she had been mixed up in another sort of racket. It had been diamond smuggling in those days."

"She didn't recognise you?" Taryna asked.

"No, I took good care not to let her see me. So I put two of the Sûreté men on to her, and as soon as I had got the film from you they told her to get out of Cannes and to stay out. The French are not as soft-hearted as we are with undesirables."

"What am I to do about Mr. Newbury?" Taryna asked. "I was going to get a job and try to pay back the money I owe him."

"I'll do that," Michael said. "And actually you needn't worry. Newbury is far too shrewd a business man not to know when he's beaten. When you meet him again, which you undoubtedly will as Kit's father, you will find he's just as genial and just as charming to

267

you as he's been in the past. And make no mistake about it, he won't suffer unduly. For every one of his projects that fails there are half a dozen that succeed. 'He's as clever,' as the saying is, 'as a cartload of monkeys.' "

"And Kit? I must tell Kit."

"You can ring her up tonight and tell her you are engaged to me," Michael said. "That will be a surprise but it wouldn't astonish me if she had similar news for you about herself and Ted."

"Oh, I do hope so!" Taryna exclaimed, and knew, as if she had already been told, that Kit would marry Ted and that the four of them would always be friends.

"But what about Irene?" she asked aloud.

"I am afraid she won't be very pleased with me," Michael answered. "But, after all, there's always Billy and Eric—and perhaps even Jim might do as a stand-in until one of them arrives."

Taryna laughed.

"You have an answer for everything, haven't you?"

"I agree to that—so why bother to ask questions?" Michael answered. "The one question I want to ask is, do you love me?"

He put his arm round her as he spoke and drew her close to him again.

"You know I do," Taryna answered. "Are you quite, quite sure you don't mind my being poor and unimportant and an impostor?"

"Money doesn't worry me particularly," Michael said. "I daresay we shall scrape along. And as to being unimportant—well, to me you are the most important person in the whole world. As for the third thing, I will forgive your being an impostor on one condition only."

"What is that?" Taryna asked, her lips very close to his.

"That you never, never pretend to me again,"

268

Michael answered. "That is the one thing I could never forgive. If you pretended to love me when you didn't."

"I will promise you that I will never pretend to do that," Taryna answered, "because I do love you. Oh, Michael! I love you so terribly."

He didn't answer that because he couldn't. His lips found hers and they clung together quite oblivious that the door had opened and the Reverend William Grazebrook had come into the room.

He stood staring at them for a moment in mild surprise, and then the door closed in the draught from the window and they started, almost guiltily, apart.

"Daddy!" Taryna exclaimed.

She got to her feet and ran across to him.

"Oh, Daddy! This is Michael, and we're engaged."

"So I somehow gathered," the Vicar said, holding out his hand to Michael as he walked towards them.

"How do you do, sir," Michael said. "I'm afraid Taryna's introduction is not very explicit. My name is Tarrant—Michael Tarrant."

The Vicar shook his hand and then said:

"Tarrant! Now let me see. There was a Tarrant up at Oxford with me. Stephen Tarrant by name. Are you any relation of his?"

"He was my father, sir. And now I come to think of it, I've heard him speak of you. I somehow never connected the name with Taryna."

"Yes, Stephen Tarrant was a very great friend of mine," the Vicar said. "In fact we made plans at one time to go round the world together. We were going to do a kind of walking tour and see everything there was to see; and then at the last moment your grandfather died and Stephen came into the title. He had to go off and look after those estates of his in Dorset. He was very disappointed, I remember, and so was I."

"Yes, that's right, sir," Michael said. "I remember his telling me about it."

"I saw that he died two months ago," the Vicar said. "It was years since I'd seen him and yet I felt that if we had met again our friendship would have been quite unchanged."

The Vicar turned and looked from Michael to Taryna.

"So this is the young man you want to marry, is it, Taryna?" he said.

"Yes, Daddy."

"Well, we'll have to tell your mother about it," the Vicar said, happily shelving all responsibility in his usual manner. "In the meantime, I daresay Sir Michael could do with some tea. I know I could."

Taryna turned to Michael, wide-eyed.

"Sir Michael?" she questioned.

"I'm afraid so," he answered. "Do you mind very much?"

"Mind . . ." she began, and then her hand went up to her lips. "Tea—oh, and my cake! I'd forgotten all about it. It will be completely ruined."

She rushed from the room into the kitchen, and then a moment later, as she was drawing a rather overbaked cake from the oven, she found Michael beside her.

"I've come to help you," he said. "Your father thought it was a good idea."

"Oh, Michael, you oughtn't to be here," Taryna said.

"Why not?" he asked. "If it comes to that, I'm an extremely good cook. Better, I expect, than you are."

"But look who you are," she said. "You've never told me. I don't think I want to be the wife of a baronet. I shall be frightened."

"You needn't be frightened of anything so long as I am there to look after you," Michael answered.

He took the cake out of her hands and put it down on the table.

"I love you," he said. "I love you so much that I can't think of anything else except that I want you. Oh, Taryna! Marry me quickly. We've got so much to do together."

She tried to speak, but somehow it was difficult, with his lips so close to hers and his arms round her, with that strange and exciting thrill running through her, making her quiver against him.

"Say you love me," he commanded. "I can't hear you say it too often. Do you remember the lights of love? I'm so afraid that they won't come true, that you will change your mind. Tell me, Taryna."

"I love you," Taryna whispered, and the Vicar, in the sitting-room, waited in vain for his tea.

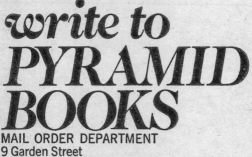